THE NYTE PATROL

NYTE PATROL, BOOK 1

ALEX P. BERG

I swung. My bat whistled through the air. A tenth of a second later it struck. The bat pinged as the softball cracked off the barrel, a few inches above the taper. A ripple flew up my arm from the impact, reaching my shoulder at the tail end of my swing. I gritted my teeth as a blip of pain snapped at my surgically repaired AC joint. I snarled and hung my arm at my side, shaking it to dull the sting. Meanwhile, the ball dropped uneventfully in the dirt fifteen feet from second base, retaining all the momentum of a marble dropped into a vat of molasses.

"God *damnit*," I said.

I stormed off toward the dugout, ripping my helmet from my head as I did so. A cool March breeze whistled past me as I stomped down the steps, wicking away the touch of sweat at my brow. I crammed my helmet onto a spot on the burnt orange and white shelf above the bench and let my bat clatter to the floor.

The pain in my shoulder had already dulled to a far off ache, a ghost of its former self, but it was nonetheless enough to put me on edge. Every time I felt it, it sent me back to the moment I'd torn it. The searing pain. The audible pop. The numbness. It had been months, but I still thought about it, much as the sports psychologists told me not to. Sure, it was easy not to focus on it when I felt no pain, but when the muscles supporting the joint snarled and hissed, how the hell was I supposed to ignore it?

I closed my eyes and took a deep breath. I forced air in and out of my lungs. Clear the mind, they'd told me. Relax. Unclench your muscles. Let the body and mind reach a state of quiet ease and the memory of the pain will disappear.

A perfect, lilting laugh shot through me, shattering the calm I'd been collecting. My eyes snapped open, and I spotted Janie Nguyen half doubled over, arm on Carrie Fletcher's shoulder as she relished in some meaningless anecdote. Her songbird laugh carried across the dugout, light and airy and free. It grated at me like a chisel.

"What the hell are you laughing at?" I said.

Janie looked up at me, her laugh melting away. "What?"

"You don't have anything to be chuckling about," I said. "You were screwing up your position in the outfield again. You were at least twenty feet too far in on most of my swings. You were practically up on the longhorn."

Janie straightened, her smile disappearing. "I was right where I needed to be."

Janie had that perfect sort of body—not regular girl perfect, but softball perfect. Five foot nine, lean muscular legs, shoulders just wide enough that she could get a solid amount of power out of them during a swing. I'd never suffered much from body issues, but next to her, I always felt like my thighs were a touch too thick, my hips too wide, and my teeth not white enough, not to mention I hated having to look up at her.

"No, you weren't," I said. "If I'd hit a good one, it would've sailed over your head."

Janie planted a hand on her hip. "I was in the right spot, Lexie, same as I always am. I adapt to the batter."

"Excuse me?"

Carrie looked like she wanted to be anywhere else all of a sudden. "Guys, come on. Relax. It's just practice."

I took a step toward them and jabbed a finger in their direction. "No, it's not *just practice.* If we screw up in practice, then we screw up in game, and if we screw up in game, then we *lose games."*

Janie rolled her eyes and looked away. "Yeah, well, we also lose games if we don't score any runs..."

I took another step forward. "You want to say that again? To my face, maybe?"

A stern, weather-worn voice cut across the dugout. "Rodriguez. Need to talk to you."

Coach K's head hovered at the far end of the dugout, her sunglasses pushed onto the crown of her head and her short gray hair framed by the afternoon sun. My nostrils flared, but I pushed my anger down and skirted Janie to join her on the steps by the fencing.

"What's up, Coach?" I said, trying to keep my voice level.

Coach K leaned on her right leg, her back leg two steps down from the front. She pushed her sunglasses into place as she glanced at the mound where Heather was still chucking change-ups across home plate. She spared me a quick glance without moving her head much. "How're you feeling, Lexie?"

"Okay."

Heather pitched. Valentina swung and missed.

Coach nodded. "And your shoulder?"

"What about it?"

"How's it feeling?"

"It's fine."

Coach stepped onto the back step, pushing her glasses up onto her forehead. This time she looked all the way at me. "It's *fine.*"

"Yeah. Fine."

Over on the mound, I spotted Heather looking our way. She gave me a nod of her head, as if to say, What's up? I shrugged in reply. Who knows if she saw it.

Coach K shook her head, and she let the sunglasses fall back into place. "You know, Lexie. About last weekend..."

"I know, okay? You don't have to remind me." I'd gone oh for eight in my plate appearances over the doubleheader. "It's not going to happen again."

"I know you don't *mean* for it to happen, but sheer force of will isn't going to make it so."

"Which is why I'm out here practicing, Coach."

"And hitting nothing but grounders and pop flys."

I swallowed back the lump in my throat. "I'm getting better, Coach. I can feel it."

"I know you are, Lexie. I have no doubt you're going to break out of this funk, trust me. But in the meantime, we're two games back of Oklahoma and four back of Baylor already. We can't afford to lose any more easy ones, so until I see you improve on the practice field, I'm moving Janie into your spot."

I felt like I'd been slapped in the face. "You're *benching* me?"

"I think you need to be honest with yourself. We brought you back too soon. Your shoulder needs more time to heal. It's nothing to be ashamed of. It'll be good for you."

The anger lingering in my stomach rushed up my throat, frothy and thick. I felt the heat building in my cheeks. "You're kidding me, right? This is *bullshit*. I've busted my ass for this team for two and a half years and you're stapling me to the bench? *Are you fucking shitting me?*"

Coach K drew herself up to full height, which was the same as mine but felt about a foot taller. She pulled her sunglasses all the way off and fixed me with a granite stare. "Don't start with me, Rodriguez. You know play time is earned, not given. It's as simple as that. So get it together and earn some."

My fists clenched into balls at my side, and I felt my nails digging into my palms. My teeth squeaked as I ground them together. I shouldn't have said anything else. Technically I didn't, but the muffled shriek of agony that forced itself out of my throat as I turned and headed back into the dugout wasn't much better than dropping an extra couple f-bombs.

My feet were leaden bricks, thumping off the dugout floor like artillery shells. My muscles were coiled and tight. The sound of grunts of exertion, yells, and balls clinking off bats faded behind the violent rush of blood in my ears. Darkness crept in at the edges of my vision.

Me? *Benched?* It seemed like a bad joke. Worse. A *nightmare*. I wanted to scream, to punch something, someone, to lash out, to break things.

Before I knew it, I'd reached down and grabbed a bat. My hands wrapped around the grip, squeezing it with every ounce of my strength. A green Gatorade jug stood on a pedestal in the middle of the dugout. I howled with rage and lunged toward it, whipping the bat through the air at fastball speed. Plastic cracked and ice water flew as I blasted the jug in the side. I heard screams, but all I saw was the jug. I swung my arms and again I smashed it, bellowing with anger as I hit it again and again. Somewhere in the recesses of my mind I logged the screams around me, especially a sharp, poignant one nearby, but I didn't let it stop me. I kept swinging until I was soaked and my arms ached and my AC joint wanted to kill me.

I stood there, huffing and puffing as the rage bled from me like air from a balloon. That's when I felt it. The weight of two dozen sets of eyes searing into my back. I turned, taking in the horrified looks of my teammates, but it was the look of fear on the girl who lay on the dugout floor that hit me the hardest.

Janie Nguyen lay almost completely underneath me, as soaked as I was and her eyes wide with fear. For a moment I didn't understand it, but as the anger fled, memory flooded back. I heard Janie's shriek above all the others, saw the whip of her black ponytail in the corner of my vision, and heard her thump to the floor as my bat had whistled past her, inches from her face.

Christ. *What had I done?*

2

I SAT AT MY LAPTOP, CLICKING IDLY AT THE SEARCH results without really looking at them. Buds filled my ears, blasting my eardrums with Disturbed and Dark Tranquility and anything else I could find in my playlist that was angry and depressing and fit my mood. My phone buzzed again as it logged another message, but I didn't look at it. I'd silenced it and put it face down on my desk for a reason.

I'd never been in a traumatic accident, but I finally understood how car crash victims felt. My entire afternoon was a blur. I only vaguely remembered running from the dugout, pushing people away as they looked at me in horror or tried to talk to me. Racing to my '94 Chevy Suburban and turning the keys in the engine, hitting the gas, and getting the hell out of there. I didn't remember any red lights, any stop signs, any crosswalks. I didn't remember a damn thing until the sound of my dorm room door slamming shut behind me signaled I'd reached my safe space.

Thank god Tanya wasn't around.

I kept clicking on the listings, but I barely read a thing in front of me. *God, how had everything fallen apart so fast?* Four months ago, I'd been on top of the world, batting in the three hundreds, feeling great about the prospects of my upcoming season, and one *stupid* swing, a silly, errant swing like any other had thrown it all into chaos. I hadn't done anything differently. Used a bat of a different weight. Overextended or taken a hack into a dirt. There hadn't been any reason for the tear, nothing I'd done to deserve it. It had just happened.

I'd gotten it repaired. The doctors at St. David's and at UT Sports Medicine had done a great job. After the rehab I'd gone through, it should be fine. For the most part it was, but every now and then the injury reached out and pinched me, reminded me it was still there, smacking me down any time I thought I might've crested its steep peak. Even if it wasn't physically affecting me anymore, it still had a place in my head, poking, prodding, sapping my confidence. Playing to my insecurities. Building within me anger and resentment.

It had finally gotten the best of me. I mean sure, Janie Nguyen was a catty bitch and there was no way in hell she was deserving of my spot, but that didn't mean she deserved to get blasted in the face with twenty ounces of aluminum. If I'd been a half a foot to my left when I'd started swinging, I could've knocked her unconscious. Broken her face. I could've *literally* killed her.

And now I was going to pay the price. The look on Coach K's face as I'd run to the parking lot had said it all. She wouldn't just staple me to the bench now. She'd use glue. Straps. She'd weld me there if she had to. Hell, I might never play again. I might get kicked from the team, not just for being a crappy hitter, a bad teammate, and an increasingly sour grump but for misconduct. For *attempted assault.* And then what the hell would I do? How would I pay my tuition and room and board if

I lost my softball scholarship? To say that my parents were middle class would be stretching the truth. They had a hard enough time pitching in the half my scholarship didn't cover.

I scrolled through another page on my laptop. Whether consciously or not, I'd started searching for help wanted ads. Anything that was close to my dorm and let me work odd hours. I wasn't sure if I'd need a part-time job. I didn't know if I'd *really* be kicked off the team and forced to fend for myself, but I sure wasn't going to crawl to my parents and tell them I'd let my anger get the best of me, screwed up the most important thing in my life, and jeopardized the degree that might earn me the living softball almost assuredly never would. Regardless, it gave me something to do. Something to mindlessly click while I avoided interacting with the real world or, even worse, starting on the statics problem set I was in no way ready to tackle at the moment. If I couldn't concentrate on a webpage, I sure as hell couldn't focus on moments of inertia.

As I switched over to Craigslist, a pop-up ad appeared in my browser. It didn't feature ten hot tips for whitening teeth the natural way or fifteen childhood celebrities that I'd be amazed to see now, but I closed it anyway.

I scrolled down the Craigslist home page, looking for the help wanted section, but another pop-up ad blinked to life. Again I clicked on the red button at the top left corner, but as soon as I closed the window, it reappeared. I thought it might've been one of those scam pop-ups and that I'd have to reboot my browser, but strangely enough the window didn't have any flashing banners and threats about viruses. Instead, it was a help wanted ad, for a business nearby no less. Since when did Craigslist have user-tailored pop-ups?

My brow furrowed as I read the ad. It was extremely vague,

something about a secretarial position, but the hours seemed right and I actually had the requirements listed, even down to the fact that it wanted someone with a large car. Did Google know what I drove? Corporate data gathering efforts were getting out of control.

Over the blast of heavy metal in my ears, I heard the crack of the door behind me. A moment later, Tanya descended into the beanbag at my side. "Oh my God, Lexie. I had the *worst* day."

I glanced at her. Tanya was one of the more perpetually upbeat people I knew. She was a great roommate and one of my better friends. Any other day, I would've been interested to know what qualified as a terrible day for someone like her, but not today. Not when I'd literally gone through *the worst day* myself.

Tanya didn't ask if I cared though. "So first off, I was sure I'd lost my phone. It wasn't in my pocket. It wasn't in my backpack. I looked *everywhere* for it after class. And then I remembered I'd been using it in the bathroom on the second floor of the Cockrell building, and I was like, *oh my god,* did I leave it there? But when I went back to look for it, it was gone, and I was like, did someone steal it, or did I *flush it?*"

I pulled my headphones from my ears. "Tanya. Seriously. Not now."

She cocked her head, but she wasn't put off. "Are you alright? What's going on?"

What's going on was that my world had been turned upside down and I DID NOT want to talk about it. I sure as hell didn't want to talk about it with Tanya, who would tell me everything was going to be alright and that I should look on the bright side and that every shower had a rainbow, but if I even hinted at what was going on, Tanya would do her darnedest to pull it out of me. She'd poke and prod and insist and I just couldn't right now. I simply couldn't.

Tanya's eyebrows drew together in concern, and she leaned in a little. The popup ad on my computer blinked, drawing my eye. It flashed again as I looked at it. Not the whole thing. Just the address.

Tanya's lips pursed. "Lexie..."

I grabbed my keys. "I'm fine, Tanya. I've got to go."

3

I LEFT THE MOTOR ON MY SUBURBAN RUNNING AS I PULLED up to the address on West 21ˢᵗ Street. I wasn't sure exactly what I expected, but a run-down shack painted four different colors wasn't it. Boards covered the front door as well as the windows, and cracks laced the mortar. An industrious vandal had painted "Keep Austin Weird" on the plywood, and someone else had added "Politicos can suck it!" alongside a crude depiction of a phallus. Strangely enough, someone had recently mowed the lawn—or weeds, really. I pulled up my phone to make sure I had the right place. Unfortunately, I did.

Across the street, a dilapidated co-op blocked the setting sun. Cinderblocks and cigarette butts littered the dirt in front of the sliding glass apartment doors. Someone had scrawled graffiti across the front of those, too, but of a less vulgar sort. At least the housing complex next door didn't resemble a crackhouse.

I slipped a can of mace from my glove box into my letter jacket's pocket. Any normal person would've gunned the engine and gotten the hell out of dodge, but as my friends and family always joked, I suffered from congenital audacity. It was a way of saying I was headstrong and reckless. I'd always contested the former, which in a way proved them right, but there was no doubting the latter. Not after today.

With vivid memories of practice in my head, I killed the ignition and hopped out of the truck. Every step I took went against my better judgement, but I approached the shack regardless. Perhaps the brand new twenty-story condo building fifty feet away on Rio Grand gave me confidence. I couldn't imagine anyone would try to rape me in broad daylight, but should anyone lay a finger on me, one scream would attract a half-dozen well-intentioned hipsters armed with chihuahuas and righteous indignation. Nonetheless, I kept a hand on the mace, and I longed for my softball bat, unwieldy as it might be for self-defense.

The online ad had said to head to the back. I followed the cracked paving stones around the side of the house, avoiding the discarded lawn furniture, and stopped at a weathered door with peeling paint. A doorbell with a speaker unit hung to the right of the jam—literally, *hung*. Exposed wires kept it in place, and a blackened smudge darkened three-quarters of the speaker panel. It looked like it might've been struck by lightning at some point, yet a laminated sign taped to the door obstinately read 'Please use doorbell.'

I shook my head, wondering why I'd bothered coming, but after reminding myself that it might be this or waiting tables while wearing a tight shirt and a fake smile, I pressed my finger against the button.

I didn't hear a chime, but a few seconds later, the box squawked. "Hello? Who is it?"

"Uh... the name's Lexie. I'm here about the Craigslist ad."

The voice had a gruff quality to it even after accounting for the crackle of the dying speaker. *"The Craigslist ad?"*

"That's right. It said I should ask for Dawn."

The speaker sparked, and a tiny puff of smoke drifted out of the cavity. "Oh. Right. Give me a sec."

My grip on the mace tightened as footsteps approached the door. I told myself if I heard the rattle of more than three deadbolts and latches, I'd run and send my application to Pluckers instead, but before I could move, the handle twisted and the door swung open.

The man who stood there was maybe six feet tall and broad in the shoulders, but a looker he definitely wasn't. Wavy unwashed brown hair fell to his jaw, brushing against his three-day old beard bristle. For some incomprehensible reason, he wore a heavy knee-length leather duster and a matching hat that would've made Indiana Jones proud. Never mind that he was indoors and it was roughly seventy degrees outside. He scanned me with dark eyes. "You're Lexie?"

I didn't let go of the mace. "Yeah."

He shrugged. "Alright. Come on in."

He turned and headed into the house, leaving the door wide open. I stood there at the step, wondering if I should follow him. On the one hand, bad things tended to happen inside boarded up homes inhabited by weird dudes in leather. On the other hand, as I leaned in to take a gander, the place didn't look particularly threatening. Not only had the door not been locked, but there didn't appear to be any deadbolts with which to lock it, and rather than crack house chic, the home had more of an aging grandmother vibe, with a little too much dust and way too much paisley upholstery.

The guy's voice echoed around a corner. "You coming?"

"Uh... yeah."

I stepped inside and closed the door behind me. Walking cautiously, I followed the guy's trail into a living room. A couple people sat with their backs to me on a couch with a faded sail-cloth slipcover, watching reruns of *Project Runway* on an old cathode ray TV. Meanwhile, Door Guy leaned back in a swivel chair, his shoes propped up on the corner of a huge wooden desk that had been pulled straight from a 1940's private eye movie. It didn't really fit in the living room, but given the size of the house, I'm not sure where it would've.

Door Guy gestured to the chairs in front of his desk. "Go on. Have a seat."

"I'm good standing, thanks. But if you could point me in the direction of Dawn...?"

"Whoops. Sorry." One of the people on the couch stood and turned—a woman with long, straight, raven dark hair and exotic features. She wore a black tank top and faux leather leggings and, I noticed, was *freaking hot*. Like, unfair hot, the kind who didn't even need to try, with a CoverGirl face and a toned gym body that said she'd never eaten a carb in her life. She skirted the armrest and rested against the back of the couch, her body taut but supple, like a reed ready to crack you over the knuckles. "Lexie, was it? I'm Dawn Blayde. This is Tank by the way—"

The second occupant of the couch, a black guy with a shaved head, leaned back and waved. I couldn't see much of him, but the wave sent a ripple down the bulging muscles in his arm. He looked like he could bench five hundred pounds. I was surprised his shirt fit.

"And you've already met Larry," continued Dawn. "I set up the ad, but he'll conduct the interview. He doesn't type his own posts for... *reasons*."

"That's right." The guy from the door raised and tipped his hat. "Larry Stuttgart, at your service—or at least that's the name you can call me by."

"The name I can call you by?" I lifted an eyebrow as I took a second look at Dawn and Tank. *"Oh god.* This is a porn thing, isn't it? I knew I never should've responded. Look, I want nothing to do with this. If you try to coerce me into some disgusting casting call—"

Larry leaned forward in his chair. "Whoa. Slow down. *Porn?* What the hell are you talking about?"

I gave the guy my fiercest glare. "Seriously? *Look at her.* And look at him. She's insanely hot, and he's probably packing serious heat down under. You're filming amateur smut in this run-down shack, and you're the disgusting sleazeball with the camera who uploads everything to the internet."

"Disgusting sleazeball?" Larry balked. "I take offense to that. But no. This isn't a porn operation."

"Then why did you introduce yourself that way? *You can call me Larry Stuttgart.* Like it's an assumed name."

"It's my real name, I assure you—at least part of it. I have a lot of middle names. Hundreds, actually."

I blinked, suddenly caught off guard. "What? Why?"

Larry squinted at me. "Uh... so the demons don't eat my soul. *Duh.*"

I glanced at Dawn. *"Huh?"*

She shook her head. "We're not in the adult entertainment industry, sis. Though you're right. Tank *is* packing serious heat. I know from personal experience. Besides, I told you Larry doesn't do computers."

"Why's that?"

Larry snorted. "Let's say electronics don't relish my touch."

"You mean you possess the tech savvy of an eighty-year old?"

"I mean they burst into fiery balls of death if I so much as brush against them."

I rolled my eyes. *"Right..."*

"Don't believe me?" said Larry. "Give me your cell phone."

"No thanks. I think I'll hold on to it—in case I need to make any emergency calls."

Larry shrugged. "Suit yourself."

"Relax, Lexie," said Dawn. "Nobody's keeping you here against your will. Just have a seat and let Larry conduct the interview." She returned to the couch.

Larry waved to the chairs again. "Well?"

I eyed the seat as if it were made of spiders, but eventually I acquiesced. "Okay, fine. But if you're not running a porn operation, then what are you doing here?"

Larry's brows furrowed and he glanced at the couch. "Dawn? Didn't you put it in the ad?"

"I kept it intentionally vague," she said over her shoulder. "You know. Like you told me to, so it wouldn't interfere with your spell."

"Spell?" I said.

Larry clicked his tongue and peered at me in a less than trustworthy fashion. "Yeah, uh... don't worry about that. It's neither here nor there. The point is it's hard to find good help, which is why you're here, isn't it?"

"The only reason I'm here is because the ad said I could work nights and that the pay is competitive. Also because this place is close to my dorm and because there's a good chance I'll be footing the better part of my own college tuition soon. Other than that, I have no idea why I'm here." All of which was true. I couldn't bear the thought of telling my dad the extra shifts he'd taken on to help support me might not be enough, but beyond the money, I wasn't sure why I'd come. Impulsive I might be, but I'd never answered an online help wanted ad before. Certainly not one leading to a dilapidated bungalow. "What do you need a secretary for anyway?"

"Secretary?" Larry leaned over the desk again. "Dawn, you said we needed a *secretary?*"

Dawn waved a hand. "Vague, Larry. *Vague.*"

Larry slapped his hat on his desk and ran a hand through his rat's nest of hair. "Okay. Given that *Dawn* didn't explain things properly online, I guess *I'll* do the talking. What you're here to interview for isn't a secretarial position. It's more of a junior partnership role. Someone to help us with our more mundane tasks, provide support when necessary, and potentially to offer the odd bit of advice. Oh, and to drive us around to meetings. That was in the ad, right? That you needed to have access to a large vehicle?"

I nodded. "I have a Suburban. So you're looking for a personal assistant and a chauffeur?"

"That's a very narrow-minded way of looking at things," said Larry. "There's much more to this job than that. Besides, I said you could join as a junior partner. There's room for growth. Quite a bit, actually. Rapid advancement, if you show yourself to be as capable as I hope you are."

"So... you're a law firm?"

Larry scoffed. "Law? *Please.* We're in the confidential consulting business. We also offer retrieval and specialty services. Together, Dawn, Tank, Bill, and I are... *The Nyte Patrol.* That's with a 'y', not an 'i.'" Larry beamed at me.

The man exuded a strange child-like innocence, which

made it all the more odd that he was interviewing me and not Dawn, who'd come across as much more matter of fact. Still, he must've been in charge for a reason. I tried to hide my smirk as I nodded back. "*Cool.* So who's Bill?"

Larry blinked. "Oh. Right. I should probably introduce him. Bill. Say hello to the young lady."

Larry turned toward the wall and snapped, and that's when I saw it. In a jar on a side table by the wall was what appeared to be a *severed human head.*

"*Oh my GOD.*" I jumped in my seat. Who the *hell* had put that there? I would've sworn to the police, God, or anyone who cared to listen that the thing hadn't been there a moment ago.

Larry mistook my surprise for something else. "Don't worry. Bill's harmless—at least while he's in his jar. He must be sleeping. Bill? *Bill!*" Larry clapped his hands a few times.

The head's eyes fluttered and snapped open. This time I jumped *out* of my seat. I might've screamed a little, too.

The head stretched his jaw, looked around, and focused his eyes on me. "*Hello.* What's your name, toots?"

The fear and horror faded quickly, replaced instead with embarrassment and anger. "Okay. *Ha Ha.* Very funny, *assholes.* Do you prank everyone who comes to interview this way?" I looked under the end table. It was only a half foot thick, and there was nothing below it. "How are you doing that, anyway? Is he in the wall? Seriously, who the hell does this? I thought this was a job interview, not *Candid Camera.*"

Larry and Bill looked at each other. Bill spoke first. "What's her problem?"

Larry spoke in a low voice, like he thought I wouldn't be able to hear him. "I don't know. She's been jumpy since she got here." Then louder. "Dawn, you put in the ad that we were a *supernatural* consulting business, didn't you?"

Dawn shrugged, and Larry sighed.

"Supernatural?" I said. "So you consult on, what? Ghost hunting?"

"We've done that before," said Larry. "Not terribly fun if I'm being honest. The spirit realm can be spooky. But yes. We do that, as well as perform a variety of services related to the paranormal, supernatural, occult, and other assorted dark and mystical arts."

"And that's somehow supposed to explain *that?"* I pointed at Bill. He clacked his teeth at me and made his eyebrows dance, like a douchebag at a club might.

"Well, sure," said Larry. "He's a disembodied zombie head, and I'm a wizard."

"A *wizard."* I said it slowly. "Which explains the exploding computers and hundreds of middle names, I'm sure."

"Naturally." Larry said it without sarcasm.

"And Dawn? She's what? A succubus?"

"Don't be silly," said Larry. "She's nothing more than a blindingly-hot nymphomaniac who spent her entire youth training in the Philippine martial art of *Kali,* where she learned the skills necessary to slice and dice vampires and demons into tartare."

"And Tank?"

"Tank's a, uh..." Larry cleared his throat. "Well, we'll get to him later. Suffice to say, he earns his keep."

Tank shot me a thumbs up from over the back of the couch. I glanced from him to the goth bombshell next to him, past them to Heidi Klum and Tim Gunn on the TV, then back to the lunatic in the beat-to-hell leather duster and the creepy head in a jar that kept starting at me like he wanted to get my number.

My head swam. "I'm going to have a seat, if that's okay."

"By all means," said Larry.

I took a few deep breaths to slow my heart. "So let me get this straight. A wizard. A martial artist sword chick whose last name happens to be Blayde. A bodybuilder who does... *something*. And this thing."

"The name's Bill," said the zombie head when I pointed at him. "And you still haven't introduced yourself."

"Uh... Lexie." I couldn't believe I was talking to a zombie head in a jar.

"I think I understand your confusion," said Larry. "You're trying to figure out what Bill brings to the table."

"Right. Let's go with that."

"You want to take this one, Bill?"

The head shot me a yellow-toothed smile. "I can bite people and turn them into zombies."

"From your jar?"

"Hey, sometimes people try to pet me. I can also be thrown at enemies."

Larry scratched his head. "That's not really where I thought he was going. And don't worry about the biting. He only does that to people he dislikes, and I can tell he's taken a shine to you. No, we keep Bill because he's our navigator."

"And friend?" said Bill. "You forgot *friend*."

"A navigator?" I said.

Larry nodded. "Yeah. Believe it or not, Bill's about three hundred years old. In life, he sailed the Caribbean from Barbados to Cuba. He's great at telling us how to get places."

"So he's like that head from *The Secret of Monkey Island*."

Larry blinked. "The what now?"

"Never mind."

The phone rang—not my phone, but the one on the corner of Stuttgart's desk, a black unit with grey buttons that looked as if it came straight out of a late nineties call center. I hadn't noticed it until now, just as I hadn't noticed the presence of Bill until Larry pointed him out, a fact which still freaked me out.

"Well?" Larry stared at me. "Aren't you going to answer it?"

4

THE PHONE CONTINUED TO RING. "I THOUGHT YOU SAID this *wasn't* a secretarial position."

"Just answer the phone," said Larry. "I'd do it myself but—"

"You can't because it'll violently explode into small pieces. Yeah, I got it." I pulled the receiver off the hook and held it to my ear. "Uh... You've reached the Nyte Patrol."

The voice that spoke had a thick accent to it, probably Russian but maybe some other eastern European variant. "Hello? Who's this?"

"I'm Lexie. I'm the, ah... junior partner. Or I will be. Maybe. Nothing's decided yet."

Larry hissed at me. "Put it on speakerphone."

"Which button?" I asked.

"The round one, on the side," said Larry.

"What you mean, which button?" said the mystery voice.

"Not you. Hold on."

I found the button and returned the receiver to its home as the man's voice sprouted from the base. "Miss Lexie? I have urgent need to speak with Mr. Stuttgart. Can you find him for me?"

"I'm right here, Mr. Romanov." Larry did that soft talking thing to me this time, even though I'm sure the man on the phone could hear him, too. "Ivan Romanov. He's a regular client of ours." Then louder again. "Good to hear from you. Still enjoying that amulet we obtained for you?"

"Yes, Mr. Stuttgart, no complaints I have," said Romanov. "Very pleased am I with results of expeditions on my behalf."

"Glad to hear it," said Larry. "So, what can we do for you this time? Something different, perhaps? An exorcism? Brewing a love potion? Do you need us to dispatch a group of trespassing gnomes?"

"No, Mr. Stuttgart, nothing of that nature," said Romanov. "I require of you to procure one more item for collection."

Larry, in that soft voice. "This guy's a total hoarder. We've located all kinds of crap for him." Then louder again. "And what are you looking for this time, Mr. Romanov?"

"A tome of extreme rarity, Mr. Stuttgart. One by name of *Librum de Virtute.*"

Larry steepled his fingers. "Ooh. *Latin.* Books in Latin are always more tempting and mysterious than those written in other languages, with the possible exception of those written in Celtic tongues. I stay away from those. Or at least I have since the time I read a tome in Welsh, accidentally coughed, and nearly summoned a Cyhyraeth."

Romanov put words to my own thoughts. "A what?"

"A death spirit, of sorts. Nasty creatures, nothing but bones and tattered robes with a howl that would make the bravest mastiff hide under a bush and piss itself. Whoops. Hold on a moment, Ivan. I've got another call coming. Can you hold?"

A light on the receiver had started to blink red. Larry gestured at the button underneath it. "Well. Go on."

Not a secretary position, my ass, I thought. Romanov protested, but I cut him off in mid-squawk with a punch of the button.

"Larry Stuttgart, Nyte Patrol, speaking," said Larry. "How can I help you?"

The guy who answered sounded like a used car salesman. "Hey, Larry. It's, ah... Barry Mealer."

Larry's jaw tightened. *"Barry.* You've got a lot of nerve calling..."

"Listen, Larry. I'm really sorry about last time. For the tenth time, I swear to God I didn't know about the leper colony inside that cave. And I'm going to get you your money, I promise. I'm working on it right now. Had almost all of it saved before my car broke down and needed repairs."

With a buildup like that, I figured Larry would give me the quiet-voiced CliffsNotes version, but he just ground his teeth instead. "What do you want, Barry?"

"I've got a tip for you. Something hot off the presses. And I'm not trying to trade it for what I owe you, hear? Think of it as a down payment to cover whatever interest has built up on my tab from the last job."

"Spit it out, Barry."

Barry's voice relaxed ever so slightly. "Alright, so listen to this. Ever heard of a biker gang by the name of *Los Desalmados?"*

Barry mangled the Spanish. I got the impression his bilingual skills extended about as far as the end of the Taco Cabana menu.

"Never heard of them," said Larry. "Should I have?"

"Maybe," said Barry. "They're some bad mothers. Word is they're responsible for half the heroin that makes it over the border."

"What do you think I am, Barry, DEA? What's the bit that makes me care?"

"I'm getting to it. What I heard is they hired a *bruja*, a really nasty one, and now they're expanding their illicit drug trade into fae drugs."

Barry mutilated the Spanish word for witch, too. It didn't seem to bother Larry. "I don't see how this *hot tip* helps me in any way, Barry. Look I've got an actual client on the phone, so—"

"Hey, wait, man. What about your friend, Connors? The cop? You could trade it to him. You can never have too many get out of jail free cards, right?"

A buzzer sounded, not from the phone. Larry pointed to a scorched speaker box on the wall in as good a shape as the one outside. "Can you get that? But switch me over to Romanov first. Bye, Barry."

"Larry, listen—"

I punched the call waiting button and moved to the intercom. Dawn and Tank were still glued to the TV. No wonder Larry needed hired help.

I depressed the button, hoping the thing hadn't broken after the last use. "Who is it?"

A soft, tentative voice spoke. "Ah, yes. I'm looking for the Nyte Patrol?"

I glanced at Larry. He waved at me idly, listening to Romanov prattle on about the ancient Latin tome.

I shook my head as I walked to the back of the house, struggling to understand how I'd already started taking orders from a guy who was friends with a talking head in a jar. Maybe upon opening the door I'd finally find the camera crew headed by a preppy co-ed who'd toss confetti in my face and tell me I'd been punk'd. It would really make my day.

I had no such luck. I threw open the door to find a young guy standing there. His weight rested on his right leg while his left foot tapped nervously at the concrete. He held his arms in front of him, hands grabbing the elbows of the opposite arm.

"Can I help you?" I said.

He looked at me and blinked a few times. "Yeah, uh... Are you Dawn?"

The guy was cute, if you could overlook his too-hairy arms and beard scruff. He was tall, with great hair and some obvious muscle tone underneath his Skeletor T-shirt. The shirt I didn't mind, but his thick-rimmed, taped-together glasses might've been too nerdy even for me.

"No. I'm Lexie. I'm not with the Nyte Patrol. At least, not yet. I answered an online ad. To be honest, I just got here, and I don't really know what I'm doing."

The cute guy's brow furrowed, but he nodded anyway. "Oh. Okay. Is Larry around?"

"He's on the phone. You want to come in and talk to him?"

The fingers gripping the guy's forearm twitched. "No. It's fine. I don't want to disturb him if he's busy."

"It's no big deal. He's just gabbing with some Russian dude about pilfering an old book."

The guy stepped off the stoop. "No, really. I... don't want to interfere. With you here, and... you know. It's fine. I'll come back some other time."

The young man was having a hard time making eye contact. "Suit yourself. Want me to leave a message?"

He'd retreated to the discarded lawn furniture. "Uh... sure. Tell them Anthony stopped by. Well, you can call me Tony. Not that they'd know me by that name. Or the other. I don't know any of the Nyte Patrol, to be honest. I'm just... looking for some help." He stuck up a hand in goodbye and darted for the driveway.

I closed the door. After mulling it over for a second, I decided my conversation with Tony had been the *least* weird one I'd engaged in since arriving.

I returned to the living room to find Larry jabbing the phone receiver with a pointy stick. The dial tone sounded as Bill gave him pointers. "A little to the left. *A little more.* That's it."

I stormed up and pressed the end call button. "Seriously? Are you kidding me? Stop it with the exploding electronics shtick."

"Easy for you to say," said Larry. "You're not the one who's picked bits of plastic out of his teeth after hanging up on a customer."

I glanced at Dawn and Tank, who still hadn't moved. "Why didn't you get one of them to help?"

Larry gave me the fisheye. "If there's one thing I've learned in this business, it's to never think you're out of the woods until you see the bad guy dissolve into a pile of denatured proteins before your very eyes. But if there are two things I've learned, it's *that* and not to interrupt Tank in the middle of a *Project Runway* marathon. Besides, I can't turn the TV off."

"At least not in a way that it could be turned back on." Bill laughed, the sound like a dying donkey. His jaw looked like it might fall off. If I wasn't so damn confused, I might've remembered I still should've been horrified.

"So," said Larry. "You in or out?"

"In or out of what?" I said.

"The team, girl. I took Romanov's offer. As soon as I can pry Tank away from the tube, we're headed out in search of the mysterious, powerful book he refused to tell me much about."

"Refused to tell you? And you didn't ask... Never mind." I was having a hard time wrapping my head around the fact that Larry seemed to be missing several key character traits that would be required for someone who was in charge of *whatever* the Nyte Patrol was, but it didn't seem like the right time to challenge him on it.

"Well?" Larry looked at me eagerly. Bill looked at me with what I could only describe as lust or hunger—maybe both. Dawn and Tank didn't even turn my direction.

I took a deep breath. "Look, Larry. You seem... *interesting* enough, I guess. But I don't know about all this. I mean, Bill alone is still freaking me out."

Larry looked at the head. *"Stop dressing her down with your eyes, you lecher.* I'm sorry about him, Lexie. He means well."

Bill grunted. "I don't, actually..."

"It's not his personality that bothers me," I said.

"What then? Is it something about the job? I've been totally honest with you about me, the team, the requirements."

"That's what I'm afraid of." Although even if I granted him his honesty, I got the feeling there was something he *wasn't* telling me.

I should've left then and there, but I didn't. I'm not sure why. It might've been morbid curiosity. That or desperation.

"Why don't you give it a try?" said Larry. "Just for the night. I'll pay you a hundred dollars, cash up front."

I snorted. My dad didn't raise a mark. "Make it two-fifty and you've got a deal."

Larry slapped his desk. "You drive a hard bargain. Dawn? Tank? Turn that off. We've got ourselves a driver."

5

It took us five minutes to pry Tank away from the TV, by which I mean it took that long for the *Project Runway* episode to finish, during which we sat and listened to Bill complain about how he never got to come along with everyone else. Larry claimed he was too much of a hassle to drag around and too big of a distraction to random bystanders, which Bill forcefully disputed. All in all, it was a very believable performance for someone whose body was secretly hidden in a wall, though the more I looked at him the more it seemed he really *was* a free-floating head in a jar. Whoever was doing the special effects and makeup for his performance deserved an Oscar.

When the credits rolled, Tank stood and turned the knob to the TV off. It was the first time I got a good look at him, and if anything, I'd underestimated him. He was *huge*. Defensive end sized. Dawn said she and Tank needed to grab supplies, so Larry waved me toward the door, saying we'd wait in the car.

Larry hopped through the passenger side door as I settled into the driver's seat. I stared at him as I fingered the three large bills in my pocket, hoping we wouldn't come across any of my softball teammates on the night's ride-along. I didn't need rumors of me transporting hobos in my Suburban added to the already explosive gossip I'd created at the last practice.

God, what the hell was wrong with me? Part of me had known it was coming, so why had I lashed out? And why had I run away afterwards?

Larry wised up to my dead stare. "What?"

I blinked away thoughts of softball. "Nothing. How is it neither you, Dawn, nor Tank have a car? How do you run a business without anyone knowing how to drive?"

"Oh, Dawn and I know *how* to," said Larry. "Tank doesn't, but he's a special case. Obviously, I can't drive because of my proclivities with machinery, and Dawn refuses to because she grew up in Manila and has permanent PTSD regarding traffic."

"I thought it was only electronics that blew up when you touched them."

"Mechanical systems don't fare much better. It makes life a bitch, trust me."

"So how did you get around until now? Don't tell me you've been riding magic carpets around town."

Larry snorted. "Please. We had another driver, but there was an extenuating circumstance during our last mission that required me to take the wheel. Given that we don't offer commercial drivers insurance, he ended up leaving in a huff."

"So you're saying I should never let you drive my truck."

"You'd be better off having Tank take the wheel, and that's saying something."

One of the back doors opened. Tank hopped in and tossed a duffel bag into the back of the 'burban. The whole thing shook as the bag landed with a clatter.

"What the hell's in that?" I asked.

Tank replied without an ounce of emotion on his face. "Weapons."

"Weapons. Of course," I said. "Because we'll need them to track down a *book*."

"Don't dismiss the value of arms," said Larry. "You brought a can of mace with you, after all."

My brow furrowed. "How'd you know about that?"

He talked right over me. "Personally, I never leave home without this baby." He reached into his duster and pulled out a pistol—but not a modern one. Rather a wooden-handled flint-lock wrapped in brass that, as Indiana Jones would say, belonged in a museum.

"What are you going to do with that, Captain Jack?" I said. "Club somebody over the head if they besmirch your good name?"

"Laugh all you want," said Larry, "but this is the only gun that's never failed me in combat. Or at least it doesn't fail me any more than it fails anyone else. Now if only I could get the reload time below seventeen seconds..."

The other back door opened and Dawn climbed in. She tossed a couple large knives onto the bench seats and placed a pair of sheathed blades next to them as she sat. "Alright. Let's go."

I glanced in the rear view mirror. "Is that a *katana?*"

"It is," said Dawn. "But you won't get any credit for recognizing it unless you also know what the smaller one is."

"A *wakizashi.* Come on. I read manga. Seriously though, is everyone here packing? And didn't Larry say you'd practiced *Philippine* martial arts?"

"Kali is a martial style that teaches the use of all weapons," said Dawn. "Japanese blades happen to be better made than those of the Philippines. Are you saying you're *not* armed?"

"I mean... I have my mace."

"We're going to have to do something about that if you decide to stick around," said Larry. "No time to worry about it now, though. Let's roll."

I turned the key and the engine roared to life. "Might be useful for me to know where we're going."

"Not far. Head over to Guadalupe to cruise the Drag. I'll keep my eyes peeled for an informant who hangs out there. He's something of an expert on hard to find items. He might be able to point us in the general direction of Romanov's book."

"The only people who hang out on the Drag are bums."

"The politically correct term is panhandler, but they can be great informants," said Larry. "Now hit the gas, Tentative Tammy."

I grumbled under my breath as I executed a flawless five point turn and headed back toward campus. Technically, the Drag only extends from the north edge of the University of Texas to the southern edge, barely more than half a mile, but I gave Larry the benefit of the doubt, took Rio Grande up to West 29th, and started there. I took my time, not that traffic gave me much of a choice, while Larry leaned halfway out the window scanning the sidewalks. We'd passed the Dobie Mall and were headed toward Martin Luther King Boulevard when Larry pointed.

"There he is. In the Taco Bell parking lot. Pull in."

I hated parking my Suburban anywhere near campus, wishing my parents had passed me down a nice mid-90's Honda Civic or Toyota Corolla instead, but beggars can't be choosers. Speaking of beggars, Larry instructed me to pull into a spot directly in front of a guy who was about three and a half feet tall, wearing a battered green jacket that looked as if it had been stolen from one of those drop boxes for homeless veterans. Hell, maybe he *was* a homeless veteran. Did the US Army accept little people?

I killed the engine as Larry hopped out the side door. "Darragh! How've you been, my friend?"

I followed Larry out of the truck, but Dawn and Tank didn't bother. *"Darragh?"*

"It's Irish," said Larry. "Means 'oak,' I think. How are you doing pal? *Buddy?"*

Darragh sat there, a beard that could've hidden a raccoon's nest stretching down his chest and an empty bottle of Boone's Farm in his hand. He smelled like a fraternity after an all-night beer pong tournament. He was also snoring.

Larry prodded him with a foot. "Darragh!"

The little guy woke with a start, screaming obscenities and lashing out with his bottle. It took him a second before his eyes focused on my new employer. "Harry?"

"Larry, but close enough. How've you been? Still beating the ladies off with a shillelagh?"

Darragh shaded his eyes despite the fact that the sun had long since fallen behind the rooftops. His voice slurred as he spoke, his Irish accent thick. "Whaddya want?"

"Straight to business, huh?" said Larry. "I can respect that. We're looking for something. A book. An old one, by the name of the *Librum de Virtute*. It's Latin."

"I know dat," snarled Darragh. "Don't petron... patron... *patronize* me."

"Sorry. Didn't mean it that way. Ever heard of it?"

"'Course I haven't." Darragh peered at his bottle, upturning it to make sure it was empty. "But I know who might've."

"I'm listening."

"Nice try. What do you tink I am, a gabhdán? Ya know mah price."

"Two fifths of Jameson's. I remember."

"And a bottle of Bushmills ten year single malt, ya gombeen. No exceptions."

"Jesus, Darragh. What do you think I am, made of money?"

I wasn't exactly the world's foremost expert on informants, but I'd coached enough fellow teammates to get a general feel for how to convince people to come around to my way of thinking. It seemed to me Larry was going about it all wrong. His conversation with Darragh had barely started, and he'd already given up the power position. "Larry, can I talk to you for a second?"

"What is it?"

He came over to me and I dropped my voice. "Look, far be it from me to tell you how to do your job—whatever it may be—but seems to me plying this sixty-five pound homeless leprechaun with enough alcohol to kill a Russian arm wrestler isn't exactly the best way to get credible information out of him."

Larry's brow furrowed. "How did you know Darragh was a leprechaun?"

I blinked and shook my head. *What?* I meant it as a pejorative, because he's tiny and Irish and drunk. You're not suggesting he's actually...?"

Larry planted his hands on his hips. "Yeah. He is. And like all leprechauns, he's an expert at finding items that are otherwise well hidden. Ever found a pot of gold at the end of a rainbow?"

"Of course I haven't. Rainbows don't have—"

"Shut up. They do have ends, but leprechauns are the only ones talented enough to find them. That's why they hide their gold there. And drunk or not, Darragh is our best bet for getting a bead on that book, so don't blow it for me by insulting his sobriety. Speaking of which, are you twenty-one?"

"Six months shy," I said. "Why? Are you going to tell me you're incapable of buying booze, too? What happens? Your driver's license turns into a flying monkey any time you take it out of your wallet?"

"Cut the sarcasm, Grasshopper. Obviously, I don't have a driver's license because *I don't drive*. Neither do Dawn or Tank, and I doubt Dawn brought her passport." Larry sighed. "Okay. New plan. Darragh might drive a hard bargain, but that guy would drink used motor oil if it could give him a buzz."

"Are ya gabbin' about me, mister?" said the leprechaun.

"Nothing, Darragh, be there in a sec." Larry dropped his voice. "As I was saying, it doesn't have to be whiskey. So why don't you mosey into that Taco Bell, get me a soft taco and a large Mountain Dew Baja Breeze, no ice, and I'll do the rest."

"I fail to see what your dinner order has to do with Darragh's demands. And you didn't hire me to be your delivery boy."

"Not delivery boy. *Junior partner*—if you can ever stop hassling me and get to work. Snap to it, girl."

I sighed and walked into the Taco Bell. Ten minutes later, I emerged with Larry's order. I shoved the items at him, interrupting his small talk with Darragh. "You owe me three dollars and forty-four cents. And no, I'm not paying for it out of my salary."

"Relax. I'm good for it." Larry unwrapped the taco, ripped the edge off, and held the rest out to the supposed leprechaun. "Want a bite, Darragh?"

The bum snatched the taco out of Larry's hand with viper-like speed. He crammed it into his mouth, speaking through mouthfuls of ground beef and shredded cheese. "Don't tink I'm givin' ya anyting fer dis, boyo. Ya offered, and I accepted. Simple as dat."

"Oh, I wouldn't *dream* of altering our arrangement." Larry turned his back to Darragh and popped the bit of tortilla he'd appropriated into his mouth. As he chewed, he snapped the top off his Baja Breeze, then spat the chewed ball of dough into the drink.

I almost gagged. *"Ugh!* What are you doing?"

"Speeding up some natural processes, that's what."

Larry lifted the plastic cup with his left hand. He brought his right hand up to it, the fingers tense, arched into a makeshift claw. His face tightened, his eyes narrowed, and he bore into the cup with his gaze. I was about to tell him it was the worst David Blaine impression I'd ever seen when, as if by magic, the chewed up tortilla ball floating in the Mountain Dew disintegrated, bubbling as it disappeared into the neon green liquid.

"What the *hell?*" I said. "How did you do that?"

Larry took a deep breath, and his shoulders relaxed. "Haven't you been paying *any* attention? I'm a wizard. I told you. Several times."

"Yeah, but..." The fact that he kept repeating the same line made me think perhaps it *wasn't* a joke. "So what did you do?"

"See for yourself. Have a taste." He offered me the cup.

"Gross. No way. I don't want your taco spit in my mouth."

"It's perfectly safe. The fermentation process kills harmful germs. Alcohol's a disinfectant, you know. But suit yourself. More to barter." Larry turned to the hobo. "Look, Darragh. I've got some bad news. The Jameson and Bushmills isn't going to happen."

The leprechaun scowled and smashed his empty bottle of Boone's Farm on the concrete. "What? Ya feckin' gobshite. How dare ya?"

"But," continued Larry, "if you play your cards right and tell us what you know about that book, you can still earn yourself the finest malt liquor that Mountain Dew and an accelerated fermentation process can provide. What do you say?"

"What da hell are ya talkin' about, ya bleedin' tick?"

"Go on. Give it a try." Larry held out the cup.

Darragh looked at him as if he'd lost his mind, but he took the drink and sucked on the straw regardless. His eyes bulged as the green liquid hit his tongue, and he pulled back from the straw, coughing and sputtering.

"Jesus, Mary, and Joseph, dat's a strong brew! What in bloody hell did ya do to dis ting?"

Larry smiled. "I guess we have a deal, then. A name, please."

"Fine, fine," said Darragh. "But next time I want da Bushmills. Da person yer lookin' fer is a bloke by da name of Adric Wallow. He's a librarian over at da Perry-Castañeda Library."

"Wait a sec," I said. "We're looking for a mystical book of power, and the *hot tip* you have for us is to *ask a librarian?*"

"Oh, sod off, ya rugby hugger. He ain't no mere librarian. He's a *bibliomancer.*"

Larry oohed and nodded.

I glanced from Larry to Darragh and back, and I felt myself frown. If Larry and his friends were pranking me, they'd done an incredibly thorough job of it. Not only had Darragh gone along with Larry's fermented Mountain Dew bit, but they'd invented a brand new language to go along with the schtick. What exactly had I stumbled into? Some sort of fantasy role playing thing? "So I've got to ask... what the hell is a bibliomancer?"

Larry nodded toward the 'burban. "Someone who might be able to help us find that book, that's who."

6

THE PERRY-CASTAÑEDA LIBRARY STANDS AT ROUGHLY THE southern edge of the University of Texas campus, just to the west of the Jester dormitories. Otherwise known as the main library, PCL is both the university's flagship research institution and one of the single ugliest buildings I've ever seen. Five stories tall and made of countless tons of flat grey concrete, I guessed the architect who'd designed it had been paid off by the Texas Cement Producers Association. It doesn't even have windows, except for one weird angled part that juts to the north toward East 21st Street.

I'd managed to find parking in a pay lot across the street, which I'd only taken because Larry assured me he'd reimburse me. This time, Dawn and Tank joined us, the latter with his enormous duffel bag slung over his shoulder, clanking and rattling with each of his steps. Despite giving her my best look of disbelief, Dawn had also strapped up, using one of those long Japanese sashes to tie her katana and wakizashi around her waist.

To say I was self-conscious as we walked through the PCL

entrance would've been a ludicrous understatement. I couldn't decide if I was more mortified by the idea of being seen by a classmate in the presence of the three weirdos or more terrified of being set upon by a SWAT team with rifles drawn and being screamed at to get on the ground. Amazingly enough, no one stopped us as we walked in, despite the fact that several students stared at Dawn with mouths open as we passed them. Maybe they thought she was a cosplayer.

We stopped at the checkout desk. Larry tapped on the counter to get one of the librarian's attention. "Excuse me? Ma'am? We're looking for someone who works here. Adric Wallow. Know where we can find him?"

The elderly woman looked up and to her credit didn't even flinch. She turned her eyes back to her computer as she spoke. "Sixth floor. Probably near the engineering collection."

We headed to the elevators and punched the up button. Larry, Dawn, and Tank stood there waiting, Larry with his arms crossed, Dawn calm and cool with a bit of a slouch in her posture, and Tank looking as if he were ready to jump out of an attack helicopter in 'Nam. I stared at them.

Dawn noticed. "Something on your mind?"

"Yeah. How the hell is it nobody seems to notice how bizarre we all look? I mean, how *you* look. I blend right in."

Dawn shrugged. "People see what they want to see. That means they also ignore what they want to ignore."

"Like the fact that you have two swords from feudal Japan strapped to your hips?"

Dawn smiled, and even though I'd never batted for the other team, I still felt myself get a little weak in the knees. "If you shake your hips right, no one notices what's strapped to them."

The elevator dinged and we piled inside. "So, that's it?" I

said as the doors closed. "Am I really supposed to buy that explanation?"

"Would you believe I've cast a spell over everyone that makes us invisible to the naked eye?" said Larry.

"Given that I can see you? No."

"What about a spell that makes people immediately forget us after they've seen us?"

"Hard pass."

"Well, there you go," said Larry. "Hiding in plain sight it is."

The elevator dinged again, and we stepped out onto the sixth floor. Seeing as I was majoring in mechanical engineering, I knew where the engineering collection was, so I led the way toward the help desk. There, organizing books on a movable cart, stood a man who was a dead ringer for Ben Stiller's cameo in *Tenacious D and the Pick of Destiny*—complete with frizzy hair, black-rimmed glasses, ludicrous amounts of jewelry, and a faded Led Zeppelin t-shirt.

"Let me guess," I said as we approached. "Adric Wallow?"

He looked up. "Can I help you?"

Larry gave me the fisheye again. "First you out the leprechaun, now this? Do you have hidden supernatural skills you failed to report on your resume?"

"I didn't give you a resume."

"Touché." Larry stuck out his hand. "Adric? The name's Larry Stuttgart. We're with the Nyte Patrol."

Adric tilted his head. "I'm sorry?"

"Don't ask," I said. "They're a motley group of supposed spell casters and supernatural badasses for hire."

"*They?*" said Adric. "You're not with them?"

"She's trying to pretend she's too cool for us." Larry glanced my way. "Yeah. I see you over there. Anyway, we're here because a mutual acquaintance told us you might be able to help source a rather hard to find book. The *Librum de Virtute*. Ever heard of it?"

"Have I *heard* of it?" Adric's face hardened. "We're talking about the same *Librum de Virtute,* aren't we? The book that allowed Julius Caesar to consolidate Rome's power in his hand and ultimately led to his death upon its discovery by Gaius Cassius Longinus? The book that unleashed the black plague in the fourteenth century? The book that vanished mysteriously from the deck of a Spanish galleon off the coast of Barbuda some four hundred years ago? *That Librum de Virtute?*"

Larry stared at the man. "Uh..."

Adric erupted in laughter. "Hah! I'm just yanking your chain. I've never heard of it. Come on, we'll check the computer catalog."

We headed with him toward a desk with a couple computer stations on it, but both were occupied, so Adric instructed us to follow us to his office instead. Of course, his 'office' turned out to be a janitor's closet that had been cleaned out and furnished with a cot, a hot plate, a bunch of canned food and granola bars, stacks of fruit crates filled with paperback books, and a tiny desk with a severely outdated library computer on it—a first generation iMac with orange plastic casing, if I wasn't mistaken.

"You *live* here?" I said.

"Librarian's salaries aren't what they used to be. Don't tell anyone. I'm trying to keep it on the down low." Adric sat at the desk and started typing. "Alright, let's see. *Librum de Virtute*. Well, it doesn't seem to be in the library's main stacks. Let me try the larger University system. Hmm... It's not showing up there, either. It does sound familiar, though. *Librum de Virtute*... Like I've heard about it recently."

"What about those? The restricted sections?" Larry pointed at the screen to one of the side bars on the library catalog. As he did so, his finger barely scraped across the monitor. The screen flickered and dimmed. I heard a crackle and a hiss followed by a pop. Despite myself, I jumped back and brought my hands up to shield my face, but the thing didn't explode. It just fizzled and died, though a puff of black smoke escaped from an air vent in the top of the monitor.

Larry hung his head. "Aww, damnit."

"What the hell happened?" said Adric. "What did you do to my computer?"

Larry sighed. "I'm a wizard."

"Oh. Right."

I couldn't help myself. *"Oh, right?* Like that's a normal explanation for why your computer died? What the hell is going on? I feel like I'm taking crazy pills."

Adric gave Larry a nod. "I thought she was with you."

"She's new. Give her a chance."

Out of nowhere, the computer burst into flames. Adric shot back in his chair, rolling the whole three feet to the other side of the closet. From somewhere, Dawn procured a fire extinguisher and doused the flaming computer with compressed CO_2. I coughed and waved away the spray. As it cleared, it revealed the warped, charred remains of the iMac, now looking like some demented Halloween decoration.

"Well, that's bad," said Adric.

"I am *so* sorry," said Larry. "I should've stayed in the hall."

"At least it was your personal computer and not one of the library ones," said Dawn as she set the extinguisher on the floor.

"About that," said Adric. "I actually stole this from one of the group study rooms. Somebody's probably wondering where it went..."

Larry winced. "Again, my *sincerest* apologies."

"There's always eBay," I offered.

"No need," said Adric. "I can probably fix it."

I looked at the computer. The melted plastic and glass had barely stopped smoking.

"Well, not *fix it* per se. But replace. What was your name?" Adric pointed at me.

"Lexie."

"Right. Could you head to the third floor, section R? The periodicals. You'll be looking for an old *Macworld* magazine, circa nineteen ninety-nine or so. Find it and bring it back up."

"Uh... I guess. Why?"

Adric looked at my companions. "You guys know I'm a bibliomancer, right?"

"We know," said Larry. "As I said, she's new."

"I don't even know what to say right now." I threw up my hands in frustration and left, heading down the stairs to the third floor. I followed the signs on the aisle end caps, searching for section R, when out of the corner of my eye, I caught a glimpse of a couple familiar looking burnt orange jackets. They could've belonged to any number of UT scholarship athletes. Baseball. Swimming. Basketball. But they didn't. They belonged to softball, and not any two softball players. None other than Carrie Fletcher and Janie Nguyen.

I cursed my luck and dove into the nearest aisle, hoping they hadn't seen me. It was probably because I was too busy looking over my shoulder that I didn't realize I wasn't the only one there. I slammed into someone, tackling them to the floor with a mutual grunt.

"Oh my gosh, I'm so sorry," I said as I picked myself up off the carpet. "I—*Tony?* What are you doing here?"

The cute, nerdy, overly hairy guy I'd met outside Larry, Dawn, and Tank's place sat up, adjusting his taped-together glasses. "I go to school here same as you. I'm an EECS major."

I glanced over my shoulder to make sure Janie wasn't on her way over. "You're in electrical engineering? No way. I'm mechanical."

"Go figure." Tony stood. "Don't tell me you're in my History of Computing class and I've never noticed."

"Nah. I'm just looking for an old *Macworld* magazine. Like from the turn of the century."

He nodded, although that didn't explain anything. "That's cool, I guess. I like vintage computers, too."

I glanced over my shoulder again, sure that the noise would've attracted Carrie and Janie.

"Is everything okay?" asked Tony. "Is someone following you?"

I looked back at him. "No. It's nothing. I saw someone I didn't want to confront right now."

Tony smiled halfheartedly and lifted an eyebrow. "An ex-boyfriend?"

"Huh? No. Girls from my softball team. I did something dangerous at the last practice that I'm angry and embarrassed about, and my coach is *majorly* pissed. Like, I'm not sure if I'll even be able to keep my spot on the team. Whatever. I don't want to talk about it, okay?"

"No, no. I get it." Tony averted his eyes, and he started to adopt that bird-like stance he'd held outside the door to the Nyte Patrol house. He tilted his head and pointed at the stacks. "Hey. Check it out. *Macworld,* January two thousand."

I followed his finger and grabbed the magazine off the shelf. The cover read '2000, Fun! Fun! Fun!,' where the o's in the date had been replaced with vintage iMacs. "Close enough. Thanks, Tony. I'll be sure to tell Larry about you."

"You haven't yet?"

I grimaced. "Slipped my mind. See you round. Maybe."

I took off before he could shuffle his feet and smile at me awkwardly some more. Checking the hallway for signs of the softball girls and seeing that the coast was clear, I headed back up the stairs. When I returned to Adric's makeshift office, I found the desk to be totally clear. The mangled remains of the computer wouldn't have fit in a wastebasket, so I assumed Tank had carried them out.

"Hey." I flashed the magazine. "Not sure why the library bothered keeping these, but I found one."

Adric took it and glanced at the cover. "Not orange, but good enough. Thanks."

"No problem," I said. "But if you don't mind my asking, what are you planning on *DOOOING?!?!*"

My voice grew into an uncontrollable shriek as Adric flipped open the magazine, pulled his arm back, and plunged it into the pages. Not through them. *Into* them. The magazine stretched and expanded as radiant blue light shot out from the glossy pages. Adric plunged his second arm after the first. He leaned over, grunted, and straightened, pulling a vintage iMac with a purple plastic case from the glowing portal. The magazine fell to the floor, shrinking back to normal size, and the eerie blue glow winked out of existence as Adric set the computer on his desk.

"There we go," he said. "Good enough. I doubt anyone will

question the color, even at an orange obsessed college like this one."

My tongue and lips worked when I moved them, but the proper words refused to come out. "I... but... I mean... *what?*"

"Sorry, Lexie, but this one's on you," said Larry. "I mentioned he was a bibliomancer more than once. Although on second thought, you did ask what they do. Maybe that's my fault. I guess I thought everyone knew. You see, a bibliomancer..."

I think he started to explain it to me, but I barely heard him. My mind was running a mile a minute. Adric had literally pulled an eighteen-year old computer from the faded pages of a trade magazine. *With magic!* Which implied everything crazy ass Larry had told me was actually true. The wizard thing, Bill being a severed zombie head, Darragh the leprechaun, Larry's ten-second distillation process. All of it. And while part of me wanted to run into the hallway screaming, to call 911, call the FBI, call *somebody*—an even larger part of me was... *intrigued*.

I mean, I'd always been technologically inclined. It was why I'd chosen engineering as a major. Even as a young girl, I'd enjoyed running my own experiments, like what happens when you squish an ant with a rock, or how hot is fire? The burn scar I'd acquired from that one still reminded me of the answer, in case I ever forgot. So if all my senses indicated Adric had created something out of nothing, and I was sure I wasn't on any mind altering substances— I hadn't eaten or drunk anything that Larry gave me after all—then maybe magic was a logical explanation for it. But how did it work? What fueled it? How did you access it? What were its limitations?

My curiosity didn't stop my heart from racing or my finger-tips from tingling, however. "Okay. Alright. Sure. Fine. *Magic*."

I don't think anyone paid me any mind. Adric had plugged the iMac back in, booted it, and the conversation had shifted back to the mysterious Latin book *du jour*.

"Let's see, where were we?" said Adric. "Your book wasn't in the library catalog, but I do remember hearing about it. Maybe if we do an internal document search. Give me a sec..." He tapped away at the keyboard. A string of search results popped up. He clicked them one at a time and scanned the results. "No. *Wait.* Here we go. I knew I'd heard of it. The *Librum de Virtute* was brought here ten years ago as part of a collection on loan from the *Biblioteca Nacional de España*. That's the Spanish national library for you non-bilingual folks."

"So it's here?" said Larry. "Or was it returned to Spain?"

Dawn crossed her fingers. "Trip to Spain. Trip to Spain. Please say trip to Spain."

"Just a moment," said Adric. "Uh... Nope. I think it's still here. Apparently, the University tried to send it back and the Spaniards didn't want it."

"Why?" asked Larry.

"Beats me."

"So where is it?"

"Well, the press release doesn't say, but it looks like the book was initially stored in... *the Harry Ransom Center.*"

The tingling in my extremities had started to fade. "The university archive down the street? Dang. That makes things easy."

Adric turned to me, his face frozen. "You don't get it. The Harry Ransom Center's underground archive is an impenetrable fortress. Dozens have tried to break into the subterranean vault over the decades. All have failed. Some have even lost their lives in the attempt."

I snorted. "You're kidding, right? Like you were with the Romans and the black plague and the Spanish galleon?"

Adric swept his glasses off. "I wish I were. I knew a man who tried to break in once. He was a good friend..." A tear formed in his eye. He wiped it away before returning his glasses to place. "The point is, you should turn back now. If the *Librum de Virtute* is housed at the HRC, for all intents and purposes, it's lost to the world. I'm terribly sorry, but your journey ends here."

7

We stood in the bushes outside the Harry Ransom Center, another of the university's artfully designed oversized concrete blocks. Well—*I* stood. Larry, Dawn, and Tank crouched, the latter comically so because the bushes couldn't come close to hiding him. They peered through the first floor windows, trying to catch glimpses of activity within, which were few and far between due to the late hour. The museum had frosted an exhibit onto the exterior windows—something to do with women's suffrage, at the moment—but as engaging as it was, it couldn't hold my attention forever.

"This is ridiculous," I said. "It's open to the public. We can walk in."

"And be caught off guard for what we find within?" said Larry. "Not on my watch. Preparation is the key to success. If this place is the fortress Adric says it is, we'll need every advantage we can get."

"It's not a fortress," I said. "It's a museum. Seriously. I've been inside. They have rotating exhibits with books and artwork and film memorabilia and an original printing of the Gutenberg bible that they never take down because it's the most interesting thing in the place. But that's it. A high-security garrison it isn't."

Dawn glanced my way. "Do you have any experience breaking into highly secure facilities?"

"Of course not. I'm a college student. A *law-abiding* college student."

"Then maybe your input isn't as valuable as you think." Dawn shook her head at Tank, who gave a sympathetic nod in return.

Her criticism came across as harsh, but fact of the matter was, I didn't know the first thing about robbing a museum. What I *did* know was that I shouldn't be a part of it. I needed a way to keep Larry from doing anything stupid that would incriminate me.

I checked my phone. "It's ten till. This place closes at the top of the hour. If we're going in, now's the time."

Larry huffed. "Fine, but we're performing reconnaissance, nothing else. I think I saw a guard or two. Speaking of which, it'll probably be best to leave the firepower outside."

Tank looked like Larry had insulted his mother. "No weapons?" That brought his vocabulary up to a grand total of two words.

"None. That goes for you, too, Dawn."

She snorted and shook her head. "Don't blame me if this goes sideways. Tank?" She gestured at the big guy's duffel bag, half hidden in the bushes.

He unzipped it as Dawn removed her swords. My eyes might've bugged out. Despite the fact that I'd started to believe Larry about the magic and the supernatural stuff, I hadn't really trusted Tank when he'd mentioned what was in the bag, but damn it if he hadn't been telling the truth, too. The thing was jam packed with firearms. I wouldn't have called myself a gun nut, but I played enough *Call of Duty* to have some idea of what was before me. On first glance I spotted a Browning Hi-Power Practical .40, a Glock 29 10mm Auto, a Mark XIX Desert Eagle .50 Action Express, a SIG Sauer 516 Tactical Patrol Rifle, a Heckler & Koch MP5 submachine gun, and a Mossberg 500 pump action shotgun. Dawn lay her swords in the duffel bag atop the guns, Larry tossed his flintlock in beside them, and Tank zipped the mess back up before shoving the bag deeper into the bushes.

Larry straightened, dusting a couple holly leaves off his shoulder. "Alright. Let's check the place out."

We walked into the museum. Larry and Dawn promptly shuffled off in opposite directions, leaving me and Tank at the front near a Frida Kahlo painting.

I nodded toward the big guy. "So, ah... what are we supposed to do?"

He shrugged.

"You mean you're not a trained art thief, either?"

He shook his head.

"You know, seeing as we're alone, you want to dish the dirt on Larry? What's with his magic? Like, is it for real? No joke? How does it work?"

Tank just stared at me.

"Not much of a talker are you?"

"Not until I get to know you." He frowned and showed me the broad side of his back. I wasn't sure how he intended to get to know me without speaking to me, but I took the gesture as an invitation to wander. Barely had I read half the inscription on another piece of Mexican folk art when someone came on the

PA. "The center will be closing in five minutes. Five minutes until closing."

Rather than feel irked that Larry hadn't followed my advice sooner, I felt relieved, mostly because I figured we couldn't get into enough trouble to be arrested in five short minutes. As I waited, I checked my phone to make sure I didn't have any messages from the girls on the team and tried to look like I was enjoying the art.

"Hey."

I jumped at the sound of Larry's voice in my ear. I spun to find him at my elbow. "Jesus, dude. Don't creep up on me like that."

"I wasn't creeping. You weren't paying attention. Anyway, I gave the place a once over, and on first impression, Adric is right. Security looks tight. Electronic locks on the doors. Security cameras everywhere. I think I might've even seen a pressure sensor under one of the exhibits. And unfortunately, I think the guards are onto me." He looked over his shoulder at a guy in a suit that almost certainly worked here. He wasn't looking in our direction.

Tank leveled a frown his way. "Want me to eliminate him?"

"*What?*" Larry sputtered. "We can't kill him. He hasn't done anything wrong."

"Not kill. I'd only torture him a little. For information on the underground lair."

I squinted at him. "I'm not sure if I should be more shocked that you're suggesting we torture an innocent man who's standing *right over there* or that you spoke several whole sentences in a row."

"Not *we* should torture. Me." Tank tapped his chest.

Larry patted the big guy on the shoulder. "*Kidding.* He's

kidding. He's a very gentle soul once you get to know him. But seriously, no torture, okay? We'll get in, but we'll do it the Nyte Patrol way, with magic and wits and when there are fewer security guards around."

Dawn's voice sounded behind me, close to my neck. "Yeah. Later at night, when the place is quiet."

I spun and stared at her. "How do you guys keep doing that? Sneaking up on me, I mean. Well, come to think of it, I sort of expected it out of you, but not Larry."

Larry smiled. "Dawn may have natural ability on her side, but I cheat with magic. Oh. Hold on a second."

Something buzzed from within Larry's duster. With my luck, I suspected it would be a swarm of ensorcelled bees, but what Larry pulled from his pocket was something much more mundane. In fact, it looked like a busted flip phone that had been patched together with twine and duct tape. It vibrated in Larry's hand.

"What's that?" I asked.

"This," said Larry with a flourish, "is an ingenious device of my own creation. It's a magical two way sonic portal which lets me communicate with an individual at long distance, at any time, no matter where they might be."

"So... it's a phone."

Larry snorted. "Of course it's not a phone. I told you, I can't use electronics. You saw for yourself in Adric's closet. This device is one hundred percent magical in nature."

"So it's a magic phone."

"Ah... no. It's a magical auditory portal device. It only works with the paired portal which happens to be owned by my police buddy, Frank Connors."

"So it's a crappy, nearly useless magical phone."

"IT'S NOT A PHONE!" Larry flipped it open and held it to his ear, huffing as he collected himself. "Hey, Frank. Sorry about the wait. I've got some new help that's slow on the draw. How are you doing?"

A tinny voice shot out of the *magical portal device,* which unlike a phone, apparently didn't have a volume button. "Larry! What took you so long? I've been trying to get a hold of you for the past half-hour."

"Sorry," said Larry. "The call didn't go through. Spotty magical coverage, I guess."

Only through an epic exertion of self control did I manage not so slap my own forehead.

"What's the problem?" Larry continued.

"Do you know someone by the name of Barry Mealer?" said the tinny voice.

Larry responded slowly. "Yes..."

"He called me recently," said Frank. "Told me this story about—"

"A Mexican witch and a drug cartel and fae drugs. Yeah, I know. He told me, too."

"And you haven't done anything about it?" said Frank. "Why the hell not?"

"Frank, I hate to break this to you, but we're not employed by the city. We're a for profit business, remember? As a matter of fact, we're currently working a job for a patron who's paid *very well* in past missions."

I spotted the security guard approaching us, which gave me confidence in my ability to keep regular people from creeping up on me. "Excuse me? Miss? The museum is closing. You and your friends are going to have to leave."

I was about to tell him they weren't my friends, but that would've created more problems than it would've solved.

"Right. Sorry." I plucked at Larry's sleeve and nodded toward the front.

He followed Dawn, Tank, and me, talking animatedly into his not-a-phone. "Alright, Frank. I'll look into it. But only because I need a chance to ponder the next steps on our current case. Don't think this'll become a regular thing. And I'm not going to make any citizen arrests, mind you. I'll try to locate the guy and talk to him, that's it. Got it?"

I didn't hear Connors' response, but Larry snapped the portal device shut and stuffed it in his pocket as we exited the building.

"What was that all about?" I asked.

"Don't worry about it," he said. "Frank can be a real ball-buster. Not like Dawn, who's a literal ball buster, but still."

Dawn looked over her shoulder and gave us a wicked smile. "I only employ the art of *pagkasira ng nuwes* as a last resort—or when I'm trying to force the man in my bed to get up and leave already."

"Pag-what?" I said. "Sorry, I don't speak Filipino."

"The ancient, sacred art of testicular destruction," said Larry. "It's not fun, trust me."

"*Testicular destruction?* Wait, are you saying you and Dawn...?"

"I told you she's a nympho," said Larry. "She'll sleep with anyone."

"But in Larry's case, only once," said Dawn. "He had a hard time accepting that."

"I'm sorry I asked," I said. "Oh wait. *I didn't.* I asked about Frank Connors."

"Right. Frank," said Larry. "He wants us to track down the guy Barry told him was distributing fae crank. Given that I'm not sure how to crack the Harry Ransom Center and it's always useful to have the cops in your pocket, I figure we should give it a shot. Especially since Frank already has a bead on the guy. Ever heard of Saint Marque's?"

"Is that a church?"

"Only to those who pray to an empty bottle. Come on. Let's get back to that truck of yours and I'll point you in the right direction."

8

DESPITE HIS BLOVIATING, LARRY DIDN'T ACTUALLY KNOW where St. Marque's was, so I punched it into my phone's GPS and followed the instructions, which the phone read to me in an Australian accent that I happened to think was much sexier than the boring standard American one. I took Dean Keaton Street across I-35 to Austin's east side, which had a reputation for sketchiness that to me seemed overblown. Perhaps once upon a time the neighborhoods had suffered from gang violence and drug use, but like every other area of Austin's rapidly expanding core, gentrification had forced out the dope pushers and *esés* and largely replaced them with young working class couples.

You wouldn't know it by looking at St. Marque's though. The place was a dump. Made of painted cinderblocks and with thick bars over the doors and windows, it looked more like a pawn shop than a bar, though the flashing neon sign advertising cold beers and tequila tried to make the distinction as clear as possible. There were a couple decked out Harleys parked in front, and the grungy sound of punk-rock drifted over from an open air patio in back. As I pulled into a spot across the street, I noticed the fencing had been covered with graffiti of the intentional kind, displaying the bar's name in an elaborate script, with lots of skulls and daggers and other manly things thrown in for good measure.

Larry spoke as I killed the engine. "Alright. Tank and I will check around the back. Lexie, you and Dawn scout the bar itself. The guy we're looking for goes by the name Melondrious Funk. I don't know any more than that, so don't ask. Let's make this quick. If he's not here, I want to tell Connors we tried and wipe my hands of it."

I felt a twitch of apprehension as I headed toward the dilapidated bar, but the mace in my pocket gave me confidence, as did having Dawn at my side, who'd left the swords in the 'burban alongside Tank's arsenal. Given the look of the place, I didn't think anyone would check my ID at the door, and I wasn't disappointed.

Night had fallen en route from the Harry Ransom Center, but a more intense darkness swallowed me as I stepped inside. Maybe the owners thought by keeping the place black as crow's wings customers wouldn't see how grungy it was. They were wrong. The flickering light of a TV and the glow from the beer fridge illuminated the peeling paint, smoke-stained ceiling, and a balding pool table in the corner. ZZ Top's "La Grange" played on the radio. A couple bikers talked in hushed tones at a corner table, a pair of old Mexican men smoked at the bar, and a trio of young hipsters in flannel drank their beers while watching the basketball game on TV—Texas versus Texas Tech.

I didn't see any women, though. That wasn't a great sign.

Dawn made a beeline for the bar, and I stuck close to her. The bartender gave her a nod as she approached, and his eyes widened, probably as he got a good look at her. Guys almost never reacted that way to me, though come to think of it, there was a bit of the same 'whoa' look when I opened the door at the Nyte Patrol house to find Tony standing there. And he *had* asked me about having a boyfriend at the library...

The bartender recovered quickly. "What can I get you?"

"Do you have any *lambanóg?*" asked Dawn.

The bartender blinked. "Any what?"

"Didn't think so. Shot of Bombay Sapphire, then. You?" She pointed a finger at me.

"Ah... no thanks." I didn't want to get busted for being underage, not to mention I was driving. "You drink shots of *gin?*"

"It's a Filipino thing. Don't ask."

The bartender grabbed a glass and started searching for the right bottle.

I slid into a spot next to Dawn. "Can I ask what *lambanóg* is?"

"Coconut vodka," said Dawn as the bartender set her shot before her. "Distilled from the sap of the unopened coconut flower. It's divine and kicks like a donkey."

"So you're from the Philippines?"

Dawn tilted her shot glass in my direction before downing it.

"I'm guessing Dawn Blayde isn't your real name."

"You've guessed right. Trust me, it's easier to pronounce than the real thing."

"So what made you pick Blayde? 'Cause you like swords so much?"

"Actually, I stole it from the *Saints Row* franchise," said

Dawn. "You know? Nyte Blayde, vampire-hunter-turned-vampire? God, I love those games."

"Sorry. I'm more into first-person shooters and RPGs, though I've played some of the *Grand Theft Auto* games."

Dawn shrugged and slid a ten dollar bill toward the bartender. As he made change, she asked him, "Ever heard of a guy by the name Melondrious Funk?"

"Is he a basketball player?" The bartender came back with some change, but Dawn waved him off.

"No. Thought he might be a regular."

"Can you describe him?"

"Wish I could. Thanks though."

As the bartender moved toward the wrinkled smoking *caballeros* at the end of the bar, I heard a voice behind me. "Hey, girl."

I figured one of the hipsters had decided to hit on Dawn, but when I turned, I found that the closest of the bunch, a guy with an undercut hairdo and a full beard, was looking right at me. "Uh. Hi."

"I'm Dave," he said. "What's your name?"

I couldn't fathom why Dave would hit on *me* when Dawn was beside me. Maybe he figured he could use me as a warmup, or he correctly figured Dawn was out of his league and decided to take a shot at me, instead.

"Look, I'm sorry," I said. "I'm not interested."

"Aw, come on. Don't be like that," he said. "I'm just trying to get to know you."

I'd heard the same speech word for word many times before. "I heard you, and I'm not interested."

He took a seat next to me at the bar. "You're being pretty

rude, you know? Are you this harsh to every guy who introduces himself?"

I felt a bit of nervous fear creeping in. I did *not* want to deal with this right now—or ever, for that matter—and I was reminded why I never went out to clubs.

"Excuse me," said Dawn. "You said your name was Dave?"

Dave perked up, perhaps thinking he'd misjudged his chances. "Yeah, that's right. Dave. What's your name?"

"Ever heard of Melondrious Funk?"

Dave smiled. "Is that a band? What do you like to listen to? 'Cause I'm really into art rock right now, but I've got a super open mind."

Dawn smiled back, her teeth radiant and white. "Oh, you have an open mind, do you? Well come over here, then. I've got an idea for something fun."

Dave couldn't believe his luck. "Yeah, girl, you bet."

I wanted to hurl. I mean, Larry said Dawn was a nymphomaniac, but was she really about to hook up with Creepers McGee? Here? *Now?* Barf city.

"So here's what I was thinking," said Dawn, her voice low and sensual as Dave closed in. "I was *thinking*, if you want, that we could slip out back, and if you're up for it, I could maybe slip my hand somewhere fun—"

Dave nodded. "Uh, yeah. Okay."

"—and then I could *rip your fucking balls off.* Or you could leave us the hell alone like my friend asked you to. How's about that?"

Dave scowled, hurled a particularly nasty insult at us, and stormed off back to his buddies. I looked at Dawn. Despite the darkness, I saw her in a whole new light.

"Thanks."

"Don't sweat it. That guy was ginormous douche."

I laughed, though it felt forced. "You know, for a second there, I thought you were into him."

"Please. I love sex, but I've already got an asshole. One is enough."

The back door opened. Larry stood in the doorway, some of the light from the outdoor patio lights flooding in. He waved at us. "Hey. We got Melondrious. Found him trying to sneak off in the shadows."

Dawn and I followed Larry to the patio, where we found Tank holding onto a midget by his jacket collar. The guy was barely taller than Darragh, though he put a much greater emphasis on hygiene. He wore a salmon-colored blazer, dark jeans, and two-tone suede shoes, and his hair had been coiffed into a perfect pompadour. He didn't look particularly happy about being restrained by Tank.

"Let go of me, you damned oaf," he said.

"Another leprechaun?" I said. "Is there a secret Irish contingent in this city that I don't know about?"

"*Leprechaun?*" said Melondrious. "Surely you jest. Do I look like a blasted leprechaun?"

I looked to Larry for help. "Uh..."

"He's a fairy," said Larry.

"What does his sexual preference have to do with anything?"

Melondrious laughed, despite his situation. "No, you twit. He's speaking to my status as one of the pure blooded fae children of the Erzorwyn clan, not my sexual proclivities, accurate though the assessment might be."

I'd taken a wild guess based on the color of his jacket. "Hey, doesn't bother me any. Practically half my softball team is gay."

Melondrious struggled against Tank's grip. "Would you kindly unhand me, you cad? None of you ruffians have even informed me what this is about. I have my inalienable rights, you know, not to mention you're wrinkling my jacket."

"Relax, Melondrious," said Larry. "We're here to talk business. Your business, specifically."

"I'm not discussing anything until I know who you are and what you intend of me, you ne'er-do-wells."

Because of Melondrious's eye-catching blazer, I hadn't inspected the rest of the patio, but now I noticed a biker from a group of five stand and adjust his leather jacket. He was staring right at us.

"Hey, guys," I said. "Maybe we should move this conversation somewhere more private?"

Larry followed my gaze. "Yeah. Good thinking. You're coming with us, Melondrious. To the Nytemobile!"

"Oh, hell no," I said. "You do not get to name my Suburban."

"Come on," said Larry. "It sounds so snappy. Don't tell me you prefer The Patrol Car. That sounds like we're with the police."

Another one of the bikers stood, and I felt a bead of cold sweat form at the back of my neck. "Look, let's just get out of here, okay? We'll figure it out later."

9

WE PILED INTO MY TRUCK, LARRY IN THE PASSENGER SEAT, same as before, and Dawn and Tank in the back. Tank crammed Melondrious between him and Dawn, his fist still gripping the fairy's jacket. I stuffed my keys in the ignition, but I didn't turn the engine over. The bikers had followed us around the edge of the bar, but they'd stopped at the street. After giving us the evil eye, they'd popped back into the building. Nonetheless, I didn't think we should test our luck by sticking around.

"Where to?" I asked Larry.

"Beats me." He turned to face the tiny, well-dressed fop. "So, Melondrious. Your name's been making the rounds. Care to guess why?"

"I can only assume the legend of my sexual prowess has reached peak saturation."

"Oh, cut the crap," said Larry. "If that were even remotely true, Dawn would've tracked you down months ago and put the rumor to the test."

"As if I'd be interested in her offerings." Melondrious

snorted. "Well. Come now. You're the ones who've accosted me. Out with it. Tell me what it is you want."

"The drugs, Melondrious," said Larry. "We're here about the drugs."

The fairy sighed. "Well, why didn't you say so, you buffoon? What is it you desire, then? The white cross? Big flakes? Black rock? Dancing shoes?"

"Not the traditional narcotics," said Larry. "We need to know about the fae stuff. The supernatural crank."

"Ah." Melondrious sniffed. "Of course you do. That one's in high demand of late. Unfortunately, I've run into some supply concerns, and I'm afraid I won't be able to help you with your request. So if you don't mind..." He flicked his hand at the door.

"We're not here to buy, you idiot," said Dawn. "We're here to... actually, what *are* we supposed to do with him, Larry?"

Larry shrugged. "Beats the hell out of me. Frank told me to locate him. I didn't actually think he'd be here. I guess we should deliver him to Connors."

"Restrain yourselves," said Melondrious. "I don't know any Connors, and I certainly don't want to be delivered to him, unless he's handsome and hung like a horse, of course. Hmm! I made a rhyme." He twittered with sudden glee.

"He's not a playboy," said Larry. "He's the head of the APD's paranormal crimes division."

"That's a thing?" I asked.

"Well, I certainly don't want to meet him then," said Melondrious. "He sounds dreadful."

As everyone argued, two bikers exited the bar and hopped on their choppers. I heard a rumble, not from the bikes in front but from around back. By the roar, it must've been more than two.

"You know what? I'm just gonna drive." I started the engine and took off, taking a right followed by another quick right, heading toward what I hoped was downtown. I checked the rear view mirror as I drove. I'd put about a block and a half of East 7th behind me and had just started to feel good when I heard another rumble and spotted a herd of bikes turning onto the boulevard from the direction of St. Marque's.

"Guys," I said, interrupting the conversation about what to do with Funk. "I don't want to startle anyone, but those bikers from the bar are following us."

Melondrious straightened and peered out the back. "Damn it all! You, in front at the wheel. I don't think I caught your name, but you might want to speed it up a tad."

"Oh, great," said Larry. "Just what we needed. Are these the guys you've been working with? Your distributors? Now they're angry because they think we've kidnapped their cook?"

"Well, to be fair, you have abducted me, but no, you don't have it quite right."

I turned onto a side street and gunned it, hoping to lose the bikers. "Go on," said Larry.

"Well, you know how this large gentleman to my side snagged me as I was trying to sneak out of Saint Marque's? Well, I didn't have any idea who you were at the time, so I wouldn't have any reason to slink away from *you*, would I?"

"The bikers are after *you?*" said Larry. "What did you do?"

"It's more what I *didn't* do. I told you, I've had supply issues with my product."

"How much do you owe them?" asked Dawn.

"Thirty kilos, give or take."

Larry swore. "Well, this keeps getting better. Tank, the next time I see Barry Mealer remind me to kick his ass."

Tank shot Larry a thumbs up.

Adrenaline seeped into my body. My fingertips tingled, and I was having a hard time focusing. Someone laid on their horn as I absentmindedly blasted through a red light.

"Christ," I said. "Larry, what do you want me to do?"

"Quick, turn here." He pointed at a darkened park. I saw the entrance and yanked on the wheel, the back of the Suburban fishtailing as I pulled onto the drive.

I regretted it almost immediately. "Crap. This is a one lane road."

Larry ignored me. "You know, Melondrious, when Connors called me to locate you, I wasn't into it. But now? I'm going to enjoy handing you over."

"There's no need to be rash," said the fairy. "We can cut a deal. How about instead of turning me over to the constabulary, I provide you sole ownership of a side business? I may be short on Mystical Mellow, but I have plenty of supply of other narcotics."

"Mystical Mellow?" said Dawn. "That's the name of your fae crank?"

"Crap," I repeated, my eyes on the road. "This isn't a park. It's a *cemetery*. And I'm pretty sure it's fenced in. Why did you tell me to pull in here, Larry?"

"How the hell should I know?" he said. "I told you, Bill's the navigator. Just park, cut the lights, and wait a few minutes before backing out. I'm pretty sure we lost them."

I pulled to the side as the others argued, cutting the lights as Larry suggested. I hadn't heard the roar of the choppers in a minute or two, so maybe the wizard was right and we'd lost them. Given how the night had progressed, I figured at some point the law of averages would kick in and normality would once again reign supreme. While the engine idled, I pulled my phone to check where the hell we were. Turns out I'd pulled into the Texas State Cemetery, resting place of city namesake Stephen F. Austin, which had thirty-one reviews with a four and a half star rating on Yelp. Seriously? Who reviews a cemetery?

A dozen high beams flared to life, cutting through the back windows of the Suburban and drenching us in light. I might've been blinded if they'd hit us straight on. As it was, I had to shade my eyes to see what was going on.

A gruff voice yelled across the expanse. "Out of the car, now!"

I squinted, making out the shape of one of the bikers from the bar standing next to his hog, its high beams on full blast.

"Crap, crap, *crap*," I said. "How'd they find us? Better yet, how'd they creep up on us?"

"Who knows," said Larry. "Could have something to do with that *bruja* Barry mentioned. Or maybe they drove real slow and quiet-like."

The biker yelled again. "Give us the fairy and maybe we'll be nice to the rest of ya'll. I ain't gonna ask twice."

"Okay, new offer," said Melondrious. "You turn me over to this Connors fellow after all. You're beloved by the police for performing your civic duty, I don't get tortured by angry bikers, everyone wins."

"Or we shove him out the window and get the hell out of here," I offered.

Larry rubbed his chin scruff. "Connors would want him... And that's a friendship worth cultivating. I can't tell you how many jams he's gotten us out of."

A sharp crack rent the air. My side mirror exploded as a bullet tore through it. I screamed.

The gruff voice followed. "That's the only warning you're getting. Next one I aim for the head."

Given that I was only a *junior partner,* I probably shouldn't have been the one making big decisions. Then again, I was the one behind the wheel, I was the one who presumably was going to get shot, and more importantly, I was *scared out of my goddamned mind!* So instead of asking for permission or waiting to see what happened, I squeezed the steering wheel with vice-like force and slammed my foot on the accelerator.

10

THE TIRES SCREECHED AND THE SUBURBAN LURCHED forward. The bikers yelled as gravel sprayed from the back tires, ricocheting off their polished hogs. My body jerked as I hit the cemetery's roadside ditch, then again as the truck roared into the grass. Another couple gunshots tore through the air. I didn't hear them ping off the car's body, but I couldn't hear much of anything over the sound of blood rushing through my ears.

I did hear the resounding crack of metal on stone as I rammed into the first gravestone, however. I screamed as chunks of granite bounced off the hood and fell into the darkness, yet I refused to take my foot off the gas. The Suburban jostled and tilted, the wheel fighting me as a tire careened off another tombstone. Melondrious, who wasn't buckled, went flying, slamming into the roof of the truck before bouncing off the center console and back onto the bench seat. Momentum smushed everyone to the right as I swerved around a sudden tree, the tires skidding and sliding.

"Christ almighty, girl! Seat belts!" Larry jammed his hand

against the dash and his boot against the footwell to wedge himself in place. "A little warning would've been nice!"

Somewhere behind us, the sound of motorcycles backfiring followed along my path of destruction. My nails gouged the steering wheel from the force of my grip, and the vehicle accelerated as we hit a downslope. "How's this for a warning? *Do something about those bikers before I kill us all!*"

I screamed again as light from the street illuminated a three foot drop in front of us. I didn't have time to react. The Suburban dropped. I slammed against my seat belt. My head whipped forward. Melondrious went flying again, grunting as he smashed into the seat. Based on the spike of pain in my forehead, I must've hit my noggin on the wheel. The Suburban didn't slow, then or when we plowed through the surrounding fencing with a violent shriek of tearing metal. I skidded across the street, horns from cross traffic blaring as cars screeched to a halt in the opposite directions. I'd lost my phone in the commotion and had no idea where I was going, so I hooked the first right I could and stomped on the gas again, hoping to put some miles between us and the bikers.

The hope didn't last for more than an instant. The roar of bikes sounded behind me, and in the rear-view I spotted a group of motorcycles round the corner. "Larry? Some help?"

"You know, I would've come up with a plan if you'd given me a moment," said Larry. "If you're going to work for us on a permanent basis, you're going to have to practice your self-control."

"*Seriously?*" I said. "Do not attempt to lecture me right now. This is *your* fault! I showed up at *your* doorstep, from *your* ad. It's your responsibility to get me out of this safely. *YOU'RE* the leader here. I'm an honors student, for God's sake!"

"Technically, that wasn't my ad," said Larry. "Dawn posted it. And as for me being the leader—"

"DO SOMETHING!"

"Fine. No need to yell. Tank?"

"On it." The big guy turned and rummaged in the back. When he pulled around, he held the SIG Sauer tactical patrol rifle in one hand and Dawn's swords in the other. Dawn took the blades and unsheathed the wakizashi, dropping the larger katana at her feet. What she planned on doing with the swords from the confines of my truck, I had no idea.

I swerved through traffic and blasted through another red light. I still wasn't sure what street I was on, but I was definitely heading toward downtown. I could see an I-35 overpass ahead and the Frost Bank tower in the distance.

Fear lanced through me at the sight of the weapons. What exactly had I gotten myself into? "Guys, we need to lose the bikers, not kill them!"

"That's still to be determined," said Larry. "I mean, how do you propose we get away from them in a vehicle with a top speed of sixty-five miles an hour?"

"You're the magician. Think of something!"

"Really? I told you I'm not good with machinery. I mean, this baby's old enough that it doesn't have a ton of electrical components, but still."

"I don't mean supercharge the truck. I mean lose them. With magic!"

"Supercharge the truck." Larry rubbed his chin. "Now, *that's* not a bad idea. I mean, if I can compress the air coming into the combustion chamber..."

"What? No. I said *don't* supercharge the truck."

"No, this could totally work," said Larry. "If I had to touch the thing, all bets would be off, but if I simply manipulate the air? Hold on. I'm not sure how much of a kick this will give us."

"Kick? What do you mean—"

The engine roared as if it had been replaced with that of a Shelby Mustang, and it bucked like one of those muscle cars from the *Fast and Furious* franchise. A sudden burst of acceleration smashed me into my seat, and the speedometer jumped to eighty-five in the blink of an eye—which might've helped it I hadn't been on a side street approaching a busy intersection under I-35.

I laid on the horn and barely managed to swerve around a line of cars turning onto the expressway. A car pulled out ahead of me in slow motion. I jammed on the brakes, but whatever Larry had done to the engine kept right on going. My life flashed before my eyes. I screamed. Melondrious sneezed, and we flew.

I mean—I think we did. The rumble and vibration of the road left the steering wheel. The car in front of me disappeared, and the underbelly of the overpass grew large in my field of view. Then the truck shook and rattled, the wheel vibrated again, and we were back on the ground.

Larry turned in his chair. *"Melondrious!* You sly dog. And here you had me thinking all you had on you was cocaine!"

"I have no idea what you're talking about," said the fairy, who still hadn't managed to buckle himself in. "I'd rather not die is all."

My mind whirled, trying to understand what was going on, but I didn't have time to think traveling ninety miles an hour down...? *Oh, god.* I saw the sign. *East 6th Street?* Home to half the bars and ninety percent of the drunks in Austin? We were doomed.

That's when I noticed the bikers were still behind us. The traffic at the intersection hadn't slowed them, and they didn't seem intimidated by our newfound speed either.

"Screw it," said Tank. "I've got this."

A light blinked on the dash and I felt the rush of air as Tank popped the side door and leaned out, wrapping his leg over the back seat for purchase. His tactical rifle snickered and cracked, the machine gun-like cacophony only slightly muted by the oncoming rush of air.

I'd never been particularly religious. I wasn't sure if I even believed in God, at least not the way most people did, but I was raised Catholic, and my parents had impressed upon me that, no matter how dire the situation might be, someone was always listening. So with gunfire in my ears, my Suburban screaming along at nearly a hundred miles an hour, bikers fast approaching from behind, and people yelling, pointing, and running on the sidewalks, I said screw it and gave it a shot.

"Lord Jesus," I said under my breath. "I come before you, just as I am. I am sorry for my sins. I repent of them. Please forgive me. In your name, I renounce Satan, the evil spirits, and all their works. I—"

Larry snorted. "Really? *Prayer?* That's a little excessive. We're going to be fine. Aren't we, Melondrious?"

A biker approached on the left side of the 'burban. Dawn kicked open the door and slashed at the guy with her sword.

My pious pleas evaporated in a mist, replaced instead with hot anger. *"Fine?* How are we going to be *fine,* Larry? Even if by an act of God we don't die, we're all going to prison for the rest of our lives! *How do you not see that?"*

The machine gun continued its ear-splitting battle cry.

Larry muttered something under his breath about needing

to put more qualifiers on the spell. "Sorry, Lexie. I keep forgetting you're not familiar with this sort of thing. But you have to remember, I'm a wizard. Remember when you asked me how nobody was giving Dawn crap about her swords at the library? Part of it is because she's a badass and nobody in their right mind would mess with her—"

"Damn right," she yelled from the open door.

"—but the other part is that to a certain degree I *can* make people ignore the present and forget the past, just as I said I could. You didn't want to believe me. Besides, if things get out of hand, I can always ask Frank Connors to soothe things over with the police."

Dawn yelled and hopped back into her seat. The Suburban rocked and the wheel fought me. Out of the corner of my eye, I spotted a blur. Something cracked. The blur coalesced into a leather clad arm and the butt of a pistol as shards of safety glass flew through the cabin.

"Son of a bitch!" Dawn lunged, wakizashi in hand, through the hole where the window had been and slashed at the biker who'd dared ram us. He didn't scream, but his bike did. I heard a loud *pop*. The bike swerved and veered onto the sidewalk before crashing through the front of the Blind Pig Pub.

"Jesus Christ!" I said.

"It's fine," said Larry. "I'll hand wave it away with magic."

An enormous fireball shot out of the hole created by the out-of-control bike, engulfing the front of the pub in flames.

Larry frowned. "On second thought, I might need help to quash this particular problem. Speaking of which... Tank. Dawn. Enough with the counterattack. Lexie. Take a right into that parking garage!"

"At a hundred miles an hour? *Are you insane?*"

"Right. Sorry." Larry snapped his fingers. The engine whined, clunked, and practically died, slamming me forward against my seat belt. At least Melondrious had learned his lesson. The lap restraint punched him in the gut as I yanked on the wheel, sending us careening into the concrete parking structure. Dawn and Tank barely managed to close the doors without flying off during the turn.

"Why am I doing this?" I asked.

"Go up, trust me," said Larry. "I have a plan this time."

I suspected he didn't, but rather than voice my opposition, I sent another silent prayer to the Lord above. The bikers turned in after us as I wheeled the Suburban toward the third floor arrow.

"Alright, Melondrious," said Larry. "It's your time to shine."

"My time?" said the fairy. "What in blazes are you blathering about?"

"Come on. Don't be coy. You said you'd rather be handed to Connors than taken by the bikers. Now's your time to make it happen."

"Perhaps all this erratic driving has addled your senses," said Melondrious. "In case you've forgotten, *you're* the spellcaster."

The tires screeched as I swung onto the fourth floor.

Larry cast a wary glance out the back window. "We don't have a lot of time to screw around, Melondrious. Cut the crap and bust out the high-grade nose candy."

I nearly burst a gasket. "Your master plan is to *get high?"*

"For the last time," said Melondrious. "I told you, I've had a supply issue and—"

"I'm not playing around, pipsqueak," said Larry. "The dust. We're out of time."

I pulled up a ramp and turned the corner onto the roof. My heart dropped as I let off the gas. "Christ. You're right."

"What are you doing?" said Larry. "Faster!"

A sense of calm fell over me. I wasn't really that scared anymore. I'd accepted my fate. "There's nowhere to go, Larry. Game over. We're dead."

"Bullshit." Larry flicked his fingers. Something kicked my foot off the brake. The truck lurched and started to accelerate.

"What the...?" I tried to stomp the brake but something invisible stopped me, a compressed block of nothingness. The same thing protecting the brake seemed to be pressed against the accelerator. "*Larry?*"

Larry held out his hand. "The dust, Melondrious."

"I swear to you, I don't have any—"

The concrete edge of the parking structure rushed toward us. "*LARRY!*"

"The dust, man! *The dust!*"

"*Fine!*" The fairy's hand flew inside his jacket. The concrete shot toward the Suburban's front wheels as he whipped his hand out. A fine white powder boiled through the air, coating the dash, the seats, our clothes, my face and hands. I sneezed and felt a bit woozy, but we never crashed against the edge of the parking structure.

We flew.

11

Until that moment, some part of me had resolutely held out in disbelief. Even after having witnessed Adric pull a first generation iMac from the pages of a magazine, a portion of my mind had reasoned that maybe, *just maybe,* it was an elaborate act, and I'd been tricked into seeing what someone wanted me to see. But as I gazed out the window of my flying Suburban at downtown Austin, I was a believer. Magic was real—either that or the special fairy cocaine I'd just snorted was the *best shit ever*.

"You sneaky sack of crap," said Dawn. "You've been holding out on us this whole time."

Melondrious crossed his arms and scowled. "To be fair, I did not deceive you. I am in *very* short supply. Fairy dust is extremely hard to produce in large quantities, and now I'm almost completely depleted."

"Considering you're going to jail, I don't think your supply matters much," said Larry. "You could've saved us all the trouble and done that sooner."

Melondrious snorted.

I tested the wheel, then the accelerator. Amazingly enough, the controls still worked even though the tires didn't have anything to push off of. "So, uh... where to?"

"South," said Larry. "Across the Colorado River to Auditorium Shores."

"Okay. Shouldn't be too hard," I said. "Though I don't know how to put her down."

"I'll handle it," said Larry. "But don't dawdle. Fairy dust isn't the most long lasting of drugs."

Melondrious's frown softened, and he sniffed a little. "That's what *he* said..."

"Oh, shut up," said Dawn.

I glanced at my dash, hoping the magic had also added an altimeter. No dice. "Why are we going to the river shore? I thought we needed to dump the fairy, not hit an open air concert."

"Trust me, I'm as eager to do that as you are," said Larry. "But between the assault rifle fire, the flying Suburban, and the fiery explosion in that bar, we'll need to do some cleanup first."

"And you know a good mop vendor who frequents the park?"

"Stick to driving the flying car," said Larry. "It's what you're good at."

I skirted the edge of the Austonian condo complex, wondering if anyone had spotted us through their thirtieth story window, and headed toward the river. Without traffic or having to worry about bridges, we'd be at Auditorium Shores in no time. Although I could do without the freaky stuff and the constant threat of death, *this* kind of magic I could get used to.

"You know, speaking of my truck," I said. "I'm going to need a good body shop guy who knows how to keep his mouth shut.

I've got a side mirror missing, scratches and dents along the side, the window's busted, the interior needs vacuuming, and I haven't even looked at the front bumper yet. I can't imagine it's going to come cheap."

"Don't forget the bullet holes in the back," said Tank.

"Bullet holes?"

"The bikers were good shots. Plus I missed a few times."

"Don't worry," said Larry. "A little bit of duct tape, everything will be fine."

"Yeah, the duct tape will throw the cops off our scent for sure."

"I'm kidding. We'll take care of everything, cops and car included." Larry waved toward the oncoming shore. "Put her down on the dirt path next to the trees."

I aimed the flying boat in the right direction and Larry took care of the rest. We landed on the reddish dirt light as a feather. I instinctively pulled the keys out of the ignition, though the engine wasn't running any more. Hopefully it would once the magic wore off.

"Alright," I said. "We're here. Now what?"

"It's obvious, isn't it?" said Larry. "Now we amplify."

Everyone filed out of the 'burban, leaving me dumbfounded at the wheel. "Right. Amplify. Like that makes any sense..."

I hopped out and slammed the door behind me. The shore-side path wasn't lit at night, but the moon was out, almost full, and the night was clear, so there was plenty of light to see by. The front bumper of my truck looked even worse than I'd expected, practically folded in half with the side hanging on by a thread. I wouldn't need a body shop. I'd need a miracle worker.

Larry and the rest of the gang—including Melondrious, who

seemed resigned to his fate—walked forward and stopped in front of a bronze monument near the water's edge. "And this," said Larry, "is where we amplify."

We stood in front of the statue of blues rock legend and guitar virtuoso Stevie Ray Vaughn. "I don't get it. Are you making a terrible electric guitar joke?"

"No," said Larry. "This is where we amplify my mind control magic to make everyone forget about the craziness on Sixth Street. We'll also patch up your ride while we're at it."

"And we'll do that next to the Stevie Ray Vaughn statue?"

"Well, yeah," said Larry. "He's buried here after all. That makes the power well crazy strong."

I looked at the rest of the group. "Okay, I literally have no idea what he just said. And more importantly, Stevie Ray Vaughn isn't buried here. He died in a tragic helicopter crash. His remains are in a cemetery in Dallas, if I'm not mistaken."

Melondrious gave me a sideways look. "Come, young lady, you don't believe any of that tripe, do you? That was the cover story the Magician's Guild put out to cover for his untimely death at the hands of the demon Astralgoroth."

"Magician's guild? *Demon?*"

Larry put a hand on my shoulder. "Sorry. Again, this is my fault. We're used to dealing with folks who are steeped in magical subculture like the rest of us, and when you showed up at the door, well... it sort of threw a wrench in everything. You see, Lexie, Stevie Ray Vaughn wasn't just a musician. He was the strongest wizard of our era. Playing the guitar was more of a hobby for him. His true talents lay in mind-control magic and in defense against the dark arts."

My first reaction was to reject the notion as complete balderdash, but as I thought about it, I found myself nodding.

"You know, that actually makes sense. I always thought his level of talent was superhuman."

"Exactly," said Larry. "The sad part is he barely had to try. He simply funneled magical energies into his fingertips and the rest is history. For the record, Yngwie Malmsteen is a wizard, too."

"What about Steve Vai?"

"No, he's just crazy talented," said Larry. "Anyway, the point is, as the final resting place of SRV, this spot possesses great power, specifically in the areas of magic he was most proficient in. Trust me, if I ever had to fight a demon, I'd choose to do so right here, but more pertinent to our current interests is this spot's power with respect to mind magic. I'm not strong enough to make half of downtown Austin forget our impromptu Hollywood action chase, but with a little boost and the right additive, I think we'll be fine. Melondrious?"

The fairy sighed. "Fine. It's not as if I have a use for it." He reached into his jacket and produced a plastic baggie. "This is the last of it, mind you. I swear, I don't have any more."

Larry hefted it. "It'll do. Now stand back. I don't want anyone getting any second degree contact burns."

I turned to Dawn. "Is he serious?"

She took me by the arm and we took several steps back. "Probably. Better safe than sorry when it comes to magic."

Larry opened the baggie, dumped the fairy dust into his palm, closed his fist, and whispered something into the clenched fingers. His arm whipped forward, and he flung the dust at the base of the bronze statue. For a moment, nothing happened, but then a strange crackle filled the air. Tendrils of cyan light appeared at the statue's feet, swirling in the night air. They whirled faster and expanded before shooting off in all directions. They flew past me, pushing me back and fluttering my hair. On the wind, I heard a whisper. Not a voice, but a melody. "Texas Flood," I think.

I let out a sigh, realizing I'd been holding my breath. "Is that it?"

"Almost." Larry pointed behind me.

I turned at the sound of screeching metal. The bumper on my truck bent and popped, plumping as it returned to form. I raced back in time to see the scratches on the side smooth out. A fog formed around the back passenger window and the side of my door. When it lifted, the glass and side mirror were back in place, good as new.

I blinked. "Whoa."

Tank make a cross with his fingers, kissed them, and lifted them to the sky. "Rest in peace, Stevie. We miss you."

"You know," I said. "While we're at it, maybe we could update the Suburban a bit. Make it a newer model. Give it some rims."

"Don't push your luck," said Larry. "Now come on. We've still got to drop Melondrious off."

I found the downtown police station on my phone and hit the road. When we arrived, Dawn exited with Melondrious in hand, but she told us to go ahead and head home without her. She'd find a ride on her own after delivering the fairy to Connors. She gave us a bit of a wink as she said that, and I think we all knew what her intentions were for the evening.

When I pulled back up to the dilapidated house on West 21st, I couldn't believe it was only eleven P.M. Apparently, I'd lived an eternity in five hours.

Tank waved as he hopped out the back, duffel bag of guns in

hand. Larry lingered behind, fingers tapping at the center console. He gave me an awkward glance. "So..."

"So... what?" I said. "Please tell me we're done for the night. I'm not sure how much more crazy I can handle."

"Oh, yes. We're done. And you more than earned your keep, so no worries there. I just wanted to talk to you. About the job."

"What about it?"

"Well... you did better than I expected. We hit a few hairy spots this evening, and you handled yourself well for a newbie, especially one who's not familiar with magic and the supernatural. Not to mention your driving skills are top notch. So I guess what I'm saying is, the position's yours if you want it."

I couldn't tell if he'd insulted or complimented me. Maybe both. "I thought you'd already offered me the job."

"Well, sure, but it was conditional. Upon you. Being capable and whatnot."

I took a deep breath and let it out slowly. "Okay, Larry. Whatever it is you're not telling me, just spit it out already."

Larry rubbed a hand against his forehead. "Damnit. Am I that obvious? I've never been good at this sort of thing."

"What sort of thing?"

"Being deceitful. Not that I've lied to you. Not directly. I simply might've failed to mention that... your showing up at our doorstep wasn't by chance."

"I'm guessing this has to do with that spell you cast?"

Larry blinked. *"What?* Yes. How did you know?"

"You and Dawn mentioned it when I first arrived, not to mention you were mumbling about it in the car. I'm not dumb, it simply took a while for me to accept that *maybe* magic spells are a real thing."

"So you understand, then."

"No. Not even remotely. I have no idea what's going on."

"Right," said Larry. "Sorry about that. As I said, I never lied to you. I need assistance with the Nyte Patrol. As you might have noticed, Dawn and Tank excel at what they do, but they lack some of the administrative and office skills our team requires, and Bill? Love him to death, but he's hard to include in everything, being a zombie head and all. Can't answer a phone, either. Which brings me to the help wanted ad. I had Dawn write it up and then, to make sure it attracted the right applicant, I cast a spell that would help it do just that. And lo and behold... you show up."

"Your spell chose *me?*" I said.

"It would appear so, and no offense, but you're not exactly who I was expecting. I mean, you're not even one of *us*. A voyager of the supernatural realms. So forgive me if you caught me off guard. But I know magic well enough to understand that it sometimes works in strange and mystical ways, so I was at least willing to give you a shot, and I'll admit that you've impressed me. It would seem that whatever you have to offer is what the Nyte Patrol needs."

"And what is that?"

Larry shrugged. "Beats me. Apparently it's not your supernatural talents, and it doesn't sound like you've done a lot of secretarial work before. Maybe it's your fresh perspective on life? Or something else. You have any experience leading a team of mercenaries or black ops commandos or anything like that?"

His mention of a team brought me back to practice, and that in turn drew a dark cloud over my head. "No. Nothing like that. Look, Larry, I think you're going to have to accept the fact that maybe your spell picked the wrong girl."

The wizard shook his head, sending his unwashed locks

dancing. "After what I saw tonight, I'd say that's highly improbable. Besides, my magic rarely fails me. So what do you say? Same time tomorrow? We've still got to procure that tome for Romanov, after all."

I surprised myself by actually considering the offer. On one hand, I couldn't imagine going back to fluid dynamics and heat transfer lectures after coming to grips with a world fundamentally different than I'd always presumed it to be. On the other hand, I'd never been shot at attending class or going to softball practice.

"Honestly, I don't know, Larry. I'm going to have to think about it. See how things shake out."

He opened the door and hopped out. "Well, don't think about it too long. Romanov offered a hefty bonus if we could locate the book within seventy-two hours. And we share bonuses equally around here—even the junior partners."

He shut the door and waved. I nodded and started the laborious process of trying to turn around.

12

THE BUZZING OF MY ALARM CLOCK FORCED ME TO CRACK my eyes. I hit the snooze button on my phone and blinked a few times, trying to get my bearings. Morning sunshine streamed through the window of my dorm room. Obviously, I'd made it home, but I didn't totally remember how. My brain felt fuzzy, like I'd drank too much, and the events of last night had that indistinct haziness to them of a bad dream.

I grabbed the remote and turned on the TV, clicking to one of the local news stations. A chipper anchorwoman sat next to a handsome middle-aged man, smiling as she talked. "—but while the second annual Central Texas Veteran's Association Ride for the Kids was ongoing, a fire broke out at the Blind Pig Pub on Sixth. Firefighters responded immediately, and while the damage to the bar was minimal, it did delay the end of the charity ride by a good forty-five minutes. Nonetheless, the ride was a success, raising over twenty-five thousand dollars for charity. I just love it when the community gets together to do something special for the kids, don't you Jim?"

"Absolutely, Veronica," said the anchorman. "I wish I could

take part in that ride myself, but it's hard when we have to get up so early to report the news. Now here's Tom with the weather."

The broadcast switched to a young man in a navy suit in front of a map of central Texas. "Thanks guys. It's shaping up to be a warmer than average day, with patches of rain across the hill country, but before we get to the forecast, believe it or not we had a bizarre weather phenomenon that took some Austin residents by surprise last night. It's called a Southerly Norther, strange as that may sound. It's when a gust of warm southern air mixes with cool air near the ground leading to higher than normal releases of *marsh gas*. When that marsh gas rises, it shimmers in the light of the full moon and can lead to some *strange* sightings. In fact, it was this shimmering marsh gas playing off a weather balloon that led some folks in downtown Austin into thinking they'd spotted a *UFO*. Can you believe it? Anyway, current temperatures are in the low fifties, but as the day goes on—"

"A weather balloon? *Marsh gas?*" I said. "That doesn't even make any sense!"

My door creaked. Tanya walked in, her wet hair hanging to her collarbone, with a towel around her midsection and a smaller one over her shoulder. "Hey, Lexie. You snuck back in late last night. Do anything fun?"

I turned off the TV. "Not really. In fact, I kind of had the craziest fucking night ever."

Tanya sat on her bed, drying her hair with the smaller towel. "Did you drop acid? I did that once. *Not* a good idea."

"No, there weren't any drugs involved." I thought about Melondrious and the fairy cocaine. "Well, not really."

"What then? Boy drama?"

I shook my head. "No. Though I did meet this guy at the library. He was kind of cute, if really awkward."

"So what made the night so crazy?"

"Well, uh... it's hard to say. I met this guy, Larry. He's like an... entrepreneur, I guess you'd say. And this chick Dawn, who's a total badass, and her friend Tank, who I still don't have a good read on. And we had an adventure together. At the library. And at this janky bar on the east side."

Tanya smiled. "I was wondering when booze would enter the picture."

"No. I didn't drink. At all. Trust me, it's *really* hard to explain." I grabbed my phone. I had sixteen unread messages and a couple voicemails. Most of them were from my teammate Heather, but there were others from the rest of the softball girls as well. Social media would probably be a war zone. I turned it off, not wanting to deal with it.

Tanya was still looking at me when I glanced up from my phone. "You doing okay, girl? You seemed like you were kind of in a bad place yesterday, and then you just ran off."

"I'm okay." I stood up and threw on clothes from a pile that I thought was clean. "I had a rough day, and I didn't want to talk about it. And now with everything that happened last night... Never mind. It'll all be fine, I'm sure."

That was a lie, of course. I didn't know any such thing, either about softball or about what I'd gotten myself into with the Nyte patrol.

I grabbed my book bag. "I've gotta go. See you later."

Tanya waved, and I headed out. Given that I had afternoon practice, I'd always scheduled as many classes as I could in the morning. Most of the time it didn't bother me, but today as I sat through back to back lectures on engineering mechanics and differential equations, I found I couldn't concentrate one whit on the subject matter. It wasn't because I was tired, though I did find myself yawning more frequently than normal. Rather, I couldn't force myself to care about free body diagrams or whatever the integral of f(x) plus y was.

Strangely enough, it wasn't the lunacy of having driven a flying Suburban hopped up on magical crack with a bunch of people I'd just met riding alongside me, one of them unloading clip after clip of assault rifle rounds at angry bikers, that got me. Rather it was the potential aftermath of my outburst at yesterday's softball practice that camped in the front of my mind. I couldn't help it. Angels and demons and goblins and witches might exist, but they'd never bothered me until yesterday. Softball on the other hand was my *life*—or at least it had been until I'd thoroughly screwed the pooch.

Through sheer force of will, I dragged myself through the classes. When they were over, I headed to the lobby on the main floor of the mechanical engineering building, found a free table, and hunkered down to do some homework. I was severely behind, mostly because I'd spent the previous evening chauffeuring people and fighting off bikers. I told myself it might have to become routine—not the high speed chases, but the middle of the day homework. I didn't see where else I'd be able to fit it in.

An eleven o'clock lunch came and went, followed by my noon lab and more homework. The clock ticked toward afternoon practice, but I stayed at my table, working through chapter seven of my thermodynamics textbook, all the while telling myself I could get in a few more of the end of chapter problem sets before I had to leave. Then a few more. And a few more. Before I knew it, practice had started, and I was still sitting in the lobby. I hadn't forgotten to leave, though. I'd made a choice to stay, if not a conscious one, and I hated myself for it.

I'd never considered myself a coward, yet there I was, rooted to my chair, refusing to answer my phone, not even having checked my email in the past twenty-four hours. All because I couldn't face the reality of what I'd done, the crap storm I'd kicked off through my arrogance and pride and shitty attitude. And if dealing with my own self-inflicted problems wasn't bad enough, a freaking *wizard* had cast a magic spell that picked me out of thin air to come help him. *Me.* As if I didn't have enough on my plate. Not to mention that I couldn't imagine how I could be of help to anyone at the moment. I couldn't even keep my own life from falling apart.

I sighed and rested my head on my textbook.

Eventually, I gave up, packed up my stuff, and headed back to my dorm for dinner. I didn't grab anything fancy at the first floor cafe. Just a sandwich and a chopped salad, the latter of which probably could've sufficed. For once I wasn't ravenous, in part because I'd skipped practice. Also because the pit in my stomach left little room for anything else.

I'd finished my sandwich and was picking my way through the chopped vegetables when the chair across from me screeched. I looked up to see Heather taking a seat across from me.

13

HEATHER WAS A TYPICAL TEXAN BEAUTY, WITH A PERFECT smile, blonde hair, and legs that stretched for miles. She pitched the meanest curveball I'd ever come across, which was both great for our team and for me personally as I got to practice off it all the time. She was a lot more girly than I was, preferring skirts to shorts and romantic comedies to superhero flicks, but despite our differences, she was far and away my best friend on the team. She didn't flash me her pearly white smile today, though. She gave me a curt nod instead. "Hey."

"Hey," I said.

Heather didn't bring any food. She stared at me as I prodded some lettuce with a battered fork. "Missed you at practice today."

"Yeah, I, uh... got caught up in some classwork."

"Didn't respond to any of my texts, either."

"I told you, I was busy. I had a lot of studying to do."

"And I'm guessing you were busy studying last night, too, when I tried calling you like three times."

I didn't say anything. Trying to explain the sequence of events that had enveloped me wasn't likely to help my case.

"Damnit, Lexie, just talk to me. Of all the people on the team, I'm probably the only one who's not pissed at you, but if you keep treating me like this, trust me, I can change my mind in a hurry."

I put my fork down and looked up. "What do you want me to say, Heather?"

"I want you to tell me what the hell is going on. You've never shut me out before. Why are you doing it now?"

I groaned. "Ugh. I'm sorry. It's not intentional, I promise. But the last few weeks have just... *sucked,* okay? I feel like everything I've worked so hard for is slipping out of my fingers, and I don't know what the hell to do about it."

Heather's face softened. "Have you talked to Coach K about any of it?"

"I had a meeting with Mitch Grady." He was the university's sports psychologist for the student athletes.

"Well, that's a start. But you need to bring Coach K into the conversation—*especially* after yesterday."

"Right. That'll be easy. I'll just call her up and be like, Hey Coach, sorry I went totally mental the other day and dropped an f-bomb and said you pulling me from the starting lineup is total bullshit. Oh, and sorry for going medieval on that Gatorade jug and nearly taking Janie Nguyen's head off in the process, even though that part was *totally* an accident and nobody's going to believe me it wasn't on purpose."

Heather tilted her head. "So it *wasn't* on purpose?"

"*No.* Of course not. Christ, even *you* think I was trying to kill her?"

"Not kill her. But come on, Lexie. You two have been butting heads since the fall."

I put my head in my hands. "God. This is a disaster, Heather. How did this happen?"

"You almost fracturing Janie Nguyen's orbital bone?"

"Me getting benched for a freshman! I was batting three-fifty last year, and this season everything's gone to shit."

Heather leaned across the table and rested her hand on my forearm. "Look, Lexie, don't beat yourself up over it. Everyone has ups and downs. You'll work through it. Besides, your shoulder surgery is clearly still affecting your swing."

I shook my head. "That's an excuse. I've been playing like crap, and it doesn't matter if it's because of my shoulder or because I'm stressed from my course work or who knows what else. Crap play is crap play."

Heather didn't flinch. "You're right. So do something about it."

I blinked. *"Wow.* Way to have my back. You're supposed to tell me I'm wrong, that I'm playing great but not seeing it."

"Lexie, I'm your friend and probably your biggest advocate on the team, but me blowing smoke up your ass isn't going to do you a damn bit of good. I'm going to tell it to you like it is, and yeah, you need to play better. I mean, honestly, I was afraid you'd be blind to it, and I'd have to walk you through it."

"Of course I'm aware of it! How couldn't I be?"

Heather frowned. "If you know you're not performing to expectations, then why are you surprised you got pulled from the starting lineup?"

"Because I'm not some scrub benchwarmer, I'm the damn co-captain, that's why!"

The words flew out thick and hot, and I instantly regretted them. I shouldn't have raised my voice. Not at Heather.

Heather's lips tightened. "Lexie, when you're healthy and dialed in, you're the best hitter on the team, but you know that has *nothing* to do with you being selected as co-captain. The girls voted you in because of who you are. Because of what you've meant to the team. And to be perfectly honest, it's kind of hard to lead when you're being a petty bitch who won't even come to practice."

I sighed. "Heather, please. That came out wrong. I know being co-captain isn't a guarantee of playing time. But to have worked *so hard* only to get stapled to the bench?"

"That's not an excuse. Everyone on the team works hard, and most of the girls look up to you for working the hardest—at least they did until yesterday. You can still make it up to them, show them they weren't wrong about you, but you need to suck up your pride and get your head out of your ass."

I hung my head, feeling like I'd been punched in the gut.

She stood and pushed her chair in. "See you tomorrow at practice?"

"Yeah."

"Good."

Heather walked off. I picked up my fork and looked at what was left of my salad, wondering if I should bother shoveling it in. Before I could make a decision, another shadow fell over me.

I cursed under my breath. "Great. What now?"

I looked up to find Tanya standing at my shoulder. "Hey, Lexie. Everything okay with you and Heather?"

Tanya wasn't on the softball team. She played soccer instead, but she knew most of the girls. We went to a lot of the same parties. "Yeah. It's fine. What's up?"

"Not much." She glanced over her shoulder. "Just wanted to let you know there's this weird hobo guy who's been asking around for you."

"Hobo?" I said. "Is he three and a half feet tall? Smells like rubbing alcohol?"

"Uh... no. He's regular sized, and doesn't smell like much of anything, thank God. He's got this ratty, knee-length leather jacket, though. Crap. There he is."

"Larry?" I turned and followed Tanya's gaze. Sure enough, there he was at the entrance to the dining hall, casting his head about as he looked at the tables. The students gave him a good fifteen foot berth, as if he had ebola or something.

"Wait, the entrepreneur guy? *That's* who you hung out with last night?"

I could hear whatever respect Tanya had for me melting rapidly. "No. I mean, sort of. It's a long story."

Larry spotted me, waved, and walked my way. The other dorm residents curved around him like a bubble in space-time. Then he started shouting. "Lexie. *Lexie!*"

I wanted to crawl into a hole and die. "God, this is just what I need."

Tanya looked toward Larry with horror in her eyes. "I've gotta go."

She took off. They say misery loves company. They're dead wrong.

14

LARRY PULLED UP A CHAIR AND SAT DOWN. "THERE YOU are. I've been looking all over the place for you."

"You realize I'm a college student, right?" I said. "I have classes and practice and stuff, not to mention I haven't decided if I'm accepting your job offer."

"Classes, yes. *Practice?*" Larry waggled his hand in the air.

"What's that supposed to mean? You picked up that I'm an athlete, right?"

"Yeah. Softball," said Larry. "But you weren't at practice."

"You went to my softball practice?"

"Relax. No one saw me. Or rather, they probably did, but they all ignored me. I used my mind obfuscation magic on them."

"That's not magic," I said. "That's a side effect of resembling a homeless person. No one's willing to make eye contact with you because they're afraid you'll ask them for money or start babbling about government conspiracies."

"Trust me. It works on security guards and bouncers, ergo, it's magic. But on a serious note, none of your teammates know I exist, so your reputation as a—" Larry waved his hand in the air. "—*whatever it is you're known as* remains intact. You can breathe easy. All I did was peer on from afar in hopes of finding you."

I hadn't realized Larry understood he was such an oddball. The fact that he knew actually saddened me a little.

I got over it quickly. "What do you want?"

"To die old and happy, but if you mean what do I want right now, it's the same as yesterday. I need a ride."

"Seriously? You spent half the afternoon tracking me down to see if I could shuttle you around town? Haven't you heard of Uber? There are also these things called busses."

"I don't like public transportation," said Larry. "Too crowded, too many Nosy Nancies, and you're far too exposed. Not to mention if the engine breaks down, guess who everyone would blame?"

I considered explaining to him that his unique sense of style didn't give him away as a wizard, and even if it did, that wouldn't naturally make anyone think the nearby thing that went boom was his fault, but it wasn't worth the time and effort. "And where do you need to go, exactly?"

"To the police station. I need to talk to Connors. He owes me after the delivery of Melondrious last night and I intend to cash in."

"Couldn't you call him on your phone?"

Larry frowned. "I've explained to you, it's a two way portal device. I'd appreciate it if you made an effort to use the proper terminology. And yes, I could talk to him, but some things are better negotiated face to face. Connors is a bit of a slither-outerer if you know what I mean. I want to make sure he delivers."

I glanced at the entrance to the dining hall. "Where are Dawn and Tank?"

"Dawn still hasn't returned home," said Larry. "Before you ask, no I don't know where she is, but I'm sure she's fine. She has a habit of taking her pleasures during the day and showing up for work at the last moment. Tank is currently indisposed."

"What's wrong with him? Did he eat a bad burrito?"

Larry snickered. "Nothing that unsavory. He needs time to decompress every day. Keeps his mood up."

"They have drugs for that, you know."

"They don't work on him," said Larry. "Metabolism is too high. Just gives him expensive pee. Besides, it's not the same kind of decompression you're thinking of."

"You still haven't told me what he does, you know."

Larry smiled. "Yes, I'm aware of that. You'll see if you stick around long enough."

"Is that a sales pitch?"

"Depends. Is it working?"

I sighed. "Look, Larry, I haven't had the best of days. I've got a lot on my mind, and I'm not sure shuttling you around town is the cure for what ails me."

Larry nodded. "I get it. It's that problem with your softball team."

I squinted at the wizard, feeling a bit of a chill. "I'm pretty sure I never mentioned any of that to you."

"Relax. I'm not sifting through your thoughts. Us wizards have to abide by a strict code of conduct—at least those of us who want to maintain our guild membership. But given that you weren't at practice and that tall blonde girl who stormed out of here a few minutes ago was, it's not hard to put the pieces together."

I stared at him.

"Yeah," he said. "Believe it or not, I'm not as dumb as I look."

"Fine," I said. "So you understand why maybe I don't want to be your chauffeur right now."

"Of course," he said. "So let's solve the problem."

"*Let's?*"

"Well, not me. You. Go talk to your softball friends or your coach or whatever. Squash the beef. Hash it out. Whatever you kids call it nowadays. I'm happy to wait while you take care of it."

I snorted derisively. "It's not that easy, Larry."

"Why not?"

I don't know, I thought. *Maybe because for the first eighteen years of my life I've been far and away the best player on any soft-ball team I joined, and then when I got to college that wasn't the case any more, and now I'm not even good enough to be in the starting lineup—as a junior no less—and I have no* flipping *idea how to deal with it.*

I didn't say any of that, though. I simply stared at Larry. He stared back, boring into me with his goofy eyes and genuinely perplexed expression.

I growled as I stood, my tray clattering as I swept it off the table. "Fine. I'll drive you to the stupid police station. Come on."

15

I'd parked in the Brazos garage, so Larry and I hoofed it out of the San Jacincto dorm and headed south along Jester Circle. I wasn't in a mood to talk, but that didn't stop Larry from trying to engage me.

"So did you hear about the attack last night?"

"I was there, Larry. But if you mean did I see the news, yeah. *A biker ride for kids?* Who came up with that junk? Or the marsh gas and the weather balloon? Don't tell me that's how memory magic works. People lose all common sense and their brains invent a muddled explanation that barely fits."

"Pretty much, yeah. You don't think gas mains really explode as often as people say on the news, or that fifteen car pile-ups happen for no reason? But I didn't mean our biker incident. I meant the were attack."

"What attack, where?"

"Not where. *Were,*" said Larry. "Like person turns into animal sort of were."

"How would I have heard about that?" I said. "Given how poorly the news covered our high speed biker chase, if a were creature attacked someone, the anchors would probably blame it on some poor, harmless pit bull."

"You can't get your news from local TV," said Larry. "They don't know a lick about what's going on in the world. The only accurate news they report is mindless drivel, like about old women feeding pigeons in a park. You need to tune in to a more accurate source."

"What are you talking about? Like Infowars or something?"

Larry balked. *"What?* No. Fuck those guys. I'm talking about Mystic Radio, home of DJ Firestorm and the Truth Squad. You just have to know how to tune in."

We were almost at the Suburban. We hopped in, and while I started the laborious process of backing out of the space, Larry looked around, popped open the glove compartment, and rifled through the documents inside. "You got any tissues?"

"Check the console," I said. "Why? You feel an allergy attack coming?"

Larry found the travel pack I'd stashed among the receipts, pens, and empty soft drink cups and pulled one out. "No. I'm tuning into the radio station."

"With a tissue?"

"Yes." With the Kleenex over his fingers, he reached out and gingerly grasped the knob on the radio. The speakers crackled. Voices and music popped in and out as he fiddled with the station.

"You're kidding me," I said. "All it takes to protect electronics from exploding in your presence is to cover your exposed skin? Why don't you buy a pair of gloves so you can answer the telephone yourself?"

"Because it doesn't always work." Static blasted and faded away.

"*What?* So you're willing to risk destroying my truck, but you won't do the same to your landline?"

"It's more complicated than that. After last night's spell regenerated your bumper and side mirror, I felt a change in your car. I can still feel it. I think the fairy magic won't ever totally fade. The point is, because I cast the spell, your vehicle is more magically in tune with me than most other machines. Your radio should be fine. The tissue is a safety precaution."

"That sounds like total bullshit," I said.

The radio settled into a clear stream. Instead of a station number, the display blinked a series of dashes. "Total bullshit that works," said Larry.

I caught the radio hosts mid-sentence as I pulled onto South Congress Avenue. "—downplay it all you want, Turk, but this story smells fishy to me. We've been reporting on the surge in overdoses in the para community from folks who've used too much of this drug. Phantom White, Crystal Chew, Fae Jay—"

"Bite or Flight."

"Right. Whatever you want to call it. Rumor has it the thugs involved in that high speed chase last night have been slinging the stuff to the elves, the vamps, even to the pixies. The question is, who was the rival gang in that magically juiced Suburban?"

"A gang? Marty, I think you've lost your marbles. No gang in their right mind would be caught dead in a piece of junk like that."

"Hey," I said. "The 'burban's not that bad."

"Well, if it wasn't a gang, it was someone with skin in the game. You felt the dissolution spell that went out in the evening? That was powerful stuff."

Larry slapped me on the shoulder. "Hey, that's me they're talking about. *Powerful.* It was, wasn't it?"

"I guess time will tell, Marty. In other news, we're still looking into reports of a possible werewolf attack in central Austin last night, though eyewitness accounts say the creature involved was *striped.* Three reported wounded, but no dead, thankfully. A reminder to all our listeners, be careful for the next few nights. We're expecting clear skies again tonight, and the moon's close to full. More news after the break."

The radio started playing commercials for products and services I'd never heard of, everything from transmogrification juice to Vampire Smiles, the only all-night dentistry service in the metro Austin area.

I killed the radio. Larry looked at me with surprise. "Why'd you do that?"

"I don't know. I feel like the less I know the better."

"On the contrary. You're deep in the weeds now, girl. The *more* you know the better. It'll help you stay alive."

I pulled the truck into an open street spot next to the downtown police station. Larry led the way inside, and I followed him. Given Larry's appearance and my obvious status as a college student, I figured someone would stop us, but as we sauntered by the information desk, past the patrol officer's workstations on the main floor, and over to the elevators, all while uniformed police officers walked by paying us no mind, I started to think there might be something to Larry's obfuscation magic, even without the additional magnification powers of a dead blues rock legend.

The elevators spit us out on the fifth floor. Larry led me down the hall, through a set of glass double doors etched with the words 'Special Investigation,' and stopped in front of a frosted one that bore Frank Connors' name.

Larry knocked but didn't wait for an answer before turning the knob and walking in. "Connors! There you are."

The presumed Frank Connors sat behind a desk, telephone held to his ear. He was a gruff, middle-aged guy with a thick Magnum P.I. mustache and eyebrows you could braid. His hair —dark brown and peppered with gray—had been trimmed to millimeter length precision, but whatever he'd spent on his haircut he'd cut from his wardrobe budget. His suit screamed department store and was threadbare to boot.

He scowled at the sight of Larry. "I gotta go, Gary." He slammed the phone down in the receiver. "Stuttgart. What do you want?"

"Jeez, Frank. Good to see you, too." He plopped into one of the chairs in front of the detective's desk. "How've you been?"

"Busy, what with trying to smooth things over with my superiors following vandalism of the state cemetery and a bizarre case of biker violence nobody seems to remember a damn thing about. You wouldn't know anything about that, would you?"

"Hey," said Larry a little too quickly. "Let me introduce Lexie. She drove me here."

"I don't care." The cop looked at me. "No offense."

"None taken," I said.

"Seriously, Stuttgart," said Connors. "What do you want?"

"You got my delivery last night?" said Larry. "In the form of a well-dressed fairy who surely had a lot of interesting things to tell you about some hard to locate drugs."

"If you're looking for a profuse expression of my sincerest thanks, you're barking up the wrong tree, Stuttgart."

"Please," said Larry. "The day you say anything nice about anyone is the day I renounce magic and take up knitting. I want something for my troubles."

"You mean besides me overlooking your endangerment of the public and all the property damage you caused last night?"

"I thought you said you couldn't get anyone to remember what happened."

"Anyone except that fairy Melondrious," said Connors. "Once I got him started, the little bastard wouldn't shut up."

"Hey, we came through on our end of the bargain," said Larry. "Not only did we find him, we delivered. With him in custody, the flow of fairy dust should stop. That's worth something."

"And what did you have in mind?"

"Nothing much. Just the blueprints to the Harry Ransom Center."

Connors blinked. "What? Why the hell do you need those?"

"Better you don't ask."

Connors scowled. "Jesus, Stuttgart. I'm not helping you break into a god-damned museum."

"It's not a break-in," said Larry. "More of an unscheduled visit. The library doesn't even want the item we're after. They tried to give it back to the owner a decade ago and were rebuffed."

"Shut up," said Connors. "I don't want to know. Not to mention the fact that I don't have access to any blueprints."

"You're a high ranking detective. Use your influence!"

"I'm not doing it, and that's final. Sorry, Stuttgart. I appreciate you helping me out last night—despite the reckless way in which you went about it. But I won't enable you."

Larry threw his hands in the air. "But we need to get in! Not to mention I have it on good authority that the basement of the HRC is a complex maze. How are we supposed to navigate our way through it without a set of architectural plans?"

"I don't care, Stuttgart," said Connors. "Out. Now. I have work to do."

Larry scowled. He flung himself out the door and stormed toward the elevators, where he stood until I joined him. "Hit the call button. I didn't bring my poking stick."

I punched the down button. "So, let me get this straight. To get through the Harry Ransom Center, you need a navigator, right?"

"Right."

The elevator dinged. "So, uh... what about Bill?"

16

WE STOOD OUTSIDE THE HARRY RANSOM CENTER AGAIN, only this time it was after dark and the museum was closed. That didn't mean the streets outside were empty. Students walked back and forth along the sidewalks on West 21st, but thanks to Larry's obfuscation magic, we mostly avoided a never-ending procession of dirty looks.

"Hey, watch the neck!" said Bill.

"Sorry," said Larry. "I don't want you to fall out."

Larry had removed Bill from his jar and was fastening him into a contraption made of straps and cloth, basically a baby carrier for diseased zombie heads. He'd already cinched the strap around Bill's forehead and was in the process of securing the strap underneath his chin.

"To be honest, I'm more concerned about stuff falling *off* than falling out." Bill snickered at his own joke. I winced.

Larry tightened the chin strap, cutting Bill off in mid-squawk. "Alright. Everyone's clear on the plan?"

Dawn sighed, hand resting on the sword hilts tied into her belt. "I'll take care of the lock on the front door, seeing as I'm the only one with any manual dexterity. We'll work our way to the secure door you located yesterday during our scouting mission. You'll handle the security cameras and any electronic locks we might encounter. From there, we'll follow Bill's directions and hope we don't encounter anything too out of the ordinary. Once we find the *Librum de Virtute,* we grab it and get the hell out as fast as we can, hopefully with enough time left over for a gin fizz nightcap before bed."

Larry nodded. "Good. Tank?"

Tank knelt on the ground, working the action on one of his rifles with his duffel bag set beside him. He looked up at the sound of his name and blinked. "I, uh... shoot anything that moves?"

"No, Tank," said Larry. "Come on, man. We're trying to keep this mission as quiet as possible. Nobody needs to die. Got it?"

Tank nodded. "Right. So... shoot anything that *doesn't* move?"

"What? No. Why the hell would you shoot inanimate objects? Look, unless specifically instructed to discharge a firearm by either myself, Dawn, or Lexie, keep your finger off the trigger, okay?"

"Hey, what about me?" said Bill. "I don't get any say in when the big guy starts ripping off five-five-six NATOs?"

"Hell no," said Larry. "I can't even trust *you* with a firearm, and you don't have hands. If I put you in charge of Tank, within five minutes we'd have a higher bodycount than a Quentin Tarantino movie."

"Yet you're okay trusting me?" I said.

"Of course," said Larry. "You're college educated, and based on your relentless screaming during last night's chase, you actually value your own life. That puts you in an elite group around here. Plus as I've already mentioned, the spell I cast picked you. You're here for a reason. So, Tank, just to review—when do you fire?"

I'd never seen a man his size look so glum. "When I'm told."

"And you're the lookout. Don't forget it."

"Speaking of your spell," I said. "I still don't understand why it would've chosen me. I don't bring anything to this team. I mean, apart from being the last of three checks against Tank going on a violent murder spree."

Larry pulled his ancient flintlock from his jacket and peered into the barrel, probably to make sure the ball hadn't rolled out. "Just because you're not aware of the reason for something happening doesn't mean there isn't one. I'm sure you have valuable skills you're not aware of that the spell picked up on."

"But that's the thing," I said. "I don't. I'm not a wizard or an elite martial artist or a gun happy whatever-the-hell-it-is like Tank. Even Bill has superior navigational skills, supposedly. I'm just an average college student."

Bill snorted. *"Supposedly..."*

"That's not true," said Larry. "You're a good driver."

"I don't see how that's going to help us inside a museum."

"Fair point. You sure you don't have any other hidden talents? Thaumaturgy? Alchemy? Necromancy?" Larry winced. "Ugh. I hope not. How about your heritage? You have any great aunts or uncles who never touched a cross or who delivered bizarre premonitions that ultimately came true?"

"No. Nothing like that."

Larry scratched his chin. "Well, I don't know what to tell you. There are really only two ways this could shake out. Either you have a hidden talent only an exceptionally dangerous or stressful situation can activate, or for only the third time in my life I botched a spell and you really are a useless nobody. Only time will tell."

"Hey now," I said. "There's a big gap between 'can't summon hell beasts to fight alongside her' and 'useless nobody.'"

Larry smiled. "Relax. It was a joke. I've never botched a spell. Look, are we ready to go or not?"

Dawn nodded, Tank gave a thumbs up, and Bill barked out a yes.

"Good. Let's move."

Larry, Dawn, and Tank hustled toward the Harry Ransom Center's entrance, Bill bouncing against Larry's chest as he moved. I followed the lot of them, feeling like a criminal, a fool, and a third wheel all at the same time. Dawn didn't slow as she reached the front doors, pulling a set of lock picks from her back pocket and going to work. Within fifteen seconds, she'd cracked the lock and pushed open the door. From there, we made our way along the darkened corridors, following Larry past the Mexican folk art exhibit to an oppressive-looking metal door. Cameras pointed at us from shadowed corners, but I trusted that Larry had somehow goosed the security systems with magic.

Larry played his part perfectly, too. As we reached the door, Larry pressed his hand against the fingerprint scanner to the side of it. The system sparked and smoked. A red light at the top of the scanner went dark, but somehow, instead of remaining locked, the door creaked and opened. Seemed like a design flaw, but who was I to complain?

Tank pulled the heavy door open and we shuffled through only to stop dead in our tracks.

"Well, shit," said Larry.

A series of fifty red lasers shot across the corridor before us in as many different directions. At the far end of the hallway sat another hefty metal door with what appeared to be a retina scanner beside it.

"Well," I said. "What's the problem? Can't you obfuscate your way past these and blow up the eyeball scanner like you did the fingerprint one?"

"Blow up the scanner? No problem," said Larry. "But the lasers are a no go. Obfuscation is a magic of the mind. The spell I cast out front won't affect the security cameras, only the guards who watch the footage. This is different. I can't bend light. If we step into those lasers, we'll set off an alarm, simple as that."

"Can't you make the guards ignore the alarm?"

"Alarms are loud, Lexie. They'll attract more than the night watch."

Dawn started to undo the swords at her waist. "Relax. There's a path through. There always is with laser mazes like this. I can already see the route."

"And then what?" said Larry. "You can't blow up the scanner like I can."

Tank's duffel bag thumped against the floor. "She could stab it."

"Don't be silly, Tank," said Larry. "Stabbing it wouldn't do anything. Only blowing it up will work."

"Maybe you could channel your energies through me," said Dawn. "Form a power conduit."

"*A power conduit?*" Larry snorted. "Yeah, right. Maybe if I was still standing at Stevie Ray Vaughn's burial site, but not here."

I heard a zipper.

"No," continued Larry. "There's only one option. *I'll* have to weave my way through the lasers. Don't try to dissuade me, Dawn. If you can do it, I can, too. Lexie? If you could hold Bill." He started to undo the strap over his shoulders. "Now let's see. If I go up and over the first one, then below the second—"

An earsplitting whistle tore the air as a missile flew down the corridor, followed by an equally deafening explosion as it detonated against the retina scanner. The lasers flickered and faded, and the door at the end of the hallway creaked as it swung open. Tank stood beside us, a smoking rocket launcher in his hands.

"God damn it, Tank!" said Larry. "I told you no firearms unless under explicit instruction from one of the rest of us."

"This isn't a firearm," he said. "It's an RPG."

"It did work though," I said, pointing at the open door. "And through another fortuitous coincidence, it also deactivated the lasers."

"Fine," said Larry, reattaching his shoulder strap. "But from now on, no firearms, explosives, chemical weapons, bayonets, or miniature howitzers unless specifically instructed, am I clear?"

Tank grumbled and shook his head as he gathered his duffel bag and headed down the corridor. Dawn clapped him on the shoulder and walked with him.

As I watched them go, I felt bad for the big guy—but I was also starting to have an inkling of why Larry's spell might've picked me after all. "Larry, can I talk to you while we walk?"

He was staring at Dawn and Tank's shrinking forms same as I was. "Huh? Sure."

"You asked me last night if I had experience with your sort of work. I don't, obviously, but I do have experience getting the most out of a team. Don't you think Tank deserves a little more—"

"Autonomy?" said Larry.

"I was going to say respect."

"Look, Lexie, Tank means well, but he can be a little reckless. Sometimes a *lot* reckless. He needs to be reined in periodically."

"I'm sure that's true, but that's not what you did there. We had a problem. He solved it. Instead of praising him for a job well done, you castigated him. What do you think that does to his morale?"

Larry frowned. "Are you saying I should encourage his recklessness?"

"I'm saying that if you don't want your teammates to ignore you while you try to hang up a phone with a stick then maybe you should start building them up instead of tearing them down."

Larry snorted. "Fair enough. I'll try to keep an open mind."

We passed through the open door and started down a circular stairway. Larry tapped Bill on the top of the head. "We heading the right direction, pal?"

"This corridor only goes one way. What do you think, Larry?"

"Hey, you don't have to be an ass about it."

"Hard to be an ass when you don't even have one." Bill brayed with laughter again.

We caught up with Dawn and Tank and took the lead, just in case we hit a turnoff and needed Bill's guidance. The ceiling lights dimmed as we descended the steps, fading from a bright white to a dim, barely discernible glow.

"So is that it?" I said. "Are we in the vault? Adric made it seem like it would be a lot harder to break in."

"Something tells me we're not out of the woods yet," said Bill.

Around and around the stairwell we went, dropping further and further into the earth. I lost track of time, but eventually I heard a faint hiss followed by a roar. Not that of an animal— more like wind playing over rocks. The darkened stairwell transitioned to a Texan burnt orange before eventually brightening to the color of flame. The steps ended, and the lot of us exited through the archway at the bottom.

Everyone looked about with varying expressions of shock. I was the first one to find my voice. "Uh... where are we?"

17

A NARROW WALKWAY EXTENDED ACROSS A STONE ARCH before us, the rock weathered and scuffed and dangerously thin. A hot wind whirled up from below. I peered over the edge of the platform on which we stood and spotted a slow moving river of lava, bubbling with anger as it oozed between the pillars of stone. Above, glistening stalactites hung from the roof of the cavern. Occasional droplets of water dripped from their tips and turned into steam as they fell into the superheated gas below.

"I don't know a way to ask this without sounding insane," I said, "but, ah... are we in hell?"

Bill struggled against the straps, and I realized he was trying to shake his head. "Nah. These catacombs are part of the Harry Ransom Center, believe it or not. Fun fact, that's why the Gutenberg bible was sent here in the first place. To secure the catacombs against the demonic forces below."

"Really?" said Larry. "How did you know that?"

"Don't look so surprised, Larry. I read."

"You page forward on your Kindle with what? Your nose?"

"They put everything on audio nowadays. I ask Dawn to help me with the earbuds."

"So, you're saying we're not *in* hell," I said. "Merely atop a portal that leads there."

"So it would appear," said Dawn with a sigh. "Bill, you want to do the job we brought you here to do?"

"Don't get testy," he said. "Go straight. And be careful, will you Larry? I may be a zombie, but I'm not immune to lava."

We headed over the natural stone walkway, and I thanked God—who must've existed if Hell did—that I wasn't afraid of heights. Larry led the way. When we reached the end of the arch, Bill instructed us to take the rightmost of four walkways that branched from there. We followed his instructions, going down steps hewn into the stone, over more natural bridges, back up other sets of steps, and through passageways into adjoining caverns. We followed that pattern several times, to the point where my feet ached and the pathways all started to look the same.

I guess I wasn't the only one. Larry called everyone to a halt at the next overlook. "Hold on, guys. Bill, are you sure you know where you're going?"

"Of course, I do. I have a sixth sense about these sorts of things."

I whispered to Dawn. "Speaking of, how *does* he know where we're going?"

"Didn't Larry tell you?" said Dawn. "Before he became a zombie, he was a navigator on an English barque."

As if that answered my question...

"I know, Bill, but are you *really* sure?" said Larry. "I feel like I've seen this same stone arch three times already."

Bill glanced to his right, then his left. It took him a while to respond. "Come to think of it, maybe we have been this way before."

Larry threw his hands up. "Come on, Bill! You've gotta tell me when things aren't working. Now what are we going to do?"

"Don't give up on me," said Bill. "I think the flowing lava is messing with my innate sense of magnetism, but trust me, I've got this. I just need to focus. So don't talk to me. Don't interact with me at all. I'm going to get in a zone and give it my best. Instead of calling out a route, I'm merely going to look in the direction we should go. Ready to give it a shot?"

"Hold on," I said. "Are you absolutely *sure* you've never played *The Secret of Monkey Island?*"

"I still don't know what that is," said Larry. "Is that like a tabletop game or what?"

"Never mind," I said. "Do your thing. As crazy as it sounds, I have a feeling it'll work."

With renewed vigor, we set out behind Larry. So as to not interrupt Bill's concentration, not a man or woman among us made a sound. I guess it paid off, because within fifteen minutes, after passing through another passageway hewn through the rock, we arrived upon a fresh vista. A hemispherical cavern stretched before us, one with numerous rock arches buttressing from openings in the walls toward an enormous pillar of rock rising from the churning lava in the center. There a pyramid stood, more Mayan in style than Egyptian, with big blocky steps and a flat top.

"There it is," said Bill, breaking the silence. "The *Librum de Virtute*. It's at the top of that pyramid, I can feel it."

Larry ruffled his hair. "Good work, buddy. Let's go snag it. We've wasted enough time as it is."

We headed across the stone walkway in single file. It

could've been my imagination, but as we set foot on the central pillar, I thought I felt a rumble underfoot. Then I heard a roar, this time more animal than wind-like, and I knew I hadn't imagined it.

I wanted to tell myself it was something innocuous, like an earthquake that would send me plummeting to my death in the lava below, but I had no such luck. I heard the roar again, and from the side of the pyramid I caught motion.

I spotted the horns first, gleaming white with tips like spears. The head appeared over the stone blocks of the pyramid's base, that of a massive bull, with black eyes, mangy fur, and a thick gold hoop set through its wide nose. Viscous ropes of saliva trailed from the edges of its mouth. Over its shoulder, it carried a gleaming axe with a blade broad enough to chop down a redwood. The beast stepped around the edge of the structure, revealing itself as a ten foot tall minotaur, its top half bovine, its lower half human—and completely bare for the world to see.

I grimaced at the sight of the thing's massive, dangling genitals. "Ugh. Why does it have to be naked?"

"Trust me," said Larry. "They're always naked."

"Really? You have a lot of experience with minotaurs?"

"Not minotaurs per se. Supernatural hell beasts in general. There was this one time when Dawn, Tank, and I were in Louisiana—"

The minotaur lifted its axe, roared again, and charged. Suddenly the thing's nudity wasn't close to the most alarming part about it. Larry leapt forward and brandished his arms before him, crackles of blue lightning dancing from his fingertips. Dawn swept her swords from their sheaths and twirled them before coiling like a tiger. Amazingly enough, Tank just stood there with a scowl upon his face, his tree trunk arms crossed over his chest.

As the minotaur's pounding feet shook the earth, fear lanced down my spine. I wanted to run, to hide, to scream, but there wasn't anywhere to go, nothing to cower behind, and Bill was taking care of the screaming part for me.

"Are we really doing this?" he yelled from the confines of his makeshift baby carrier. "Christ, you've gotta be kidding me. *Ohhhh SHHHHIIIIITTTTT!*"

The minotaur grunted as it leapt. Its muscles rippled as the axe swung forward, light from an unknown point source gleaming off its edge. Lightning erupted from Larry's fingers, arcing across the gap into the weapon's tip. The air crackled. Tendrils of pure energy played over the axe head, shooting into the minotaur's arm. The beast roared as hair fried and fat popped, but the bolts didn't stop the attack's momentum.

The massive axe blade slammed into Larry's side. I screamed, expecting his top half to go flying in a shower of blood and entrails. Instead I heard a dull thump like that of a sledge-hammer hitting a tire, and Larry flew back some twenty or thirty feet, rolling through the dirt and gravel as he landed.

The minotaur planted its fore leg and brought the axe around in a heaving back swing. The thing travelled in slow motion toward me. Snippets of thought zipped through my mind. Had Larry cast a protective spell over me, too? Would the force knock me into the lava? If not, would I retain conscious-ness long enough as my severed torso soared through the air to yell the foul-mouthed pile of curses at Larry that he so richly deserved, and why in God's name did my final moments have to be spent staring at a minotaur's swinging junk?

Fate never put my theories to the test. Dawn appeared out

of nowhere, her blades whistling in a tornado of steel. An ear splitting clang filled the air as her swords met the meat of the minotaur's axe. Sparks showered the pair of them. Dawn staggered under the strength of the blow, an awe-inspiring feat given that a similar swing had sent the much heavier Larry flying halfway to San Antonio.

Dawn moved at the same speed as her blades, spinning, twirling, dodging, weaving, a vortex of death with hardened razors for hands. Her swords found the minotaur's chest, thighs, and back, causing glistening red wounds to blossom across him like bluebonnets. Her katana dug deep into his ribs, her wakizashi hamstrung the back of his knee, and with a flying leap reminiscent of *Crouching Tiger, Hidden Dragon*, Dawn cut deep gouges across the beast's biceps.

None of it mattered. With an angry bellow, the creature slammed a fist into Dawn's ribcage. This time she did go flying, past Larry who'd stumbled to his feet and was rushing back into the fray. He put his hands together as if in prayer, but his face was set with determination. When he pulled the edges of his fingers apart, a bright yellow glow erupted from the middle. He screamed in a not terribly frightening manner as a torrent of flame shot from his palms toward the hulking beast.

The minotaur crouched as the onslaught arrived, shielding himself from the worst of it with the broad side of his axe. When the fire dissipated, he stood and stretched, his fur smoking, his skin steaming. He bared his inhuman yellow teeth and bellowed. The cavern shook, and the pillar of rock underneath us rumbled.

Larry spun his arms in wide arcs, the space between them having grown dark and foreboding. He shot us an angry glance. "A little help would be nice, Tank."

"Sorry, I'm not supposed to shoot anything."

"Jesus Christ, are you kidding me?" I said. "Shoot! Shoot it to death!"

I'll give him credit, Tank took his orders seriously. In one smooth motion, he unzipped his duffel bag, reached inside, and pulled the Desert Eagle .50 Action Express. He tossed the bag into the air as if it were filled with foam packing peanuts, and before it hit the ground, he'd squared his shoulders and fired a full seven rounds into the minotaur's left eye.

The beast wobbled, took one step, and collapsed face first into the dirt.

18

Tank ejected the empty magazine, stepped to the discarded duffel bag, knelt beside it as he put a fresh magazine in, slipped the Desert Eagle into the bag, and looped it over his shoulder as he stood. That's when he noticed me staring at him. "What?"

I tried to form a full sentence, but all that came out was, *"Holy shit."*

He tilted his head at me. "Sometimes the old methods work best. Sometimes they don't."

Larry walked up, brushing the dirt from his coat. "Hey, I would've dealt with him. Eventually."

Tank shook his head and rolled his eyes, a move I was intimately familiar with.

I lowered my voice. *"Larry..."* I tipped my head toward Tank.

Thankfully he got the hint. "Oh. Right." He cleared his throat. "Ah... regardless of whether or not I had him under control, good job, Tank. That was some nice shooting."

Tank's made eye contact with Larry, and his face lost some of its tension. "Thanks."

Dawn joined us, cool as a cucumber as she slipped her swords back into their sheaths. "Well? What are we waiting for?"

"Yeah," said Bill, his eyes wide and his voice shaky. "Let's snag that book and get the hell out of here before another minotaur decides to make us his love slaves."

"I don't think that's what he was after, Bill," said Larry.

"Maybe, maybe not," said Bill. "But I'm the only one here who's undead. No small wonder *you* don't care what happens to your corpse after you die."

"Eww," I said. *"Gross."*

"Exactly," said Bill.

"The point is, he's dead," said Larry. "Unless one of you has been practicing necromancy behind my back, this is a conversation we don't need to have."

With Larry leading the way, we approached the stone structure. From afar, it hadn't looked like much, but I soon realized that was more of a statement on the size of the cavern than the pyramid. By the time I set foot to the steps at the base, I'd realized the ascent up the side would make the stair workouts our softball team sometimes did at Darrell K. Royal Stadium seem like a warmup.

At least we took them slow. Larry's physique suggested he couldn't handle them at an accelerated pace, but the look on the wizard's face made me think there was something beyond the physical act of exercise that was bothering him.

I sidled up next to him. "Something up?"

He blinked at me. "What do you mean?"

"You've got this glazed look to you, and you've been staring at your feet for the last hundred steps. You afraid to see how many are left?"

Bill smiled at me from the baby carrier. "Sometimes it's good not to have legs, know what I mean?"

Larry ignored him. "I'm not studying the steps. I'm studying the symbols over them."

"Symbols?"

I followed his finger. They were faint, as if they'd been carved into the rock millennia ago and worn away by sun and rain or whatever weathering mechanisms there might be in an underground cavern such as this one. Circular carvings with images embedded in the middle, depictions of demons or warriors or hairy anteaters—it was hard to tell which.

"Right," I said. "Symbols. Are they a warning?"

"Could be," said Larry. "I'm not an expert on ancient Mesoamerican symbology. But I'll tell you what I do know. Those symbols are magical in nature."

"I'm guessing you can feel the magical energies?"

"Smell them, actually."

I wrinkled my nose. "You can *smell* magic?"

"Yeah," said Larry. "And that look you're giving me is a good representation of what these symbols smell like. A mixture of decaying flesh and a Wall Street stock trader's cologne. It's the scent of pure evil."

"Are we talking about the symbols or that minotaur?"

"That was his *real* smell," said Larry. "I'm speaking about magical aromas. Trust me, compared to these carvings, that minotaur smelled like a rose. What I'm saying is, keep your eyes peeled."

I was pleased with myself for not panting when we finally crested the pyramid's summit, something Larry couldn't claim.

As he caught his breath and Dawn and Tank closed the gap behind us, I stared off the edge into the sprawling cavern and rivers of lava beyond. I didn't have to be a vulcanologist or a student of ancient Greek literature to enjoy it, though it did strike me as odd that such a thing could exist under a city with zero tectonic activity such as Austin. Then again, I'd seen so many crazy things over the past thirty hours that I'd started to lose my ability to be shocked.

The vista of the pyramid's plaza-like top wasn't anything to speak of, but it drew Larry's attention regardless. He straightened, his shortness of breath forgotten as he stared at the stone pedestal at the center.

"That's it," he said. "That's where we'll find it. The *Librum de Virtute.*"

"Yeah?" I said. "How does it smell?"

Larry snorted. "Joke all you like, but it smells *freaking amazing.* Like chocolate and sex and crisp hundred dollar bills."

Larry headed toward it a brisk walk, a look of determination upon his face. I ran after him and grabbed him by the arm. "Whoa. Slow down."

Larry scowled. "What? Why?"

"You said it yourself. To keep our eyes peeled. This feels like a trap."

Larry snorted. "A trap? Give me a break. All I have to do is walk over there, grab it, and—"

"Not so fast!" called a strong, masculine voice.

I turned at the sound. A man crested another of the pyramid's sides, a tall, handsome guy in his early twenties with luscious, russet colored hair, muscles that bulged from underneath a too-tight cotton shirt, and dreamy green eyes. A golden sword handle gleamed over his shoulder. He smiled as he approached us, and I felt my knees weaken.

"O'Neill?" said Larry. "What the hell are you doing here?"

"Same thing as you," he called out. "I'm after the *Librum*."

I turned to Dawn, who'd joined me at my side. *"O'Neill?"*

She smiled at me. "Smitten? I don't blame you. That's Angus O'Neill, renowned druid and sword fighter extraordinaire. He's almost as good with that cleaver as I am with mine. Lucky for me I've got two. Looks pretty damn good considering he's pushing two thousand, huh?"

I squinted. "Pushing two thousand what?"

"Years, Lexie. But don't worry. It doesn't slow him down in the sack one bit."

Angus overheard and shot Dawn a smile along with a set of finger guns.

"Are you saying you and him...?" I sighed. "Of course."

"Hey, it's a reunion," said Larry. "Great. Too bad it's going to end poorly. Sorry, Angus, but you can't have the book. We have a wealthy financier who's paying us big bucks to retrieve it for him."

"So?" said Angus. "I need it to defend myself from the McGreggor clan. I think personal safety trumps a cash grab any day."

"The McGreggors?" Larry blew a raspberry. "Those guys are a bunch of chumps. I could take them with one hand tied behind my back and a—"

"Hold it right there you lot!"

We all turned to the far side of the pyramid, where a pair of mismatched individuals were approaching. One of them was an enormous gump, maybe six and a half feet tall, with a shaved head, a chin beard, and as much muscle as fat on his oversized frame. The other was a petite CEO type, a woman with an upturned nose, wearing fashionable glasses and with her hair pulled into a tight ponytail. Both of them wore flak jackets, black pants, and combat boots and had roughly the contents of Tank's duffel bag strapped to their bodies.

"Who the hell are they?" I asked.

"Ugh…" Larry rolled his eyes. "That's Otis Zachary Pacheco and Jane Fettercross, owners and operators of the black ops monster hunting conglomerate, BSI."

"*BSI?*"

"Brute Squad Incorporated," said Otis as he came to a stop near us. "And I hate to burst all your bubbles, but the book on that pedestal is officially ours."

"*Officially* yours?" said Angus. "Bollocks to that."

"Yeah," said Larry. "What kind of crap is this?"

"The best kind," said Otis. "The official kind. Jane? Care to show them?"

Jane reached under her bulletproof jacket and pulled out an envelope, which she handed to Larry with a smirk. "That's the official correspondence from the FBI giving us sole right of possession to that tome."

Larry ripped the letter open and began perusing the contents while Angus looked over his shoulder. Even knowing Angus was a dog of the loosest morals, I couldn't help but feel my heart flutter with him nearby.

Larry slapped the page. "This is bullshit of the highest order. This document is so vague as to be worthless. Any lawyer worth his salt could poke a hundred holes in it. Not to mention you mistakenly assume any of us care about the law."

"I know I certainly don't," called a sultry new voice to our right.

We all groaned and turned to face the new entrant.

"Charity Peterson?" said Larry. "Oh, you've got to be fucking kidding me."

A tan woman in a black tube top and a cropped jean jacket stood there, one hand on her hip as she struck a sassy pose. Rose tattoos covered both her forearms. She also sported a tattoo of claw marks across her ridiculously chiseled abs and another of skulls across her collarbone that dipped dangerously into her cleavage. I felt inadequate just looking at her.

"Seriously," I said to Dawn. "Does every woman in this line of work look like you two? Because it's starting to piss me off."

Dawn bit her lip as she trailed her gaze over the new arrival. "Not all of them. Charity is particularly *tasty*. She's so mysterious and cool and sexy…"

"Keep it in your pants, Dawn," said Larry. "You too, Angus. And what could possibly bring an airplane mechanic slash ghost spirit shifter such as you here, I wonder?"

Charity's voice flowed like honey wine. "I'm here for the book, of course."

"I know!" yelled Larry. "I was being sarcastic. Christ! We're all here for the book."

"And you're all going to walk away disappointed," said Otis. "Because we're the only ones with the legal standing to retrieve it."

"Legal standing, schmegal standing," said Larry. "We got here first. Not to mention I called dibs under my breath the instant I saw Angus. It's ours."

"Why should any of that matter?" said Angus. "This is clearly an issue of seniority. I'm the oldest, therefore I should get the book. Not to mention I'm the handsomest."

"And I'm the strongest," said Otis. "Who gives a crap?"

"Precisely nobody," said Larry. "Not to mention Tank is clearly the strongest, but it's not a competition. The point is—"

The ground started to shake and a high pitched screech filled the air, like that of a tanker ship rubbing against an iceberg. We all turned toward the pedestal. Perched upon the top stood Charity, the *Librum de Virtute* clutched in her hands.

She smiled and winced. "Sorry. I thought I could steal it while you were arguing."

The screech intensified, as did the rumbling. The cavern ceiling wobbled back and forth, the stalactites swaying precariously. They didn't crack and fall though, perhaps because it wasn't the ceiling moving at all. It was the pyramid that couldn't stop dancing.

The ear-piercing wail of stone on stone reached a fever pitch. I jammed my fingers into my ears to shut out the roar. After a few seconds, the painful sound receded, the rumbling of the earth slowed, and given that a giant stone sphere hadn't dropped from overhead and begun rolling in our direction, I thought maybe, just maybe, we'd gotten off scot-free.

I still hadn't learned a damn thing, apparently.

As the screech faded, a new sound filled the air, more of a whisper crossed with a moan. I couldn't quite locate where it came from. Then I saw it. A shadowy blur, climbing over the side of the pyramid. It paused a few feet from the edge. It was a wolflike thing, with black matted fur, a long eyeless head, and feet that resembled an eagle's. It stood on its back talons, uncoiled to twice its height, and cut loose with a raptor's cry.

"Well that's a relief," said Charity. "After all that rumbling, I was sure we'd have to deal with something far worse than a homeless man's griffin."

From all around us, other creatures echoed the cry. Three

more climbed over the edge. Then five from another side. Another seven clambered over before the dam broke. A teeming horde of black poured over the edge and sprinted toward us.

Larry babbled at light speed. "What do you say everyone? Let bygones be bygones? Good. Now *ATTAAACKKK!*"

I'd never seen so many people move so fluidly. Larry darted toward the creatures. Beams of white hot light burst from his hands, cutting through them as if they were made of smoke. Dawn and Angus dove toward them with swords flashing, the latter's growing is size as he swung it until it reached almost seven feet in length. Tank roared and pulled two assault rifles from his bag, cutting loose with a hail of gunfire. Jane lobbed incendiary grenades with one hand while firing rounds from a Walther P99 with the other. Otis barreled into the nearest bunch of hell creatures, an Atchisson Assault Shotgun with a thirty-two round drum barking from his hands. I lost track of Charity until a six foot hyena with markings suspiciously similar to her tattoos dove into the fray, ripping and tearing into the black furry attackers with savage teeth. Bill's fevered scream pierced the roar of action, and I couldn't tell if he was scared out of his mind or having the time of his life. Maybe both.

Through it all, I stood in the center, my feet rooted to the ground and my mouth open. I'd seen similar scenes play out in *The Lord of the Rings* or while playing *Skyrim*, but never in person.

Larry's light beams vaporized another dozen nightmare creatures. "Lexie, now's the time to show us what you've got."

"What *I've* got?" My voice sounded high-pitched in my ears. "Whatever I bring to the table, this is decidedly not it. I don't even have a weapon!"

"What about the mace?"

"I left that in my letter jacket, not to mention I don't think it would help."

A beast disappeared in a cloud of smoke. "You know I told you to arm yourself."

"Is this really the time for this conversation?"

Larry blasted a leaping nightmare while Dawn speared one approaching him from behind. "How are you with a flintlock?"

"Terrible."

"Well, what are you good with?" Three more beasts went down, two to light beams and a third to a vicious decapitation.

"In video games I usually pick an axe. In real life? I don't know. A softball bat?"

Larry paused, his brow furrowed as Tank ran by with guns blazing. "A bat for the softball player. It's fitting."

The horde continued to push in, faster now that Larry was distracted. "Yeah," I said. "Only problem is I didn't bring one."

"Way ahead of you, Lexie. Tank, cover me." Larry's palms faded back to flesh color as he knelt next to the decapitated demon head. Tank's rifles cracked and rattled. Shell casings flew as Larry passed his hands over the nightmare's gaping jaws and razor-sharp fangs. His lips moved, but I couldn't hear a word of it over the din. Then he plunged his hands into the demon's open mouth and grasped one of the protruding canines. He pulled with all his might, but the tooth didn't give. Rather it grew, lengthening as Larry drove against the stone with his legs. Eventually, it gave with a resounding pop, tossing Larry back two feet through the air. He hefted and twirled it before holding it before him. "What do you think?"

The demon tooth now measured almost three feet in length, with a tapered end where Larry had gripped it and a thicker end where it had come free. Where the end cap would normally be was still rough from the tooth's roots.

"Not bad," I said. "But it's missing a knob."

"A what?"

"A knob," I said. "The part at the thin end that keeps your hands from slipping off."

One of Tank's rifles clicked as it emptied. "Boss?"

"Oh, for crying out loud." Larry waved his hands and threw the bat into the air before turning and blasting another batch of demons with his laser light hands. As the bat flew, bits of hair from the dead demon's head swirled behind it, coalescing into a thick pad at the base of the bat.

I caught the thing by the grip in mid air. I wanted it to feel evil, slimy, or disgusting, but it didn't. It was light but strong. It had perfect balance, and the grip was ever so slightly textured. I gave it a test swing. It whistled through the air without resistance and with just the right amount of bend. There was also something about it I couldn't put my finger on. A hidden strength that flowed into my fingers and up my arm as I gripped it.

"Well?" called Larry over his shoulder.

I couldn't lie. "This is the best damn bat I've ever held."

"Great. Now get your ass in here and earn your keep!"

Larry didn't have to make room for me at the front lines. A hell beast snuck through Tank's fire and Larry's vaporizer beams and sprinted toward me at cheetah-like speed. I held my ground, planted my feet in a side stance, cocked the bat, and using the skills I'd honed since T-ball, waited for my chance. The beast lunged and flew. I uncorked on it right as it hit the strike zone. The monster cut loose with a comical wail befitting a cartoon coyote as it soared up, up, and away, at least two hundred feet through the air before disappearing off the edge of the pyramid, but the best part was that my shoulder felt fresh as a daisy.

I looked down at the bat in my hands. "Oh, *hell yeah*."

Larry's voice carried over the mêlée. "Lexie? Any time now!"

I think I actually smiled as I sprinted into the fray.

19

THE DOOR TO THE NYTE PATROL HOUSE CLATTERED AS WE shut it behind us. Larry groaned as he headed to the living room. "Christ, I'm beat. Tank, you want to grab some beers? I'll take two."

Tank split off toward what I presumed was the kitchen while Larry unhooked Bill, dumped him into his jar, and ditched the baby carrier before collapsing into his chair. He flicked his hand at one of the guest seats, but I paid him no mind. I couldn't get enough of the demon tooth bat. It had shrunk to about the size of a walrus tusk on the walk out of the catacombs, but I found that if I squeezed it, it grew back to full size within a second and a half. It was *freaking awesome*.

Tank returned with a half dozen beers. He set them on the table, popped three of the caps off, and took one. Larry helped himself to one as well, poured some of it into Bill's jar, and held the third out to me, which I accepted without taking my eyes off my tooth.

While Bill lapped noisily at the finger of beer in his jar,

Larry sighed and leaned back in his chair. "Well... That escalated quickly."

Tank shrugged as he took a long draught of his ale. "I thought it was fun. Feel bad about Angus though."

"Yeah, seriously," said Larry. "You straight up murdered him, Tank."

"I didn't murder him. It was an accident."

"Oh, really? You *accidentally* knocked him off the edge of the walkway as that last batch of hell creatures bore down on us?"

Tank snorted. "Fine. Maybe it wasn't an accident. But let me remind you he tried to sneak off with the tome when he thought we were engaged. Besides, he's immortal. He'll be fine."

Larry frowned. "Ehh... I don't know about that. I'm not sure he's ever been tossed into a river of flowing lava before. His screams sounded pretty... *final*. Either way, you should probably lay low for a while in case the rest of his clan comes looking for you."

I squeezed on the demon tooth and it shot to full size. I loosened my grip, and after a few seconds, it shrunk back down again. I couldn't help but snicker. "This is so cool. Larry, can you make more of these? My teammates would totally flip."

Larry took a sip of beer as he shook his head. "Sorry, that's a one time deal. I had to sacrifice one of my four hundred or so middle names to make it. That's how seriously I take your commitment to this team."

Bill paused from lapping up the beer in his jar to stare at Larry. "Hey. You never made *me* a demon tooth anything."

"You're a zombie head in a jar, Bill. What do you want me to make you, a demonic sombrero?"

While he grumbled, I heard the back door open and close.

Dawn stumbled around the corner, a weary look on her face, with her hair and clothes in disarray and her sheathed swords held in her left hand.

"Dawn!" said Larry. "There you are. We were worried about you. Are you okay?"

Dawn dumped her swords on the floor and walked gingerly toward the couch. She leaned against the armrest and gave a heavy sigh, her eyelids mostly closed.

Larry leaned up in his chair. "Dawn?"

Her eyes snapped open. "Huh?"

"I said are you okay?"

"What? Yeah. I'm fine. Charity and I got separated from you guys during that bit with the earthquake and the steam fissures. We made it out okay."

I looked at Dawn's stance, the relaxed manner in which her arms hung at her sides and the look of total serenity on her face. I smiled. "So... you and Charity got *separated,* huh?"

Dawn shrugged off my mirth. "Whatever. That woman is foxy as hell. If you swung that way, you would've done the same thing."

"I don't know," I said. "I think she would've had to buy me dinner first."

"What the hell are you two talking about?" Larry's eyes darted between me and Dawn before eventually settling on Dawn. "Oh. *Ooooohh.*"

"So," said Dawn. "Did you get it?"

"Get what?" asked Larry.

"*Hello?* The tome."

Larry snorted. "Give me a break. Of course we got it. Tank, you got it, didn't you?"

Tank frowned and shook his head. He set his beer on the

desk, rifled through his duffel bag, and dumped the book on the desk. A dusty cloud filled the air as the cover made contact with the wood. The beer bottles and Larry's phone rattled from the impact. The thing weighed as much as a sack of bricks.

"For the record, I'm not your pack mule," said Tank.

"I know that," said Larry. "But I was already carrying Bill, and my hands were otherwise occupied with literal beams of destruction. What was I supposed to do, shove the thing in my pants?"

Tank batted a dismissive hand Larry's way, snagged his beer, and stormed out of the living room.

Dawn lifted an eyebrow. "What did you do this time?"

"Why do you assume this is my fault?" Larry said. "He's just upset that he killed Angus O'Neill. You know how he gets."

Dawn sighed. "Give me a few minutes. I'll get him out of his funk."

Dawn left after the man, and I settled into one of the guest chairs. "I really hope *get him out of his funk* isn't a euphemism for something sexual."

Larry scowled at me. "Get your mind out of the gutter. They're friends. She's going to talk to him, that's all. Tank might look tough, but he's a big baby. Gets all worked up over the smallest things."

"Like you taking him for granted over and over again?"

"When did I do that?"

"In the laser hallway, obviously, and again just now. You never asked Tank to carry the tome. You sure as hell never thanked him for it, and you acted like a giant ass at the very thought of him losing it along the way."

Larry snorted. "We're not in kindergarten. I'm not handing

out participation trophies. Besides, what makes you such an expert on team chemistry?"

It was a painful jab, but I don't think he actually knew about my explosion at practice. "I'm literally on a softball team, Larry. Come on. Your spell picked me for a reason. You said so yourself, and I'm telling you that if you don't want your team to fall apart, you need to stop minimizing everyone else's contributions. That goes for Dawn as well as Tank."

Larry sighed. "Fine. I'll smooth things over with Tank later tonight. But in the meantime, can you stop being such a buzzkill? I mean, seriously. We got it. The *Librum de Virtute*." He flourished the hand that wasn't holding his beer. "That makes two successful missions in two nights, and this one will actually pay the bills. Not bad, am I right?"

I eyed the ancient doorstop. "Speaking of the *Librum*—can we talk about it?"

"What's there to talk about?"

"Well, there's the fact that according to your bibliomancer friend, the University tried to get rid of the book some years ago but the original Spanish owners refused to take it. So instead they buried it deep in an underground catacomb surrounded by lava and protected by a bloodthirsty minotaur, and then when Charity picked it up off its pedestal, it spawned a legion of black, furry nightmares that tried to separate our flesh from our bones."

Larry blinked. "And?"

"What I'm saying is this book is clearly dangerous. Do you even know what it does?"

"Not my problem," said Larry. "Romanov hired us to deliver it to him, not to teach him how to use it."

"Which is kind of what I'm getting at," I said. "Look, I

punched *Librum de Virtute* into Google. It literally translates as 'Book of Power,' which, yeah, after tonight with the demons and the lava and everything else, I totally believe. And you're willing to hand it over to this Romanov guy, no questions asked."

"Well... he pays really well," said Larry. "And on time, I might add."

I wanted to reach across the desk and shake the guy by the throat. *"You're missing the point, Larry.* How well do you know him? Can he be trusted? What are his motivations?"

"Not very well, I have no idea, and beats me, in that order. But I told you when we first met, we've located a number of items for Romanov over the past few months and to the best of my knowledge he hasn't done anything evil with them so far. I don't see why that would change."

"What have you given him so far?"

"Let's see... A magic sword. Some crystals that were imbued with ancient spirits or mystical energies or some crap like that. Ah... a map. I remember that one being quite mundane. And I can't remember the last one. Bill, you want to help me out?"

Bill looked up from his beer swilling efforts, his eyes glassy. Despite his efforts, a finger of beer remained in the bottom of his jar. He seemed to be losing a fair amount through the decayed holes in his cheeks every time he lapped some up, but I wasn't sure he'd made *any* progress. Then I realized the beer was leaking out through his severed neck right back into the jar. I wanted to gag.

The brew seemed to be doing the trick, though. "Whaz that?"

"The items we brought to Romanov, Bill. A sword, a map, crystals, and what else?"

"Hold on," slurred Bill. "Itz on the tip of my... on the tip of my tuh... tuh... tongue."

"Oh." Larry snapped his fingers. "An amulet. That's the last one."

"And all these items were magical in nature?" I said.

"Well, yeah. All except the map. I'm pretty sure we got that one at a gas station."

I frowned. "That's odd... but whatever. The point is, what's Romanov going to do with all these items? No. Scratch that. You don't know. Of course you don't. But what *could* he do with them?"

"Ah. Well..." Larry stuck a finger into the air. "Actually I don't know."

"Well, maybe that's something you should figure out *before* you hand this all-powerful book of ancient magic to him, hmm?"

Larry rubbed his chin and surveyed me carefully. "You know, you're starting to get awfully involved in this job given that you haven't fully committed to being a permanent member of our team yet. Hint hint, I can snag a contract real quick, nudge nudge."

"It has nothing to do with you, trust me. I'm mostly invested in not releasing a swarm of demon creatures on central Texas." I glanced at my phone. It was ten to midnight. "I've got to go. Please don't show up at my dorm again tomorrow. Just give me a call or a text like a normal person, okay?"

"But I can't use a phone because—"

"Then get Dawn to do it. Come on, Larry. I'll see you tomorrow."

I got up. As I headed to the back door, I realized I hadn't used the promise of tomorrow as an excuse to get out of his sight. I'd actually meant it. I'd be back.

Damnit. I *was* getting invested.

20

THE FOLLOWING MORNING GOT OFF TO AN INAUSPICIOUS start. I woke up late. The dorm shower ran out of hot water halfway through my lather, which helped me get out faster than I otherwise would've but not fast enough to avoid a late arrival to my eight o'clock class. That in turn meant I got a delayed start on the pop quiz our instructor assigned. It was open book—a blessing because I'd never emptied my bag from earlier in the week—but I don't think it helped enough. By the end of it, I had matrices swimming in my vision and all I could hope for was that the test would be graded on a generous curve.

My second class went better than the first, if only because I didn't have any exams sprung on me, but gosh darn it if I hadn't come down with a case of sudden onset daydream syndrome. One moment, I'd sat there while Dr. Borovyk droned on about stresses from bending moments, then a wail filled the air, the door at the front of the lecture hall burst open, and a swarm of smoky, razor-clawed demons poured inside. I'd leapt to my feet, demon tooth bat in hand, and started swinging it with wild abandon. The beasts went flying, crashing through the walls and ceiling, howling with fear as they tried to escape the blur of my bat. I smacked one across the jaw. It soared into the projection screen at the front of the hall only to fade into nothingness. Suddenly there was Dr. Borovyk again, and the presentation was about eccentric axial loading instead of moments and I had to click back several slides on my laptop to figure out what I'd missed.

Similar problems afflicted me throughout lunch and my afternoon lab. As I exited my last class of the day and headed to the study hall, I silently admonished myself for my lack of focus, something I'd always thought I'd had in spades. With self-imposed threats hovering over me, I jammed my ear buds into place, cranked up some AC/DC, and got to work on another pile of homework that I hadn't touched the night before. It was going pretty well until my screen went fuzzy and my eyelids gained ten pounds. Then I was off in Neverland again—or at least back at McCombs Field. I was in the middle of a game, but Larry and Dawn and Tank were there. Bill, too. Then my teammates magically disappeared, replaced instead with a herd of chimeras in softball uniforms. Larry's magic crackled, Dawn's blades flashed, Tank's guns rat-a-tat-tatted, and I was in the middle of it all, fighting, leaping, yelling, and having the time of my life.

I awoke with a start. I blinked a few times and worked some saliva onto the roof of my mouth. My collar felt damp as I plucked it off my skin, and I sat up, pretending like I hadn't been drooling all over myself while sawing logs in public. My earphones were still blaring AC/DC—the eponymous track from *Back in Black*. It was a bad sign given the last song I remembered was "Whole Lotta Rosie" off *Let There Be Rock*.

I tapped on my laptop to wake the screen and cursed when I saw the time. "Shit. *Shit shit shit.*"

I pulled my phone from my pocket and pushed my thumb to the scanner. Four messages waited for me. Three of them were from Heather, and they were as bad as I'd expected.

At quarter till three. *I'll see you at practice in fifteen. Hope you worked on your speech.*

Twenty minutes later. *Lexie, where the hell are you? You'd better be hauling ass to get here.*

And then the last one, from fifteen minutes ago. *Damn. Way to reinforce my trust in you. Good luck with life, I guess.*

Whatever mirth was left from my epic dream battle against the Greece Tech Mythological Bombers shriveled and died on the vine. I couldn't believe I'd missed practice *again,* and after promising Heather I'd be there and make good on my outburst to boot. The worst part was that softball hadn't crossed my mind all day, at least not until my sleep-deprived, hard rock fueled dream. What the hell was wrong with me? Did I not care anymore? Did I no longer want to be a part of the team?

If anyone had ever asked me, I would've told them 'quitter' wasn't in my personal dictionary, but I'd never bungled something this badly before, either. Over the last thirty-six hours I'd gone from a bad teammate to a nonexistent one, and perhaps worse, I'd become a bad friend to Heather. Maybe the world's *worst* one.

There was one more message on my phone, one that had arrived a minute or two before I woke up. I didn't recognize the number, but I opened it anyway. *Hey, it's Dawn. Larry says he wants to talk to you. Has some information you wanted. Also, can you pick up Whataburger on the way over? A chicken sandwich for me, a double meat burger for Larry, and a triple meat with three extra patties for Tank. Should probably get something for Bill, too, otherwise he'll get pissy. Thanks.*

My teeth squeaked as I ground them together. I hit the reply button and paused with my finger over the screen. Part of me wanted to tell Dawn to shove off, that I had much bigger issues at the moment than fetching fast food for her and the rest of the Nyte Patrol, but was it really true? Wasn't the *Librum de Virtute's* potential misuse arguably more important than anything in my disjointed personal life?

As I tried to rationalize my decision, I knew I was fooling myself. I'd gone running to the Nyte Patrol in the misguided hope of finding a team, any team, in which I'd feel as vital and valuable as I used to feel on my softball team. I hadn't found that—not yet, anyway—but I had found one whose end goal was more weighty than the number of runs on a scoreboard.

I sighed. After a moment, I typed out a simple response. *Ok. Be over soon.*

When I arrived, I sauntered into the living room to find Dawn and Tank in front of the TV, this time watching one of those home flipping shows. Bill was in his jar, quietly snoring, but Larry was nowhere to be seen.

"Hey." I tossed a couple fast food bags on the desk. "I'm here."

Dawn rose from the couch and joined me. "Hey, Lexie. Thanks. We were running low on dinner options. Figured this was easier than having you swing by the supermarket. Tank?" The big guy leaned over the back of the couch as Dawn tossed him the comically oversized sextuple meat burger.

"You guys cook?" I said.

"Tank does. He makes a mean gazpacho." Dawn tapped on the side of Bill's jar, waking the zombie from his slumber. She sprinkled some fries over him. "Dinner time, little buddy. Eat up."

I glanced at the man mountain on the couch. Between the fashion shows, the home makeover stuff, and the cooking, I had a lot of questions, but I let them slide for the more pressing one. "Bill eats french fries?"

The zombie head yawned and blinked. "Trust me, if fast food places served sauteed brains, I'd order those, but I take what I can get. And I don't really eat them. Mostly I lick the salt off."

Dawn took a seat and started on her chicken sandwich. I sat next to her and pulled out the burger I'd ordered for myself. "So where's Larry?"

"Holed up in the study," said Dawn, pointing with a fry. "He popped out to tell me to summon you, then dove back in. He's been reading that tome all day as far as I know."

"And what have the rest of you been doing? Watching TV? Baking scones?"

"Tank's more of a biscuit guy, but no. Larry assigned us research tasks pertaining to the items we'd previously delivered to Romanov. Said you had a good idea to investigate those. Probably should've done it sooner, to be honest."

I was curious and I didn't want to come across as an ass, so I simply nodded. "And?"

"I investigated the sword. Wasn't too hard, given we knew the name. *Gwyriad,* a Welsh sword from the sixteenth century. Translates to deflection or divergence or something like that, which gives you a good idea as to the magic imbued to it. I tracked the sword over the centuries and found that the wielder was always abnormally hard to strike down. Makes me think I should've kept the sword for myself, actually."

I blinked. "You traced five centuries of a sword's history? You must have good contacts."

Dawn shrugged. "I know how to Google. Tank, you want to tell us about those crystals?"

The big guy didn't turn from the TV. "They're pink, I think. They... focus power or something."

Dawn sighed and rolled her eyes. "Pretty sure *he* shirked his assignment. But Bill didn't, did you Bill?"

Bill pried his tongue off one of the fries. "Sure didn't. I made some calls. Go on. Ask me about the Amulet of Melding."

"I'd rather ask you how you made those calls."

"As I've told Larry more than once, arms aren't everything. Trust me, I can do a *lot* without appendages." He smiled in a creepier way than normal.

I grimaced. "You know, I figured you would've been the one to study the map, not the amulet."

"I didn't need to study the map," said Bill. "There was nothing special about it. It was literally a AAA map with the South Congress bridge circled in permanent marker."

"The bridge all the bats nest underneath?"

"That's the one," said Bill. "Now, the amulet on the other hand—"

"EUREKA!"

I jumped in my seat as Larry stormed around the corner. He plopped into his chair and dumped the *Librum de Virtute* on the desk. "I've got it."

"Got what?" I said.

"What the *Librum* does, of course." He opened one of the bags and stuffed his face inside it. "Did you get anything for me?"

"A burger," I said. "Should be the only one left. The fries are to share, though we might be running low already."

Bill snickered. "You can have mine when I'm done with them."

"That's okay. Knock yourself out." Larry tore into his meal, moaning his approval as he shot me a thumbs up.

I stared at him. "Well?"

"Well what?"

"What do you mean, well what? The book, Larry!"

"Oh, right. As it turns out, the *Librum* contains detailed magical instructions about imbuing objects with power. Not just inanimate objects, but non-sentient beings as well. And in a bit of serendipity, or perhaps by design, it contains magic to help the reader transfer power to said objects and beings."

"So it can be used to create, what? Golems or something?"

Larry smiled as he licked sauce from a finger. "Hey, you know what golems are. I knew you'd fit right in. But to answer your question, I *think* so. The book is really long, and I'm not much of a speed reader, not to mention my Latin is rusty."

I crumpled my wrapper into a ball and started ticking items off on my fingers. "So thus far you've provided this Romanov guy with a sword that can deflect attacks, mysterious pink crystals that focus power *or something,* a map of the south congress bridge, and an amulet..." I glanced at Bill.

"Of melding," he said. "It can meld things."

"Of course," I said. "And the book can bring objects to life, or so we're led to believe. So if you had access to all those things, what would you do with them, Larry?"

"I'm not the best person to ask," he said around a mouthful of hot beef. "My aspirations in life mostly revolve around not being homeless or starving to death."

"Bill?"

"I'd meld my head onto a new body and stab someone with the sword!"

"Dawn?"

She sighed. "Well, unlike these two idiots, I'd use the items to consolidate my own magical power, assuming I had any to begin with. Then I'd probably use them to do some nasty, spiteful shit and subjugate a bunch of people under my rule."

I blinked. "Seriously?"

"I mean, the Nyte Patrol is fine and all, but if the choice was between all powerful supreme leader for life and this? Come on. But just because I'd use the items for evil doesn't mean Romanov would. Honestly, I don't know a thing about him."

"Right," I said. "Which was the point I was trying to make last night."

"You know," said Larry as he finished his burger. "Instead of assuming the worst of others, we could always ask him what his plans for the *Librum* are."

I scrunched my face. "I don't know how to tell you this, Larry, but sometimes people lie."

He snorted. "I know that. But spells of truth can work wonders, young padawan."

"You can cast spells over the phone?"

"I wouldn't have to. Romanov has a place in town. He runs an academy for disadvantaged gifted folks."

"You mean like Professor X?"

"Not exactly. You'll see. I can give you directions. We've been there several times to drop off the other items."

Something told me heading to Romanov's place was a bad idea, but I couldn't explain why other than the fact that he already had a bunch of powerful magical items and apparently was surrounded by gifted individuals that he was training in the use of deadly magics. "Alright. But we don't take the tome with us. We need to store it somewhere safe until we're absolutely, positively sure we can trust Romanov."

"Relax, Lexie," said Larry. "I know just the man for the job."

21

"For the record," I said as I pulled onto a private drive in west Austin, "Bill was not the right man for the job. He's not even a man. He's a disembodied zombie head. What's he going to do if someone tries to steal the tome? Nibble them to death?"

"Would you let it go?" said Larry. "You've been urging me to build people up, right? Bill is far more capable than you give him credit for. For the record, I've seen him scare away a herd of possessed llamas with his gaze alone, and he won a battle of wits with a Sicilian of intellectual repute. Not to mention that nobody knows we have the tome other than perhaps Charity Peterson and the leaders of BSI. The latter are too goody goody to break into our house to steal it, and I'm pretty sure Dawn and Charity's tryst last night precludes any quid pro quo tome theft."

"For the record, it doesn't," said Dawn from the back seat. "But I don't think Charity will be coming over any time soon. I made it clear I'm a one and done sort of girl."

The trees on either side of the driveway parted, and my jaw

dropped. Romanov may not have been taking unruly mutants under his wing, but his estate sure as heck resembled the Xavier Institute for Higher Learning. The building was more castle than mansion. I parked on the wide circle drive in front of the sprawling structure, killed the engine, and hopped out of the Suburban.

I paused with my hand on the hood of the truck. "Dang. Now I understand what you meant when you said he paid well."

"I know, right?" said Larry. "This guy's loaded. He's pretty much single-handedly kept us afloat for the last six months. Whoa, whoa. Tank. You can't bring that in!"

"Huh?" Tank had hopped out the back, his duffel bag hooked over his shoulder.

"No guns," said Larry. "Dawn, you'll have to leave your swords in the car, too. This is our client. We have to show some professionalism."

Tank grunted and tossed his bag back in the truck while Dawn rolled her eyes and did the same with her swords. The sky was turning a nice shade of purple as we reached the twelve foot tall front gates.

Larry gestured to the doorbell. "Would you please? I'd rather not break anything."

I pressed the buzzer and heard a set of melodious chimes. A moment later, the latch clicked, and both of the doors swung inward on silent hinges. No one stood there to greet us, though a slight breeze whistled past me. I thought I heard a pained moan on the wind's nebulous lips.

Larry stepped inside, but I hesitated. "Did anyone else hear that?"

"You mean that voice?" said Larry. "Yeah, don't worry about

it. Happens every time I've been over. Pretty sure this place was built on an ancient Indian burial ground."

"Right," I said, following him inside. "Because if anything, *that* proves Romanov isn't evil."

"Sometimes you have to make concessions when buying property," said Tank. "Even high priced buyers have budgets, you know."

I snorted. "Alright, Mr. I've Watched Every Episode of *Flip or Flop*."

The entry hall opened into a sprawling cylindrical foyer, one with a broad staircase that split at the back of the room and curved up both walls. A deep purple runner ran the length of the stairs, and velvet drapes of a similar color hung over tall windows at the back of the room, obscuring almost all the remaining natural light. Antique kerosene lamps hung from wrought iron fixtures at the base of the steps, sending flickering shadows dancing across the polished marble floor.

I lifted an eyebrow. "Homey."

"Yeah, it's a little too *Death Becomes Her* for me," said Larry, "but to each his own. Hello? Ivan? Anyone home?"

I heard the moaning breeze again, and the kerosene lamps flickered. As the flames coalesced and returned to full strength, I heard an unfamiliar voice. "Welcome to Goatboil. Can we help you?"

I turned to find two young men standing behind Dawn and Tank. They looked like they could've been twins, each of them a shade over six feet tall, wearing black tank tops that showed off their toned bodies. Each sported perfectly coifed hair that had too much mousse in it, one pitch black and the other a dark brown. They were both undeniably good looking, though a little on the douchey side for my tastes, with sharp features, strong jaws, and smoky eyes—too smoky. They might've been wearing eyeshadow, actually. Maybe eyeliner, too.

Dawn arched a stern eyebrow at the pair. "Cool it with the surprise entrances, Hall and Oates. I may not have my swords on me, but that doesn't mean I'm defenseless."

The young men eyed Dawn with surprisingly cool indifference. "We meant no offense, Miss...?"

"Blayde." Dawn made the name sound like a threat.

"Yes, hi," said Larry. "We're the Nyte Patrol. We're looking for Ivan. It's about an item he asked us to locate for him."

"Hold on," I said. "Are we going to gloss over the fact that this place is called *Goatboil?*"

The young men looked my way. Their eyes focused as if seeing me for the first time. In a blur, they were beside me, one on each side. The one with the black hair stood in front of me, undulating in a somewhat snakelike fashion. He arched an eyebrow, puckered his lips, and gave me a Blue Steel sort of look. When he spoke, his voice had adopted a more sultry, seductive tone. "And who, pray tell, are *you?*"

"Uh... I'm Lexie." I glanced over my shoulder. The guy at my back had adopted the same look as the one in front of me. "And you guys are?"

"Tristan," said the brown haired one.

"And I'm Gavin," said the black-haired one in front of me. He ran his tongue across his lips in a thoroughly creepy way. "Lexie, I don't quite know how to say this, but I find you strangely irresistible. Intoxicating, even. Of every young woman I've ever met, you're without a doubt the one that's the most..." He paused and took a deep breath, as if he were trying to sniff the word out of the air.

"Spell-binding?" I offered.

"Plain."

I took a step back. "Excuse me?"

"It's true." Tristan spoke in my ear. I turned around and nearly smacked him. "Just look at you. There's not a spectacular bone in your body. It's glorious."

I was momentarily too shocked to tell the guy to piss off. "Larry? What kind of academy did you say this was?"

"One for supernatural youth. Vampires mostly, as you can see."

I sneered at Gavin. "Are they all as big of douchebags as these two?"

Larry tilted his head from side to side. "Eh…"

Gavin pulled off his tank top, revealing pecs that had been chiseled from stone. "Lexie. We're going to go on a date. Tomorrow morning. I'll drive. I like to drive fast. It's incredibly easy for me. I barely even have to pay attention. You'll be thoroughly impressed."

"The hell I will," I said.

Tristan spoke in my ear again. I turned to find him shirtless as well. He'd also oiled his muscles. "Lexie. After your date with Gavin, we'll go out. Maybe to a nice, exorbitantly priced restaurant. I'll barely eat, and neither will you. You'll be too busy admiring me, of course. I'll pay. That'll impress you as well."

"What the fuck is wrong with you?" I said. "I'm not dating either of you."

"Yes you will," said Gavin. "We're irresistible."

"Are you using some sort of vampire compulsion on me? Because it's not working."

Gavin looked genuinely confused. "What? No. You'll go out with us because you like being told what to do. It's very erotic. And then, once we get back from the date—"

"Okay, that's enough." Dawn stormed forward, waving her arms. "Get the fuck out of here you pricks. She's not buying your jerkwad teenage power trip fantasies. Go on, git. Before one of us sticks a boot up your ass."

In a blur, both of the guys had their shirts back on and had retreated to the base of the stairs. Gavin smirked at me. "You'll come around, Lexie. Your kind always do."

The cocky bastard blew me a kiss before disappearing. I growled as Tristan lingered behind, waving seductively.

"Hey, hold on," said Larry. "Romanov. Where can we find him?"

"Not sure," said Tristan. "Ask Administrator Cheyev. He should be in his office upstairs."

Tristan vanished, and I realized I was fingering the demon tooth in my pocket. I shook my head. "What a pair of asshats. Teasing me like that. Bet it gets them off..."

"Oh, they weren't teasing you," said Dawn. "They're legitimately into you. But don't let it get you down. You're not nearly as plain as you appear on first glance. Larry?"

"Yeah, Cheyev's office," he said. "I know where it is."

Larry led the way up the stairs, past more velvet drapes, ancient portraits of old dudes in stuffy suits, and several more smarmy youngsters with too much hair gel who gave me slack-jawed looks. Eventually we hooked a right into a study where a thin, severe man in a three piece suit stood behind a broad mahogany desk and between shelves packed with books. He adjusted his tie in a standing mirror that failed to reflect his image.

"Hey. Cheyev, right?" said Larry. "We met once before, I think."

The man turned, still fiddling with his black tie, though it looked fine to me. "Mr. Stuttgart, of Nyte Patrol. I remember." His accent was as thick as Romanov's. In fact, he sounded exactly like the man. "What can I do for you?"

"We're looking for Ivan," said Larry. "It's about an item he told us to procure for him."

"Yes, book," said Cheyev. "How goes hunt?"

"We're, uh... working on it." Larry gave me an exaggerated wink. "But we have some questions about it, and about some of the other items we've obtained for him."

Cheyev spread his thin, delicate, overly veiny hands. "I'm familiar with, ah... *employer's* affairs. Please. Ask away."

"No offense, Cheyev," said Larry. "But the spell will only work on Romanov."

"Dude." Was Larry incapable of keeping the existence of *any* spell under wraps?

"Spell?" said Cheyev. "What spell?"

Larry looked like he'd stepped in dog crap. "I mean... You know. The spell. That we're using to track the tome. It'll only work with Ivan's express approval. It's critical we speak with him."

Somewhere in the distance, a bell tolled, filling the room with a haunting melody. Cheyev perked at the sound, his eyes shifting to the open door. "I see. Well, I am terribly sorry, but Mr. Romanov isn't available at moment. Perhaps another time. Now if you excuse me, I have pressing matter to attend to. You can see yourselves out, I am sure. *Do svidaniya.*"

22

CHEYEV WALKED BRISKLY TO THE DOOR, THEN FLICKERED and disappeared. It was a little disconcerting, but not as much as Larry's idiocy.

"Nice save, Larry," I said. "You play a lot of hockey growing up?"

"Sorry," he said. "I'm not used to being all cloak and dagger. Like I said, I've always played it straight with Romanov. He's always come across as a stand up guy."

"Yes, I'm sure the Russian oligarch head of a mysterious vampire academy with a penchant for ancient objects of power is a veritable saint."

The bell continued to toll as we exited the study and headed down the stairs, its ringing filling the corridors. Not a soul bumped into us, and even the whistling moan seemed to have fled the halls.

"So, are we going to ignore the bell, too?" I asked as we approached the entrance hall. "Just like how nobody batted an eye at this place being called Goatboil?"

"To be fair, Lexie," said Dawn, "all supernatural and

wizarding academies have bizarre names. I mean, Miss Margle-cluck's Institute for Witchcraft and Wizardry? Quacknog's College for Paranormal Pedagogy? Come on."

"Yeah, I've never heard of either of those," I said.

Larry paused in the middle of the corridor. "You know, she makes a good point about the bell. It *is* ominous, and I never heard it on any of my prior visits."

"And it's kind of weird that Cheyev had to dart off like that," said Dawn.

"And that Romanov is nowhere to be seen," said Larry.

"And that the halls are suddenly empty," said Tank.

I glanced from one member of the trio to the next. "So you're saying we should investigate it."

"I'm not saying that at all," said Larry. "We're paid to deliver magical items, not to snoop."

"Oh, for crying out loud," I said. "We're here to get the scoop on Romanov, aren't we? Then I'm pretty sure we need to figure out what's up with the haunting bell that cleared the mansion. Come on. I'll lead the way."

I followed the sound toward what I presumed was the back of the house, cracking a door onto the estate grounds. The sound rang clearer through the crisp night air as I led our team down a gravel path lined with neatly manicured shrubs and oversized junipers, but I quickly realized that despite the sound being *clearer*, it wasn't particularly directional. I had a general sense of the ringing originating away from the house rather than close to it, so I followed the path, picking directions at random when it forked, and hoped Larry, Dawn, and Tank didn't call me out on my choices.

As we reached a dead end with a marble statue of a cherub circled by trees, I realized the jig was up. It also didn't help that the ringing abruptly stopped, fading from the air like a bad dream.

"Um. Yeah..." I said.

Larry held up a finger. "Hold on. Do you hear that?"

Come to think of it, silence hadn't replaced the bell's ringing. Instead, a soft hum filled the air. A chanting of sorts.

Larry pointed toward the trees. "It's coming from there."

He pushed his way into the forest, past the edge of the trees and down a shallow escarpment. Dawn, Tank, and I followed him down the gentle slope before stopping at the edge of another treeline.

"Just to be clear, Lexie," said Larry in a hushed voice. "When you called Romanov a saint—you meant that as sarcasm, right?"

I gaped at the sight before me. Not at the buffet tables in front of us, decorated with glistening ice sculptures and laid out with scores of bite-sized appetizers and a massive bowl of blood red punch, but beyond that, to a throng dressed in hooded robes crowded together in a circular plaza, humming a soft indecipherable chant. Torches mounted on long poles blazed merrily at the perimeter while in the center, separated from the crowd by ten feet of solitude, a young woman in a pink blouse and torn jeans stood tied to a wooden stake. She struggled against her bonds, and though she grimaced as she did so, staring at the crowd in wide eyed fear, she didn't scream.

"Dear God," I muttered. "I thought you said this was a training academy, Larry."

"Yeah. For *vampires,* not aspiring tennis players. What did you expect?"

"Well, after what happened indoors, I was expecting the

cute, socially-challenged kind of blood-suckers, not the murderous sort."

"Look," said Dawn, pointing at the woman's feet. "Those are the crystals we obtained for Romanov, aren't they?"

Indeed, a coral-colored set of multifaceted crystals had been carefully arranged under the woman in the shape of a five-pointed star. They glowed erratically, pulsing with a hidden energy. I presumed the flickering light was due to the power focusing magic Tank had alluded to, be it just as easily could've been the result of violent radioactivity.

A pair of hooded individuals separated from the crowd and approached the young woman on both sides. The young woman's head darted from one to the other as they closed to within striking range.

Arms flashed, and the hoods slid down, revealing Gavin and Tristan. In the light of the torches, their skin seemed paler, their lips redder, their eyes brighter. They smiled, evil white flashes in the dark of night. The woman gasped. The glowing crystals at her feet gained in strength, and her eyes widened.

"Jesus," I said. "Larry, Dawn—we need to do something!"

"Maybe if Larry hadn't insisted I leave my swords behind..." said Dawn.

"Or my guns," said Tank.

"Larry has magic," I said. "Maybe if you cast a garlic spell, or summon a shower of holy water—"

It was too late. The two vampires dove onto the young woman, teeth flashing and tongues flicking. Gavin pressed his mouth against her neck, and Tristan began tearing at her clothes with superhuman speed and strength. The crystals flashed, bright pink in color now, and the electric murmur from the crowd intensified. Scraps of clothes flew. In moments, the young woman was naked as a newborn babe.

I wanted to turn away, to shield my eyes from the violent murder of the poor young woman, but my eyes were riveted to the B-grade horror flick come to life. The young lady gasped and moaned. Gavin pulled back. I expected a gout of aerosolized blood to spray across the crowd, but nothing flew other than a fleck of spittle. From a distance, the woman's neck appeared fine, if perhaps wet and red from overaggressive sucking.

"What the...?"

Gavin and Tristan's arms shot back. Their robes dropped to the ground, revealing every square inch of their chiseled bodies. They pressed into the young woman, gyrating against her with their naked bodies. Her face appeared to be one of pleasure, not pain, and the wide eyes which I'd initially thought were a byproduct of fear might as easily have indicated she was high as a kite.

The pink crystals flared again, and bright beams of collimated light shot into the night sky, sweeping across the heavens in a coordinated rhythm. The torches at the perimeter shot gouts of flame into the air, orange and yellow and red alongside other stranger colors, too—purples and blues and greens. A thumping beat swallowed the crowd's chanting, not of drums but of dubstep. I blinked and noticed a DJ booth at the far side of the plaza, one manned by none other than Cheyev, who'd switched out of his suit into a mesh shirt, neon green visor, and comically oversized headphones.

I blinked. "Well, this is unexpected."

The music grew louder. Fog rolled in from machines hidden among the surrounding brush. The crowd threw up their hands, and all of their robes dropped to the ground. In the blink of an eye they'd transformed from a hooded mob into a naked, gyrating mass, slicked with sweat and without a shred of inhibition among them.

"*Oh god,*" I said. "This is *absolutely* not what I expected."

"Really?" said Larry. "Given how Gav and Trist came on to you out front, this is *exactly* what I expected."

Dawn perked. "Hey, is that Skrillex? I love Skrillex."

Larry snorted. "Fine, Dawn. Go ahead. We all know what's on your mind."

"I resent that," she said. "Just because I'm a nymphomaniac doesn't make me an exhibitionist. I like the music, that's all. Besides, I made my opinion of those two androcentric dipsticks perfectly clear."

I turned away from the orgy. "Well, given all Romanov seems to be using his crystals for is creating laser light shows, I think it's safe to get the heck out of here, which I'd suggest we do before any unwanted bodily fluids spray in our general direction."

"Agreed," said Larry. "Might be worth checking out the mansion in greater detail given that everyone is otherwise occupied. Lead the way, Lexie."

I blinked. Had he asked me because I'd been the one who led us into the clearing, or was it a more broad reaching statement? "Yeah. About that. I think I lost track of where we are. Can anyone spot the castle from here?"

Tank shook his head. "Should've brought Bill."

Larry pointed toward a path leading from the plaza. "Follow that. Should be safe enough. But move quick. Who knows how long this party will last—or how long the male vampires will, if you get my drift."

I groaned as I stepped from the woods onto the path—or

tried to, anyway. Before I'd taken half a step, I caught my foot on a root and went tumbling, slamming hard against the paving stones.

"Son of a...!" I rolled over and grasped my knee, which now sported a glistening scratch that stretched halfway down my shin.

The dubstep kept thumping, but something rippled through the air, as if the vampire orgy had taken a collective gasp. I looked up to find the gyrating and thrusting had come to a standstill. All the vampires were looking my way—or rather, at my bloody knee.

23

THE VAMPIRES STOOD FROZEN, STARING AT ME IN UNISON with wide eyes. I felt like Lindsay Lohan's character in *Mean Girls* after being called to the front of the assembly hall, but the vampires weren't eyeing me with hatred or even disdain. A few licked their lips, while others ran tongues across pearly white exposed fangs.

Larry grimaced. "Has anyone ever told you your timing is *impeccable*, Lexie?"

I winced as I stood. "What did I do?"

"Don't you know anything about vampires?"

"What do I look like? An Anne Rice groupie?"

"Your shin, girl. The scent of blood sends vampires into a frenzy."

As if on cue, the naked herd turned toward us, moving slowly, deliberately, with looks of absolute focus chiseled onto their faces.

Larry shook out his arms and crouched into a defensive stance. He cast me a quick glance. "Well? What are you waiting for? Get the hell out of here. Now! I'll hold them off."

"The hell you will," said Dawn. "Lexie, stay there. You've got your bat, right?"

"Dawn, I can handle this," said Larry. "Don't be a hero. Either of you."

"I'm not trying to protect you. I'm protecting Lexie." She fixed me with a steely glare. "You've seen these things move. You can't outrun them. If we split up, we die. Christ, Larry, why the hell did I listen to you and leave my swords in the truck?"

"It was a logical move," he said. "How was I supposed to know this trip would end in a violent dubstep orgy?"

The vampires picked up the pace, moving toward us at a trot. Their tongues flicked, their teeth flashed, and I saw hunger in their eyes.

Dawn leapfrogged the buffet table and ripped a carving knife and a two-pronged fork from a side of roast beef. "Tank, we could *really* use your special skills about now."

He grunted and shook his head. "I prefer guns, you know. They're much more civilized."

The vampires hissed like a quiver of angry cobras and broke into a run.

"Screw civility," said Larry. "We need brutality!"

I reached into my pocket for the demon tooth, but I was too slow. The vampires' superhuman speed turned them into a blur as I wrapped my fingers around the magical weapon, and I spoke a silent prayer as I prepared to have my throat torn to ribbons.

Larry stuck his arms out. The air rippled, and I heard a wet pop combined with a metallic ring. Vampires materialized out of thin air, bouncing off an invisible shield before us. Others were caught in the middle of it, reaching toward us in slow motion with outstretched arms.

Dawn leapt forth and slashed one of them with her carving knife before spearing a frozen vampire in the eye with her meat fork. "What did you do?"

"Stasis field," said Larry as a ball of lightning grew in his hands. "It'll only slow them. Don't get cocky."

Shaking with adrenaline, I pulled my tooth from my pocket and squeezed. As it grew, I noticed something on the other side of the barrier. "Tank! He's outside the field!"

"He'll be fine." Larry chucked his ball lightning into a group of vampires stuck in the field. They shook as electricity played over their bodies.

"Fine?" I said. "What the hell do you mean he'll be—"

Tank hunched over, his muscles bulging, his arms shaking, a pained grimace on his face. I was sure he'd already taken a deadly wound, but the vampires seemed to be ignoring him. Actually, it was the opposite. They were deliberately giving him a wide birth, maybe for good reason. Tank was *growing*.

"Lexie, move it," said Dawn as she forked and filleted another vampire. "The field slows them, not stops them."

A vampire near me stumbled and hissed, having mostly pushed through the barrier. He leapt at me, mouth wide, junk swinging in the air—god, why did every supernatural creature that tried to kill me have to be naked? Luckily, the thing's ankle remained caught. I blasted him across the temple with my bat and his limbs turned to jelly.

By the time I turned back to Tank, the big man had grown another four feet and added a half ton of mass. His clothes lay in tatters at his feet, but unlike the vampires, he'd grown fur to cover his nakedness. He'd also acquired an enormous snout, teeth as big as sausages, and paws the size of toaster ovens.

"Holy shit," I said. "Tank's a wearbear?"

Tank's roar shook the trees and sent a ripple through the stasis field. He lurched forward and slammed a meaty paw into a vampire, sending him flying into the night sky, though I probably could've done better with my demon bat.

"Were-Kodiak, to be precise." Larry bundled another lightning ball among his fingers. "He gets testy when you call him a mere bear—about as testy as when he has to turn unexpectedly and take on a horde of angry vamps."

Tank bellowed again and dove into the hoard, batting vampires to the sides like bowling pins.

I smashed another vampire over the head with my bat. "Is it the turning he hates or the vampires?"

"Both," said Larry, shooting lighting through the field. "Turning's incredibly painful, and vampires are natural enemies of werebears."

I thought that was werewolves, but I didn't have time to ask. Dawn jumped through the air, carving knife whistling and meat fork jabbing. "Guys, is it me, or is the stasis field getting less stasis-y?"

Vampires crowded around us, pushing from all sides. The field flickered and whined, and I saw the same thing as Dawn. The vampires were moving faster, as if battling a strong wind rather than a wall of molasses.

"The spell can't handle that much supernatural counter pressure," said Larry. "Maybe if I compartmentalize the field and use more localized targeting I can achieve a better result. I don't know if I can cycle spells that quickly, though."

Dawn's meat fork snicker-snacked. "Which means what, in practical terms?"

"I shoot each vampire down with an individual stasis spell."

I pictured the sweaty, naked vampires as gatorade jugs and went to town. "Are you making this shit up as you go along?"

"More or less." Larry pointed at a nearby vampire, a burst of rippling air shooting from his finger. The vampire froze and keeled over. Larry did it again and again. *"You* get a stasis field, and *you* get a stasis field. Hah! I feel like Oprah!"

"Faster, Larry," said Dawn. "The main field is failing!"

"I'm working on it." Larry kept downing vampires with stasis blasts from his finger guns. Dawn and I hacked and slashed at the hungry undead trying to break through the weakening shield, but for every head I bashed and every eyeball Dawn speared, more vampires appeared. They shrieked and howled, pushing at the shield even harder in response to the fading magic.

A vampire with a mouth the size of a grapefruit flew through the barrier. I blasted him full strength in the jaw. His head flopped to the side, but I think all I did was daze him. *"Guys...?"*

The rippling shield flickered again, more noticeably this time. The thumping music shifted to something more beat heavy and aggressive. Sweat beaded on Larry's brow as his hands blurred, spells flying. Even Dawn sported a look of concentration mixed with a splash of fear. Then she paused, blinking as she gazed toward the DJ booth. "Wait. This *is* Skrillex. "Bangarang." I love this song."

"Not the time, Dawn," said Larry.

"No," she said fiercely. "It's *absolutely* the time. Everyone, follow me! TANK!!!"

Dawn grabbed Larry by the arm and darted through the barrier as it gave. Larry cursed and fired something into the crowd, a crackling electrical stasis field combo punch he'd apparently been saving for a rainy day. It blasted the vamps back, opening a narrow path before us. Dawn didn't hesitate to sprint along it. I released the pressure on my bat and took off after her, imagining her ass as first base and the oncoming vampires as rival players. I didn't bother to check if Larry was coming, but by the continued barrage of compartmentalized mini-stasis blasts, I knew he was right behind me.

The combo punch only gave us a moment. Within seconds, the dazed vampires sprung from the ground, eying us with newfound rage. Before they dove at us, I heard an ear-splitting roar. Vampires scattered, the earth shook, and out of nowhere Tank leapt into the sky, soaring over us in his furry glory. His arms spun in giant arcs and his teeth flashed, spraying flecks of spittle from his powerful jaws—until one of Larry's mini-stasis spells slapped him in the underside of the jaw. He fell to the ground, rolling and crushing vampires underneath him like an overturned car.

"Oh, *shit!*" said Larry. "Sorry, Tank!"

I kept sprinting after Dawn, the DJ booth approaching rapidly. *"Dude.* Did you just kill Tank?"

Larry blasted two more vamps as we ran. "Kodiaks are very stout. He'll be fine."

Dawn leapt onto the DJ platform and shoved Cheyev, who was still working the turntables, into the bushes. She lifted the nearest speaker, which was at least two and a half feet tall and must've weighed eighty pounds, and pointed it toward the vampire horde.

She screamed at full volume. "Alright, Larry. Let's do this!"

"Do what?" yelled Larry as the two of us hopped onto the platform alongside her.

"Two words. *Weaponized dubstep.* I've wanted to do this

ever since I played *Saints Row IV*. Now quick, juice me! While Bangarang is still playing!"

"Weaponized dubstep?" said Larry. "I can't turn dubstep into a weapon! I mean, some of it is pretty god awful, but I can't kill people with it."

"Don't you dare criticize dubstep, Larry," said Dawn. "Now do something! Blast these fuckers with sound!"

In the distance, Tank stumbled to his feet. Half of the remaining vampires rushed him, but that left the other half in a race to see who could disembowel us first.

"Do something. Right." Larry glanced at the undead ravers. He darted to the turntable, a digital version hooked up to a MacBook. His fingers tapped frantically at the keys. Dawn grunted as she lifted the speaker overhead, like John Cusack in *Say Anything* except the speaker was blasting overwhelming bass and drum samples with hopes of murdering undead instead of finding love.

The air blurred as the vampires burst into another run. I squeezed my demon tooth bat back to full size, my heart hammering harder than any dubstep rhythm.

"Now, Larry!" yelled Dawn.

Electricity crackled through the air, and I thought the man had conjured another spell. A gout of sparks erupted from Dawn's speaker. She swore and dropped the thing as flames erupted from the other speakers. Sparks and smoke filled the air as every electronic device connected to the booth—the turntable, the computer, the amps, the speakers, the fog machines—exploded in a violent fireball.

The vampires hissed and screeched. I jumped off the DJ booth, batting at my sleeve to smother the fire that had caught there. I couldn't see clearly with the thick smoke choking the air, but it seemed as if the vampires were retreating.

"*Fire,*" I said. "Of course. Vampires hate fire. That's a well known trope, isn't it?"

Dawn waved her hands, trying to clear the air. "It's true. Why the hell didn't you think of that earlier, Larry?"

"To be honest, I didn't even think of it now," he said. "I was trying to switch the dubstep to Celine Dion. Figured that would drive them off."

One of the fog machines roared and flared again. The fire crackled as it spread into the surrounding brush, sending up a fresh cloud of smoke. The vampires hissed, backing away from the spreading flames. Some of them screeched and darted into the woods.

They weren't the only ones. Tank bellowed and dashed into the forest, trees shattering and flying as he ran. His fearful cry echoed over the moans of the vampires and the roar of the flames.

"Right," I said. "Bears hate fires, too, don't they?"

"No time to worry about it," said Larry. "He can take care of himself. Right now we need to get the hell out of here."

"Right," I said. "To the Nytemobi—I mean, to the truck."

Larry smiled. "See? It sounds good, right?"

"Shut up," I said as I broke into a run.

24

I turned onto a street somewhere in the Westlake Hills, glancing at my phone to get a sense of our direction, while Larry kept his eyes trained on the lavish homes at our sides.

I sighed. "Look. It's pretty clear we're not going to find him this way."

"And what would you suggest we do?" said Larry. "Leave him in the woods? What happens when someone calls the police to report a Kodiak bear roaming west Austin? They're not going to send animal control, I guarantee you."

"Why do you assume he's still in bear form?" I said. "If he can transform into a Kodiak at will, can't he transform back whenever he pleases?"

"Well, about that... Remember how I hit him in the jaw with that stasis spell?"

"Wait," said Dawn from the backseat. "You did what?"

"It was while you were sprinting toward the DJ booth with dreams of a dubstep cannon dancing in your head," said Larry. "Trust me, I wasn't aiming for him. I'm worried the spell might've not worn off yet."

Dawn sighed. "Now I understand why we've been driving around these hills for the last half hour."

"Can't we call him?" I said.

"Even in human form, Tank doesn't carry a phone," said Larry. "As you saw, his clothes get shredded when he transforms. As a bear, where do you think he'd carry it? In his prison wallet? Bet that would feel great when it rings."

I grimaced. "Eww."

"Even if he did have a phone, how would he answer? You saw his paws, right?"

"I get it. Bad suggestion. But you're the one who asked me to drive around looking for him. It's up to you to come up with a way to track him."

Larry took off his hat and ran a hand through his greasy hair. "Believe it or not, this isn't a problem I've had to deal with before. Tank's usually very good about staying nearby. Just head to the house for now. I'll think of something. Maybe I'll call in some favors."

I turned the Suburban around and headed back downtown. Even at night, Austin traffic could cause headaches, so it wasn't until twenty after nine that I pulled in front of Larry's place. We all hopped out of the truck, headed around the side of the house, and through the back door.

I froze the instant I stepped foot inside. While I never would've called the home clean and tidy, it hadn't been a war zone when we'd left, either. Papers, pillow fluff, and glass shards littered the floor. The side table in the entry hall lay on the floor, a deep crack running through it, and glimpses of the living room showed similar signs of furniture abuse. The light above us flickered twice and died.

My jaw dropped. "What the...?"

"Easy," said Larry, holding out his hands. "It might've been Tank. *Tank?* Buddy? You here? It's Larry, Dawn, and Lexie. Don't hurt us, okay?"

"Hurt us?" I said. "I thought he remained lucid while in bear form? He didn't come after us at Romanov's place."

"Well, yeah," said Larry. "But that was before the stasis chin tap. I have no idea how it might've affected him. He might be pissed off about it, to be honest."

Dawn's sword rang as she pulled it from her sheath. "It wasn't Tank. Look at the floor. Those are bootprints."

Larry reached into his coat and pulled his flintlock. "Damnit. Be careful." His eyes widened. "Bill? *Bill!*"

He darted into the living room, and I followed with Dawn close behind. The place was as trashed as the front. The couch spewed bits of foam, the TV had been knocked to the floor, and Larry's phone littered his desk in pieces. The side table at the wall was miraculously in one piece, but shy an occupant.

"Damnit!" shouted Larry, swinging his pistol through the air. "They took Bill. *They took Bill!*"

"And left his jar," said Dawn. "Who does that? They must've reached in there and plucked him out, rotting flesh and everything."

"I do that," said Larry.

"Yeah, but he's your friend," said Dawn. "And you still wipe your hands with antibacterial gel afterwards."

"Guys, perhaps more important than Bill being missing?" I pointed at the desk. "The tome's gone."

Dawn swore as she slid her sword back into its sheath. "We told you not to leave Bill in charge, didn't we Larry? *Didn't we?*"

"I'm not in the mood to hear it," said Larry. "We're talking about my friend here. He's gone. Kidnapped. Abducted. Who knows what kind of danger he's in, or what sort of twisted torture he's being subjected to? Christ, this night has been a disaster. First Tank and now Bill? *Shit.*"

"Hey. Slow down," said Dawn. "I didn't mean it that way. I was just upset. We'll find him, okay? Tank, too. It'll be all right."

"Yeah," said Larry, returning his flintlock to his coat. "Sure it will. I'll find some trace of the intruder's presence. Maybe a hair, or mud off one of the boot prints. If I mix goat's blood, wolfsbane, and salt peter and draw the proper sigils on the floor, I should be able to conduct a séance. Ask the spirits to show me what happened. Maybe I can even catch a glimpse of who broke in."

"Or we could read the note the intruders left in Bill's jar." I pointed at a folded yellow note card, half hidden at the bottom of the jar under a few soggy leftover fries.

Larry snatched the jar and dumped the contents on his desk. He flipped open the note and scanned his eyes across the message. After a moment, he let out a sigh. "Well, there's good news and bad news."

"What is it?" said Dawn.

"The good news is Romanov and his band of sex-crazed vampires didn't snatch the tome. The bad news is the people who did aren't going to be any easier to deal with." He held out the note for Dawn and me to see. "It was *Los Desalmados.* They want Melondrious Funk and the money they're owed—ten million dollars worth—otherwise they'll kill Bill and sell the tome to the highest bidder."

"Which is Romanov," I said, snatching the note. "And it gets worse. They want to meet at midnight. We've got to do something! We can't let Romanov have the tome."

"Correction," said Larry. "We can't let Bill's brain be turned into scrambled eggs. But yeah, I'm with you."

"Guys, I hate to break it to you," said Dawn. "But we're screwed. Melondrious is in police custody. We sure as hell don't have ten million dollars. Heck, we don't even have Tank."

"Which means we need to find him," said Larry. "Then spring Melondrious from prison, rob a bank, and save Bill, in that order."

"I'm not robbing a bank," I said.

"Change of plans then," said Larry. "No bank robberies. We'll figure out the money as we go. But we need Melondrious. We won't be able to cut a deal with the bikers without him."

"And how do you plan on getting him?" said Dawn.

"Same way we find Tank. We enlist Frank's aid." Larry pulled his not-a-phone from his pocket, opened it, and held it to his ear. "Hello? Frank?"

A tinny voice came through the device, but it was quieter than Frank's and not as gruff. I couldn't make out the words this time, but I got the gist of things from Larry's reactions.

"No? Then who the hell are you? ... *Jerry?* Well, where's Frank? ... What do you mean he's not available? Find him. Tell him this is important. ... I don't care if he told you not to disturb him, this is a matter of life and death. ... Well, then you're going to have to help me instead, won't you? I need a prisoner released to me. ... No, I brought him in yesterday. I'm telling you I need him. ... Well, what *can* you do for me, then? ... Do you at least know anyone in the canine unit? ... Alright, I'll be there in fifteen."

Larry returned the phone to his pocket and sighed. "Well, one for two. Better than nothing, I guess. Come on. We need to move."

25

I WALKED THROUGH THE WOODS, A FLASHLIGHT IN ONE hand and the leash to Betsy, a three year old police German shepherd, in the other. Dawn walked beside me, a rucksack stuffed with Tank's clothes on her back. She'd used the clothes to give Betsy Tank's scent, but as Larry had already made clear, Tank would need them once we found him, assuming he'd transformed back into human form. I didn't relish the extra dose of nakedness on a night already filled to the brim with it, but given Tank had saved my life, I figured I could overlook it. He was also easy on the eyes, if I was being honest.

After poking around the edges of Romanov's estate, we'd eventually found some trampled brush and a few broken tree limbs. It wasn't conclusive evidence of Tank's passage, but after giving Betsy a whiff of his scent, she'd started barking and darted into the darkened woods. Now she led the way, though she stopped every now and then to get her bearings.

Larry walked at my side, having refused a flashlight when we picked Betsy up at the police station, claiming that destruction of police property was a crime. Instead he'd opted to create his own magical nightlight—a foot long stick he'd found that now emitted a beam of light that could blind an airline pilot if pointed in the wrong direction.

"Any chance you could ratchet that down?" I said. "Given how you dispatched those nightmare beasts at the temple, I'm not entirely sure that thing won't cut through me if you get spooked and take a sudden spin."

"Sorry." The beam dimmed to that of a battery operated version. "Better?"

I nodded.

"Let me know if it gets out of hand again," he said. "Sometimes I'm blind to the strength of my own magic."

"Like how Dawn had to point out your stasis field was weakening during the vampire fight?"

Larry shrugged. "I'd like to say it's something about the magical forces I draw upon that have a Heisenberg-like quality to them—that I can't judge both the nature and the potency of the magic at the same time—but that's a load of horse shit. Fact of the matter is I'm not that focused. Probably something I should work on."

"You can say that again," said Dawn. "But please don't. It's a hackneyed joke."

A branch crunched underfoot, but Betsy was too focused to care. I think she'd caught a good whiff of Tank recently. "Speaking of which," I said. "There's something about your magic that's been bothering me for a while."

"Being?" said Larry.

"How does it work?"

"What do you mean? It's magic."

"Well sure, but there's got to be a rhyme or a reason to it. I mean, take tracking Tank. Why did we have to borrow Betsy from the police? Can't you whip up a spell to magically sniff him out?"

Larry snorted. "It doesn't work that way."

"Which is what I'm getting at," I said. "Your magic seems exceedingly selective, not to mention arbitrary. There are things you can do and other things you can't. You can shoot lightning from your hands, artificially accelerate fermentation, and talk to ghost spirits, but you can't track a bear through the woods? You can create a magical portal device to talk to people, and you can create stasis fields that condense air or slow time or something, but you can't figure out how to touch a computer without making it explode?"

Larry shrugged. "Magic is a mystical and unknowable enterprise."

"But there's got to be limits," I said. "I mean, if you can shoot beams of white hot light from your palms, how about bigger ones? Like nuke-sized ones as hot as the core of the sun."

"Oh, well, that's easy," said Larry. "Magic is exhausting. If I use too much, it'll knock me on my ass for a week."

"You haven't seemed particularly tired after any of our fights."

"I also lose a small piece of my sanity every time I access magic. Eventually it'll drive me insane if I don't stop."

I squinted at the man. "You're kind of a jerk, but you don't seem crazy to me."

"Magic also takes time. Preparation. Careful thought goes into everything I do."

"Which explains the compartmentalized stasis spells you came up with on the fly."

"Not to mention," continued Larry, "that the use of magic

attracts evil spirits who are desperate to consume my soul. The more spells I cast, the likelier it is they'll find me."

I shook my head. "You're so full of shit."

"Trust me, those are all very believable explanations for the limitations of my magic."

Betsy pulled on the leash, and I walked a little faster to keep up. "Whatever. Can we talk about the tome instead?"

"What about it?"

"You know we can't give it to Romanov, right?"

Larry frowned. "What makes you think I still want to sell it to him?"

"Back at the house. You didn't exactly agree with me when I said we had to keep it out of his hands. I get the impression you still don't totally believe he's a bad guy."

"Well, I don't know it for a fact. I mean, Cheyev was polite to us, if not terribly helpful. And those vampires at the rave were just having a good time until you tripped and scraped your knee. That fight was your fault, you know."

"Larry! Romanov is acquiring items of power. Lots of them! He's building some sort of vampire army, and you want to give him something that will make him stronger? You have to realize what a bad idea that is."

Larry grunted. "Fine. I won't sell him the tome. But those funds were going to pay your salary, mind you. We'll need to find other work quickly if the job's a dud."

Mention of my salary brought back thoughts of my softball scholarship and Heather and the rest of my teammates. I sighed. Up until now, I'd been perfectly happy ignoring my more mundane problems.

Betsy barked and pulled on the leash, dragging me along

with her. "Whoa. Slow down, girl. What is it? You smell something?"

Betsy didn't listen to me. She took off, pulling me behind her as she darted through the trees. She barked a few more times, clearly excited.

"Whoa there. *Whoa.*" She pulled me up a small knoll before coming to an abrupt stop. She pointed her head toward a fallen log half submerged under dried leaves, a low growl building in her throat.

I shined my flashlight over the log. Sure enough, facedown in the leaves with his bare ass sticking into the wind was none other than Tank.

"Tank. There you are," said Larry. "Thank goodness you're not hurt."

Tank grumbled and snorted in a not entirely human fashion. He pushed himself out of the leaf pile and turned to face us.

Dawn put her head in her hand and sighed.

Larry winced. "Well... that's unfortunate."

Tank had transformed back into human form—mostly, anyway. He still sported the head of a Kodiak bear, though.

He gave a restrained growl. "Rahr rarrah."

"Yeah, I hear you," said Larry. "Hold still. Let me try to unfreeze you."

Larry tapped his flashlight wand several times until the light changed to a pale green color. He mumbled something under his breath and flicked the wand at Tank. A ripple shot from the end of the stick and slapped Tank in the head.

Tank grunted. "Ruurarh."

"Okay, that didn't work," said Larry. "Let me try something different."

He tapped the stick again, this time until the light was pink-ish-yellow. He spoke a more forceful sentence in a language I didn't understand and flicked another spell at Tank's head.

This one bounced off and sent Tank tumbling into the leaves. He shot up, his head still in bear form, and belted out a menacing, *"Grrahraah!"*

"Damnit, Larry, we don't have time for this." Dawn stepped forth, pulling clothes from her backpack. "Tank, get dressed. We need to move. We'll figure this out as we go."

Tank cocked his head as he slipped into his pants. "Graah?"

"Precisely," said Dawn. "Bill's missing. So's the tome, and the clock is ticking."

26

I pulled up to the Taco Bell drive-thru intercom and turned to Larry. "Well. We're here? What do you want?"

He had his magical two-way portal device pressed to his ear. He glared and flicked a hand at me. "Not now. Can't you see I'm on the phone? Frank! Damnit man, pick up."

I snorted. *"Phone.* Yes. I can see that. Dawn?"

She sat in the back of the Suburban with Betsy sitting happily on the seat between her and Tank. After her initial shock, the police dog seemed to have taken a liking to the big guy, despite the fact that his head hadn't returned to normal.

"I don't know," said Dawn. "I'll take a chalupa, I guess. This is really about Tank. He's the one who needs food."

Tank nodded. "Ruh graurhar."

Dawn squinted at him. "Yeah, I didn't totally catch that one, but get him like fifty tacos to be on the safe side."

I sputtered. *"Fifty?"*

"Transforming to and from bear form is exhausting. Regenerating the wounds he suffered at the hands of the vampires is more so. He needs calories, specifically protein. Come to think of it, we should probably order some of those fried chicken chalupas, too."

Tank nodded his enthusiasm. "Ruhrah!"

A voice crackled on the intercom. "Welcome to Taco Bell. Can I take your order?"

I relayed the request, though I had to repeat the quantity of tacos three times before the guy taking the order was sure he'd heard it right. He told me how much it would run and then warned me it might take a few minutes.

Larry slammed his not-a-phone shut as I pulled up to the pick up window. "Damn! Where the hell is he? Doesn't he know the whole point of a *two-way* portal device is that it's only good for speaking with one other individual? Why would I want to talk to his assistant?"

"I'm guessing you haven't had any luck convincing this Jerry guy to hand over Melondrious."

Larry scowled. "Do I look like I've had any luck?"

The pickup window opened and a pimpled teen nodded to me. "That'll be seventy-nine forty-six."

I handed him a hundred dollar bill, he made change, and handed it back before closing the window again. "You owe me for the food," I told Larry. "Again."

"I'll borrow it from my 401k."

"If we can't get our hands on Melondrious, then we might as well not even show up to that meeting with the bikers," said Dawn.

"We can't not show up," said Larry. "Bill's life is on the line, not to mention the whole tome situation."

"Roaruh rahraa?" said Tank.

"Not an option," said Larry. "I'm not letting you anywhere

near the police station in your condition. We'll have to think of something else."

The pickup window reopened, and the pimply youth leaned out with a giant bag. "Alright. Here you go. Fifty soft tacos, three chicken chalupas, one regular chalupa, a caramel apple empanada, and one order of... *holy shit.* What the *hell* is that?" He was staring into the back of the 'burban, directly at Tank.

I sighed. *"Larry?"*

"Yeah, I've got it." Larry snapped his fingers a few times to get the kid's attention. "Hey. Kid. Are you familiar with the concept of a freak show?"

He blinked. "What?"

"We're with the circus. Tank there is one of our acts. Here. Let me show you." Larry cleared his throat. When he spoke, it was with a voice far more grandiose and bombastic than his own. "Ladies and gentlemen, boys and girls, gather round for a most sensational, stupendous sight, a veritable visual bonanza of brawn, bravery, and the bizarre. A creature so fierce, so ferocious, so foul that he's been forced into hiding for the past thousand years. Hailing from the little known Kodiak Archipelago off the southern coast of Alaska, feast your eyes upon the one, the only, the amazing manbearfreak!"

Tank nodded and grunted. "Roarah."

The tortilla flipper nodded. "Whoa."

"But that's not all," said Larry. "To his left, let me introduce the woman who forced an army to its knees in more ways than one, the voracious, rapacious, insatiable battleslut!"

Dawn sneered. "I will literally stab you in the neck, Larry."

"Cool," said the fast food kid. "So what does the dog do?"

"It's a dog," I said. "And before you ask, I drive and beat on things with a demonic softball bat." I passed the bag back and Tank tore into it, ripping tacos from their wrappers and tossing them into his mouth whole.

"Well, I don't know about the rest of you," said the Taco Bell kid, "but that bear guy is pretty cool. How long are you in town?"

Larry clicked his tongue. "Sorry. We're headed out tonight. On to Dallas."

"Bummer," said the kid. "You guys seem pretty cool for freaks. Normally, the only weirdos we get around here are the bums on Sixth Street."

Tank took a break from inhaling his tacos to tip his head toward the kid. He grunted, and I think he tried to smile.

Larry blinked. "Weirdos. *That's it.*" He unhooked his seat belt, opened his door, and hopped out.

"Wait, what that...?" I said. "Larry! *Son of a bitch.*"

"Don't worry about him," said Dawn, unwrapping her chalupa. "He does this sort of thing all the time."

"I'm not worried about *him.*" I pulled the Suburban into an open parking space and killed the engine. "Should we go after him?"

Tank grunted. Dawn shrugged and spoke around a mouthful of beef and cheese. "Once we're done eating, maybe. Sure you don't want anything?"

"I naively thought there'd be extra tacos." My phone started to buzz. I pulled it from my pocket and glanced at the ID. It was an unknown number, but a local one, so I took a chance.

"Hello?" I answered.

"Hi, uh...? Lexie?"

The voice sounded familiar, but I couldn't place it. "Yes. Who's this?"

"It's Tony. You know. From the library?"

"Oh. Right." The voice did have a bit of a nervous twang to it. "How'd you get my number?"

"I looked you up in the student directory," he said. "I didn't know your last name, but I remembered you said you were a softball player, and you're the only Lexie on the team."

"That's... resourceful." *And somewhat creepy,* I thought. "So what's up?"

"Oh, you know. Not much."

I braced myself for the awkward question that was sure to follow.

"So, uh... have you talked to Larry yet?"

I blinked, surprised. "Ah, no. I'd totally forgotten. Sorry about that. Things have been crazy lately."

"Oh, I totally get it. No hard feelings. But is he, ah... there now?"

I glanced at the empty seat. "Just missed him. Why? What's going on?"

Tony laughed nervously. "It's nothing really. Just a little problem I've got. Nothing serious. I got a little out of control last night and I have a feeling it might happen again."

"I hate to break this to you, Tony, but Larry's not an addiction counselor."

"Yeah, that's not the kind of problem—"

The door opened, Larry hopped inside, and slammed it back shut. "Damnit. I can't catch a break. He's not here."

"Who's not here?" I asked.

"Darragh, of course," said Larry. "Who else would I be looking for in the Taco Bell parking lot?"

"I'm sorry I asked. Look, Tony, let me put you on speaker-phone. Larry, can you talk to this guy? He needs your help.

Some sort of recurring issue he refuses to be specific about for untold reasons."

"No time for that." Larry leaned over the phone. "Sorry whoever you are. Unless you know where to find a drunken hobo leprechaun within the next thirty minutes, I'm afraid you're plum out of luck. Lexie? Hang up."

"Sorry, Tony." I lifted a finger over the phone.

"Wait," he said. "Have you tried the homeless camp in the Barton Creek Greenbelt?"

Larry froze. "Say again?"

"The Barton Creek Greenbelt. Lots of homeless people camp there overnight. It's within easy walking distance from downtown."

"*Lots of homeless people,* you say," said Larry. "Guy? You're a lifesaver."

27

With the flashlight in one hand and Betsy's leash in the other, I walked through another set of darkened woods while I suffered an eerie sense of déjà vu. The difference was this time Tank walked beside Dawn, who no longer sported the backpack full of clothes. Instead, she grasped another leash, this one loosely wrapped around Tank's furry bear neck. A cardboard sign hung from his shoulders upon which we'd written 'The Amazing Manbearfreak!' in black permanent marker.

Tank grunted and shook his head. "Grrahruh."

"Well, I don't like it either," said Dawn. "I mean, I'm the one who has to hold the stupid leash. Blame Lexie. It's her fault."

"I think what you meant to say is I'm the one who had the *brilliant idea* for the disguise," I said. "It's not like Tank can walk around in public in his current state, and since Larry is too busy or tired or is going insane a little too quickly to cast a spell to keep him hidden, I took the initiative."

Larry sighed. "As I already mentioned, a spell to take care of *that* would require too much magical upkeep, and I'm going to have to exert myself enough with a second one later on. Besides, I want to be prepared for whatever else we have to deal with tonight. Though I'll admit, fermenting a second Baja Breeze did take the wind out of my sails a little."

"You really think Betsy is going to be able to track Darragh from the scent of that boozed up Mountain Dew alone?" I asked.

"I don't see why not," said Larry. "She tracked Tank from the smell of his groin sweat. Besides, she seems to be doing a pretty good job so far."

I glanced at Betsy, who continued to lead us through the woods with a look of quiet determination. She seemed to know where she was going, but I sure didn't. I squinted at the path before us—nothing more than dirt and leaves. I would've thought a homeless camp in the middle of the woods would've had a more obvious entrance, but maybe the bums didn't want anyone to find them.

I glanced over my shoulder, wondering not for the first time if we'd taken a wrong turn. The woods all looked the same to me —for all I knew we were walking in circles—but beyond that, something didn't feel right. My danger radar beeped quietly. Were we being followed?

Betsy barked and pulled on the leash, sending me stumbling after her. "Slow down, girl. Dang."

I jogged behind her as she dragged me through a cluster of junipers into a clearing. I clicked my flashlight off as I came to a stop. Thanks to the light of the full moon, I could see perfectly well without it—even though I wasn't sure how much I *wanted* to see.

Betsy had led us into a junk yard. Trash littered the expanse, from beer bottles, soda cans, and plastic bags to bigger items that should've been close to impossible to bring into the woods: shopping carts, motorcycle engines, mildewed couches, even a rusty refrigerator. There was a weird smell to the place, too. A mixture of wet earth, urine, booze, and sweat.

"Dang," said Larry. "This place is a dump. Literally."

Tank nodded. "Gruhrah."

Betsy sat on her haunches and whined, looking from side to side nervously. She looked up to me for guidance.

"Uh-oh," I said. "I think Betsy lost Darragh's scent."

"How could she lose it?" said Larry. "This whole place reeks of week old liquor and—oh, I get it now."

"Exactly," I said. "Finding your leprechaun pal here is like trying to find a needle in a stack of needles. Poor Betsy. This is bad enough for me, girl. I can't imagine the discomfort you're in."

Dawn glanced toward the moon. "Lexie, have you got the time?"

I stuffed the flashlight in my back pocket and grabbed my phone. "Quarter after eleven. We're cutting it close."

"Grahh gur roaruah?" said Tank.

"Good thinking, Tank," said Larry. "We can cover more ground by splitting up. Lexie, you keep Betsy. Dawn and Tank, you two should stick together, obviously. I'll—"

Leaves rustled. Betsy growled, Larry spun, and we all turned our attention toward the sound.

An old guy in a ratty jacket with wild white hair and a matching beard approached, his tequila and cigarette stench potent enough to beat back the overall funk. He held his hands in the air. "Whoa, there, friends. Just looking for a smoke. Maybe you've got one?"

Larry held out an arm as if he were shielding an unbuckled

kid in the front seat of a car. "Stay back everyone. This one isn't what he seems. I can smell the magic on him."

"Yeah, that smell?" said Dawn. "It's not magic."

Betsy whined, and I couldn't blame her. I detested cigarettes. "Come on, Larry," I said. "Just because he's dressed like you doesn't mean he's a wizard."

"Wait, *Larry?*" The bum took a step forward and squinted. "Larry Stuttgart?"

Larry's arm fell. *"Wayne?* Is that you? Holy hell. I knew I recognized that magical aroma. What in the world are you doing here?"

"You know this guy?" I said.

"Sure," said Larry. "Wayne Nelson. We were roommates back at Zephyrburr Magical Academy. Christ, Wayne, what happened to you? You look like you've aged a hundred years."

"Seventy-six, actually," said Wayne with a shrug. "I got stuck in an alternate dimension fighting a race of sentient ant people. They imprisoned me and left me to rot in a cell, but I never gave up. Took nearly a lifetime, but eventually I escaped."

"That's awful," said Larry.

"I know," said Wayne. "Seriously, though, do you have a cigarette? I'm dying here. Literally. Of old age."

"And you're trying to speed up the process?" I said.

Wayne glared at me.

"Sorry, Wayne," said Larry. "None of us smoke, though we all inhaled a turntable and a few speakers earlier this evening. But since we tried our hardest to help you with your goal of hastening your eventual demise, perhaps you could do us a solid in return?"

Wayne sighed. "Seventy-six years in an ant prison wanting

nothing more than a nice long drag of sweet American tobacco and this is what I get when I return."

"I'll take that as a yes," said Larry. "We're looking for a leprechaun by the name of Darragh. A drunken, ornery little guy. Any chance you've seen him?"

"A drunken, ornery leprechaun? Can't imagine I've ever seen one of *those.*"

"I'd be fine without the sarcasm, Wayne. We're in a rush."

"Yeah, and the guy who spent seventy-six years in a hollowed out dirt hole lined with ant spit's got nothing but time." He grunted and waved. "Come on. He's got a tent near the swale."

Wayne led us through piles of garbage and thick under-brush, skirting the odd occupied hammock or leaf pile that had been lined with towels and emitted snores. Down a shallow slope we went until I heard the faint sound of water gurgling over stones.

"You said *Darragh*, right?" said Wayne. "Not Dúnchadh or Dubhghall? We've got a lot of the little treasure lovers in this encampment."

"Is that a joke?" said Larry. "Because honestly I'd take any of them. I suspect Darragh will be the most accommodating of the bunch, though."

Wayne pushed back a bush revealing a shabby tent the size of a washing machine. The mesh door was zipped half shut, and sounds of snoring leaked from within.

"I guess you're in luck," said Wayne. "Sounds like he's home."

Larry unzipped the flap the rest of the way, bent over, and stepped inside. The tent stretched and wobbled as he crammed his body in there, but it quickly dissipated back to its original size.

"Damnit," called Larry. "He's out cold. A little help?"

"How do you propose we do that?" I asked. "Despite Tank's freak show sign, none of us are contortionists."

"It's roomier than it looks," said Larry. "Trust me. Come on in."

I looked at Dawn. She shrugged, ducked, and wiggled through the flap, dragging Tank through the gap behind her. When they both disappeared, I knew there wasn't any point fighting it.

With Betsy's leash still in hand, I pulled up the flap and stepped through myself—into a tented space roughly five times the square footage of my dorm. Though he'd undersold the size, Larry had failed to mention the place was even more of a dump than the surrounding homeless camp. Piles of junk stretched to the canopy on all sides: moth eaten books, crates of National Geographics, empty liquor bottles (surprise, surprise), piles of rocks—not gemstones, mind you, but regular old rocks. By far the most prevalent item of all, however, was shoes. There were stacks of them everywhere. Ratty shoes, new shoes, loafers, high-heels, pumps, flip-flops, sandals, clogs, sneakers, high-tops, and even an original pair of Jordans in royal blue.

"What's with the footwear?" I said.

Larry knelt over a cot that contained Darragh's snoring, unmoving form. "You need to bone up on your fantasy lore. Leprechauns are cobblers. Tank? A little help?"

The manbearfreak stepped over two giant piles of junk and stopped at the side of the bed. "Gruh rurahrah?"

"We're not kidnapping him," said Larry. "We're borrowing

him. In his state, he'll barely notice. In fact, it might be better that's he's drunk as a skunk. Won't be able to contradict us."

"Ruh grawarah."

"He'll be *fine,* okay, Tank? Trust me."

"Hey, everything alright in there?" Wayne stepped inside and cast a wary glance at Larry and Tank.

"Yeah, we're fine," said Larry. "Just need to, ah... *relocate* Darragh."

Wayne crossed his arms and frowned. "You know, it occurs to me you never mentioned *why* you wanted to speak with the leprechaun."

"Come on, Wayne," said Larry as Tank hefted the halfling over his shoulder. "We're old roommates. Buddies. Did I ever try to pull a fast one on you?"

"That was three-quarters of a century ago for me," said Wayne. "To be honest, I don't remember. My gut tells me the answer is yes."

Larry rubbed the scruff on his face and got serious. "Alright. New deal. I'll buy you a carton of cigarettes and you forget all about this, okay?"

Wayne snorted. "Make it two."

"Sure," said Larry with a smile. "On one condition."

"Being?"

"You help me cast a glamour spell. I'm saving myself for later."

28

GRAVEL CRUNCHED UNDER THE SUBURBAN'S TIRES AS I pulled off an obscure FM road into a darkened parking lot in the middle of the Texas hill country. According to my phone, it belonged to a BBQ joint by the name of Bone Lickers. Given the name, I expected the place to have a giant sign in the front featuring a cartoon waitress with comically oversized breasts wearing a knotted crop top and giving the incoming patrons a sexually suggestive wink, but the place was much more subdued. A stone walkway snaked off through a cluster of trees toward an old barn in the distance. I didn't see any lights.

I squinted at the structure, trying to spot any motion. "Is this place abandoned?"

Larry unbuckled his seat belt. "You wouldn't expect a gang of murderous bikers to meet us at an *operational* BBQ joint, would you? Remember the plan?"

"I stay in the truck with Tank and *Melondrious* while you and Dawn hash out a deal with the bikers. When we see the signal, we bring our *fairy* out to the meeting site."

"Unless you want to get us killed, stop putting emphasis on his name and race," said Larry. "Actually, new rule. No talking once you and Tank bring him out. I don't want anyone screwing this up."

I glanced into the rearview. Betsy had been relegated to the far back so Darragh would fit between Dawn and Tank. He slouched there, snoring in a drunken stupor. Thanks to the glamour Wayne had cast over him, he looked like the spitting image of Melondrious.

"What about him?" I said. "You're just going to hand him to the bikers? What happens when the spell wears off? Or worse? What if the bikers buy it and start torturing him, assuming he's who he's supposed to be?"

"As I told Tank, it'll be fine," said Larry. "I have a plan. Dawn?"

Dawn and Larry hopped out of the vehicle, slamming the doors shut behind them. Gravel crunched as they headed off, the sound fading as they reached the stone path.

I turned toward the back of the truck, wondering how I'd found myself alone with a police dog, an unconscious leprechaun, and a guy with a bear head. "What do you think, Tank? Are we doing the right thing? With Darragh I mean?"

"Grooahruh."

"Yeah, I have no idea what that means. Are Dawn and Larry actually able to understand you in bear form?"

He shrugged. "Rah grugh grahrah."

I snorted. "Yeah. That's what I thought."

Betsy started to growl. I cocked my head at her. "What is it girl?"

I jumped and slammed my head into the roof as something tapped at my window. I spun around to find a familiar nerdy young man in a purple He-Man shirt standing there, waving at me.

I rolled down the window. *"Tony?* Christ. You scared me half to death. What the hell are you doing here?"

He smiled nervously. "Hey, Lexie. Sorry for scaring you. Didn't mean to." He leaned over and looked into the vehicle. "Is Larry with you?"

"He stepped out. Seriously, what are you doing here? How did you even get here?" I glanced into the parking lot, but I didn't see any other cars.

Tony grimaced and scratched his neck. "Yeah, I've sort of been, ah... following you. Not in a creepy way, I promise. I just really need Larry's help, and when you guys hung up on me after I mentioned the homeless camp in the greenbelt, I thought..."

So I wasn't crazy. Someone *had* been following us. "Right. I apologize about that. Larry was all like, We've gotta go! And my truck's a dinosaur. It doesn't have bluetooth enabled. I can't link calls. I might be reckless, but I don't talk and drive at the same time. The point is Larry knows you need help, and he's totally got your back. I think."

Tony hopped from one foot to another, as if he needed to pee. "Great. So if you could, like, call him over...?"

A burst of bright red light erupted over the barn. "Damnit," I said. "Tony, I swear you've got the worst timing. Just hang out by the Suburban. Keep Betsy company. She's the dog. I'll be back with Larry soon. Tank? Time to move."

I hopped out. Tank did the same, with the Melondrious doppelganger thrown over his shoulder. We hoofed it onto the path while Tony stayed behind, stammering his objections. The flare sparkled in the air as we walked, fading slowly, and I realized it wasn't coming from over the barn. Behind it, rather. It wasn't until the path curved around the edge of the painted red structure that I spotted our destination. A smaller building, this one with lights inside. An exterior spotlight shone on a group clustered near an outdoor stone grill. Tank and I approached them, joining Larry and Dawn on the near side.

"See?" said Larry. "Here they are. With Melondrious, as promised."

A group of four bikers in leather jackets and with bandanas on their heads stood a dozen paces from us. They were decidedly more hispanic in appearance than the ones we'd previously dealt with at St. Marque's. One of them held Bill by the hair, an ice pick pressed against his ear. Bill's eyes were as wide as saucers. He looked like he was sweating, which I didn't realize was possible.

The biker in the front nodded at Tank. "This your guy, esé?"

"That's my guy," said Larry.

The biker blinked. "He always like that? With the, ah...?" He waved his hand at his own head.

"It's a temporary thing. He's working through it."

"Could we speed this up?" screeched Bill. "Larry, they're going to scramble my brain. Don't let them scramble my brain! It's the only one I've got."

The head biker shot a finger at us. "The talking *cabeza's* right. Let's see the guy."

Tank walked forward, pulled Darragh off his shoulder, and set the leprechaun down in the middle of the lit area before stepping back.

"He ain't moving," said the biker.

Darragh chose that moment to cut loose with a ragged snore.

"He's a little drunk at the moment," said Larry. "He'll be fine, at least until you get your hands on him. Time for you to hold up your end of the bargain."

The biker nodded to his compatriot. He pulled the ice pick from Bill's ear, wound up, and chucked him at us from across the divide.

Larry caught him with both hands. "Hey, pal. Good to see you."

Bill was panting. "I knew you'd come. I knew you wouldn't leave me."

"Are you kidding?" said Larry. "How would we navigate without you? I mean, other than joining the twenty-first century like Lexie has. Come to think of it, you're getting pretty replaceable."

"*Oye,*" called the head biker as one of his crew came forth to collect Darragh. "We ain't done here, *gringo.* Where's the money?"

"We're taking option two," said Larry. "We're offering the drugs instead."

"Then bring 'em out."

"You're asking the wrong guy," said Larry. "Melondrious is the one who knows where they are."

The head biker scowled. "Nice try, *cabron.* We can ask the fairy ourselves."

"Exactly," said Larry. "You get the guy and the drugs. It's exactly what you want. So hand over the book."

The biker's scowl intensified. "No cash, no *drogas,* no book. We'll keep it. Word is someone's willing to pay a pretty penny for it, *esé.*"

"Not anywhere near what Melondrious owes you," said

Larry. "It wouldn't make a dent in that debt. It's not even worth your time. Be better if you gave it to us."

Despite the fear that tingled in my fingertips, I couldn't stand silent and listen to the exchange anymore. "Larry? *Larry!*"

He held up a finger. "Sorry. One moment. *What is it, Lexie?*"

"Have you been through one of these before?"

"One of whats?"

"Exchanges. Handoffs. Whatever. Because you seem to have no idea what you're doing."

"For your information, I've already secured Bill. And I'm close to reasoning with this man for the return of the *Librum*."

"Are you kidding me? Tell me you have a plan, Larry. You *do* have a plan, right?"

"Eh... *Jefe?*"

We turned at the sound of one of the biker lackeys, the one dragging *Melondrious* toward his buddies. The doppelganger's jacket flickered, changing color from salmon to green to violet and back. His face looked glossy, like he'd been heated under a flame. Then his nose started to lengthen, his eyebrows grew thicker, and his jaw widened.

A half dozen guns cocked, including several at our backs. Dawn swore. I would've too if I knew language foul enough for the situation.

"Hijo de puta. What are you assholes trying to pull here?" said the head biker, his own pistol drawn and aimed at us.

"Damnit." Larry pinched his fingers together. "I was *this close* to negotiating for that tome, too."

29

A HAND JABBED ME HARD IN THE BACK, PUSHING ME INTO A dark room that smelled of mesquite smoke and charred meat. Tank followed through the exterior door beside me, holding Darragh—now fully returned to his original form—in his arms.

"Move it, *pendejos.*"

Dawn and Larry followed us in at gunpoint, the former stripped of her swords. Larry stumbled as one of the armed bikers shoved him in beside us. "Hey. Watch the jacket."

"You worried about your *jacket,* holmes?" said the biker. "Damn, you're even more *estúpido* than you look."

"Hey, we can work this out," said Bill, who Larry still held in his hands. "There's no need for violence. No brains need to be scrambled."

"*Cállate,* all of you," said the second biker who'd drawn on us. "I don't want to hear another damned word, got it?"

A distant screech rent the air. One of the bikers turned toward the sound, but the other was disciplined enough to keep his eyes and his gun trained on us. "*Que es eso?*"

The screech sounded again, a pained, somewhat human,

somewhat birdlike sound. The biker who'd turned whipped back around, shoving his gun into our faces. "Well? What the fuck was that?"

"I'm confused," said Larry. "I'm supposed to talk now?"

"Don't fuck with me, *puto.*" The biker stepped closer. "You tell me what that is."

"I have no idea," said Larry. "A coyote? A pair of mating ostriches?"

The screech sounded again, closer this time, and even the disciplined biker cast a lightning-quick glance toward his buddy.

"Best not be *cagando* me," said the first biker. "Otherwise you gonna be in a world of hurt."

He nodded to his friend, and they both backed out of the room, slamming the door shut behind them. It rang with a loud, metallic clang, plunging us into total darkness.

"Great plan, Larry," I said. *"Great fucking plan."*

"Hey, my plan worked fine until Wayne's magic wore off unexpectedly." Larry snapped his fingers, and his hands started to glow. "I mean, I saved Bill didn't I?"

Larry's hands grew in intensity until I could make out the bounds of our prison. There wasn't a single window to speak of, and the walls, floor, and ceiling were dark as midnight—not from paint, but from soot. A three-sided cinderblock grill stood in the center of the room. Wood had been piled high in one corner. Other than that, the place was empty.

"Actually, Larry," said Dawn, "it's even worse than Lexie's making it out to be. Your plan didn't just suck. You didn't even *have* a plan."

"And I suppose putting the glamour on Darragh was a happy accident? Give me a break."

As if on cue, Darragh stirred in Tank's arms. "Whaza? Who's 'er?"

Tank grunted. "Ruh grah grah."

"Oh, so you're *all* ganging up on me, now?" said Larry. "Fine. Be that way. At least Bill's on my side."

Bill laughed nervously. "Yeah, I mean. Thanks, old friend. Much appreciated. But we aren't exactly out of the woods yet, are we?"

The inhuman screech rang through the air again. In the distance I heard shouting. Someone screamed.

Larry grimaced. "Admittedly, I have a feeling things aren't as bad as they could be."

"Oh, shut up, Larry," I said. "Stop trying to make it seem like this is all part of your master plan. You're bumbling your way thorough this, same as you do with everything else. God! And to think at first I wasn't sure what kind of help you needed when your spell brought me in."

"I'm not saying this was part of my plan. The screaming might be entirely serendipitous." The warbling howl intensified, muted by the bunker-like BBQ cage. More shouts followed, then gunfire. A dozen shots. "Yeah, I'm pretty sure that's not a coyote."

Dawn cocked her head at the sounds. "Larry, what the *hell* have you gotten us into?"

"It wasn't me," he said. "My plan was to get in and get out, not bring hellfire down upon the bikers. I have no idea what's going on out there."

I sighed. "About that..."

Larry's jaw dropped. "Lexie? This is *your* doing?"

"Of course not. Well... maybe a little bit. Yours, too, at least indirectly. Remember Tony?"

"The guy on the phone?"

I nodded. "He dropped by the house a couple days ago. Said he needed your help then, too. He showed up outside the truck while Tank and I were waiting for your signal. I have no idea how he got there, but he seemed *pretty desperate* for help."

More screams pushed their way through the concrete, followed by more gunfire. Lots of it. Dozens if not hundreds of shots, from automatic rifles, not pistols. The spine-chilling warble didn't stop. If anything, it grew louder. Angrier.

Darragh, hearing the sound, pushed himself free from Tank's arms and dropped to the ground. He stumbled before vomiting all over the floor. "...da hell am I?"

At the same time, a buzzing sounded within the room. For a moment, I feared we might be under attack by mutant wasps until I realized it was coming from Larry's jacket.

With Bill cradled under one arm, Larry reached into his jacket and flipped open his not-a-phone. "Frank! For Christ's sake, took you long enough!"

The cop's voice shot from the two-way portal, gruff and unhappy as ever. "This better be good, Stuttgart. And by good, I don't mean you wanting me to release the drug-dealing fairy to your custody."

"Melondrious is a moot point now," said Larry, watching Darragh wobble and vomit some more. "What we need is backup. Lots of it. We've got bikers with machine guns and some inhuman horror terrifying everything for miles."

Frank cursed. "Stuttgart, is your ass ever *not* in a sling?"

"I'm serious. Send a car or thirty. We're at Bone Lickers in Driftwood."

"Driftwood?" said Frank. "That's outside my jurisdiction."

"Screw your jurisdiction. Did you not hear me say *inhuman horror?*"

"Sorry, Stuttgart. Call me when you reach the city limits."

Larry growled, his phone hand shaking with anger as Frank cut out. "Damnit!"

Tank shook his head as the screeching and gunfire grew louder. "Roarurh grawar."

"I agree," said Dawn. "We need to get the hell out of here. This smoke room might be safe for now, but for how long?" She ran forward and tested the door. It didn't budge. "Tank?"

The big guy came forward and slammed his shoulder into the door a few times. It still didn't give. He shrugged. "Gruh?"

"Well, can't you turn into bear form?" said Dawn. "Rip it off its hinges."

Tank shook his head. "Roarurh groo."

"What do you mean you need an *external stimulus?* What does that even mean?"

"Guys, there's another door." I pointed to the back of the room. "I've been to places like this. I bet it leads to a dining hall or the rest of the kitchens."

Dawn, Tank, and I hurried to the back door, carefully avoiding Darragh's puddles of vomit, while Larry continued to stew. Dawn tested it. "Damn. Also locked." She rattled it in its frame. "Doesn't seem as solid as the front one. Tank, surely you can break it down?"

He slammed a palm against it. "Ruhgruh?"

"I don't know," said Dawn. "Give it your best shot."

"Can't you pick it?" I said. "Like at the Harry Ransom Center?"

"Yeah. If I'd brought my picks."

A voice sounded from near my knees, and someone slapped me on the thigh. "Outta da way, ya geebags."

I blinked. "Darragh?"

The leprechaun pushed his way through. He reached into his green jacket, pulled a leather tool case, and opened it. He plucked a couple pointed metal tools and jammed them into the back door's keyhole.

Dawn looked as surprised as I felt. "The *leprechaun* has lock picks?"

Darragh looked up. His face went green. He bent over and retched all over the bottom half of the door. He wiped his mouth, wobbled back up, and glared at Dawn. "They're cobbler's tools, but they work in a pinch. How do ya think so many o' us build our fortunes?"

Darragh worked on the lock as Larry came over, Bill in hand. The warbling howls continued unabated, but the gunfire and human screams were dying down. "Seriously, guys, maybe we should stay. Whatever's out there probably doesn't even know we're here."

The lock clicked. Darragh cranked on the handle. The door swung open, revealing a dark room filled with long tables, benches, and an empty display case. The lights were off, but moonlight streamed in through the windows.

"Sorry, Larry," said Dawn. "You're going have to earn back your leadership privileges after this debacle. The rest of us have voted. Move out, but be quiet."

Darragh took one step through the door, wobbled, fell flat on his face, and promptly started snoring again. Tank picked him up on his way through. Dawn and I followed, with Larry in the back.

"Aren't you all forgetting something?" said Larry as we

snuck past a greasy table. "We can't leave yet. We don't have the tome!"

"Screw the tome," said Dawn. "Our safety is more important."

"Actually, Dawn? I'm going to agree with Larry on this one," I said. "Getting that tome *is* a matter of safety. If we don't take it, those bikers will sell it to Romanov, and I have a nebulous but frightening idea of what he'll do with it."

"If there are any bikers *alive* after that shrieking horror finishes with them," said Dawn.

"And you'd rather *it* find the tome of power?" said Larry.

Dawn sighed. "Fine. You win. But how exactly do you propose we find it?"

"Look in the obvious places, for starters," said Larry. "Like, say, that office over there."

He pointed. Sure enough, at the side of the dining area an open door led to a room with a desk, a swivel chair, and multiple filing cabinets. We walked there quietly and peered inside. A cool breeze blew through an open window, rustling the pages under a paperweight. The air was oddly still, calm and quiet in a lull between howls. In the center of the desk was a massive tome. The *Librum de Virtute*.

Tank grunted. "Gruh."

"I know, right?" said Dawn. "Talk about serendipity."

"Well, don't look a gift horse in the mouth," said Bill. "Grab it and let's go!"

Tank nudged me with an elbow. "Roaruh gruh."

"Yeah, you've got Darragh," I said. "I can figure it out by context."

I took a step toward the tome. As I did so, I hesitated. Maybe it was the sudden cessation of the breeze, or the lack of screaming and gunfire, or maybe I was finally developing the sixth sense that kept idiots like Larry alive. Either way, I dropped as I neared the book, rolling into the side of the desk. I belted out a strangled warning, but it was too late. A rush of air whooshed over me as a furry, clawed blur leapt through the window. If I hadn't dove when I had, the thing probably would've taken off my head.

Instead it flew right into Tank's.

30

Tank roared and bucked, dropping Darragh with a thud as the creature latched onto his muzzle. Tank's hands shot to his face, trying to tear the beast from his fur, but the thing moved with unbelievable speed. It zipped and twirled, whipping around Tank's head in a black and grey blur, attacking the big man in a frenzy of scratching claws and flashing teeth. It screeched again, the sound filling the office, piercing my ears.

Tank spun, arms flailing as he stumbled into the dining area. Dawn and Larry dove out of his way. Bill went flying, cursing as he smacked into a wall. Tank tripped over a chair and crashed into one of the wooden tables. Splinters flew.

I leapt to Dawn and Larry's side. "Christ. Do something!"

"Without my swords?" said Dawn.

"It's on his face," said Larry, gathering energy in his hands. "If I miss, it won't be pretty."

"Tank's not particularly pretty as is," I said.

Tank roared again as the creature continued to savage him, cutting loose with an angry bellow. Cloth tore as the pile of man and bear flesh topped with a ferocious nightmare blur sprouted thick fur all over and grew.

"So *that's* what he meant by an external stimulus," said Dawn. "I get it now."

Tank rose from the remains of the dinner table, now in full bear form. He swiped at the creature on his head with his massive paws, but the thing was too quick. Tank succeeded only in smacking himself in the muzzle.

"You've got to do something, Larry," I said. "He can't get it off. If you don't help, I will."

The heat from Larry's energy ball warmed my face. "How do you plan on doing that?"

I pulled the demon tooth bat from my pocket and squeezed. "By trying."

Larry shook his head. "Fine. Here goes nothing. Sorry, Tank!"

Larry extended his arms. The ball of energy flew through the air, crackling and expanding as it went. I'm not sure what guided it, because despite Tank's bucking and flailing, it nailed him right in the face, enveloping his head with a foot to spare on all sides.

The creature attacking Tank may have been quick, but Larry's magic ball had grown big enough to render its speed moot. The screeching howl turned into a yelp as the creature shot across the room, blasting through the cinderblock wall separating the dining room from the smoke shack.

Tank lifted himself from a pile of mangled furniture and shook his head. Not his bear head, but his human head, which was now stuck onto his comically oversized bear body.

"Tank?" said Dawn.

"I feel it," he said, patting his shaved head with a massive bear paw. "It's okay. I can work with this." He flexed an arm. In a blink, it shriveled down to his overly muscular but comparatively tiny human arm. "Whoa. I'm *better* than okay. I think you've unlocked selective body part transformation, Larry."

"Uh... great," he said. "That's what I've been trying to do all along."

The creature's inhuman screech echoed through the open door and the hole in the cinderblock wall.

"Crap," said Larry. "I thought that might've been enough."

I ran with Larry to the open door and glanced at the creature that crouched, hissing, at the other end of the smoke shack. For once, it had decided to stand still.

"It's a *raccoon?*" I said.

The trash panda hissed and bared its tiny fangs.

"Strongest damn were-raccoon I've ever seen," said Larry. "Of course, weres who can't control their turning during a full moon are always the strongest—and most dangerous. Your pal Tony mention anything specific about his condition?"

At the mention of his name, the raccoon cut loose with another ear-splitting shriek. His claws played a melody on the floor as his feet spun into action, his beady little eyes full of hate and focused directly upon us.

Good thing I'd always hit the fast ball best. I planted my feet and brought my demon bat back as Raccoon Tony launched himself into the air. I connected with a crack, sending the furry missile flying. He slammed into the heavy metal exterior door, blasting it off its hinges without slowing.

Larry and I rushed to the door, where we paused in horror. Bone Lickers looked like it had been hit by a tornado. Bikers sprawled across the grounds, some moaning in pain, others still and quiet. The exterior lights were shattered, shards from their bulbs and covers littering the lawn. Branches had been ripped from trees and leaves from bushes. Even some of the barn's siding had been knocked loose.

Pounding footsteps sounded from behind, and Tank squeezed through the door to join us. He was still in bear form except for his head and the one arm. "Damn."

"Damn is right," said Larry. "Where's Dawn?"

"Guarding Darragh, Bill, and the tome," said Tank.

Larry eyed Tank's arm. "I thought you could transform your body parts at will."

Tank flexed again. "Still working on it. I'll get there."

Tony the were-raccoon hissed and darted across the lawn. Larry shot a couple quick spells after the thing, hissing missiles that blasted chunks of earth into the air, but he didn't come close to connecting with the creature.

"Stop it." I batted his arm down. "We don't want to kill him."

"Says the girl who slapped him upside the head with a demon tooth softball bat."

"That's different," I said. "You'd already proven he's resistant to impacts."

Tank glanced at the guns and empty shells littering the premises. "I think he's resistant to just about everything."

Tony darted across our field of vision, howling as he did so, but the ear-splitting call had acquired a new tone. There was a hint of fear in it that hadn't existed before.

"The point is, he needs help," I said. "He's asked us multiple times. We have an obligation to capture him, not kill him."

"Well, he's spooked now," said Larry. "How do you plan on drawing him in?"

"We need bait."

"My face worked the first time," said Tank, "but I'd rather not use it again."

"Not your face." I snapped my fingers. "That's it! *Tacos!*"

Another pained howl filled the air.

"Hate to break it to you, Lexie," said Larry, "but Tank ate all those."

"Not tacos specifically. I meant food in general. After the fight with the vampires, Dawn said Tank needed protein to recover. Tony's taken about a hundred bullets and tangled with a were-bear. He must be starving. You saw the meat locker in the back of the dining hall, right Tank?"

"Lexie," said Larry. "This place may be a BBQ joint, but it's abandoned. I don't think—"

"I'm on it." Tank took off through the door behind us.

"He's not going to find anything," said Larry.

"He'll pull through," I said. "What we need is a way to subdue him."

"Beyond asking Tank to put him in a headlock?"

"Not much of a long term solution, Larry."

"Well, you think of something. I'm into wizardry, not animal control."

Heavy breathing preceded Tank as he popped out the door, a twenty-five pound pork leg in his hand.

I almost retched at the smell. *"Oh dear god."*

"Yeah, it's been there a while," said Tank. "It's all I could find. I figured—"

Tony screeched and dove at us from the shadows. Thankfully for me, even though I was busy trying to keep my dinner down, Tank was on his game. He swung the meat, batting Tony to the side in mid-leap. Bits of rotting flesh sprayed from the ham, splattering as they hit the ground. Raccoon Tony dove on one of the larger pieces, wolfing it down in a single gulp.

"It's working!" said Tank.

I choked back some vomit. "Larry... *urgh*... use a ... *hurgh* ... stasis field."

"I've got a better idea." Larry pointed at the outdoor grill near where we'd met the bikers. "Tank, chuck it under there."

"Under?"

"UNDER!"

Tank pulled back his arm. The rotting meat flew. It bounced and rolled into the fire pit. Tony pounced in after it, hissing voraciously.

"And now," said Larry. "All we need is a little *pressure.*"

He lifted his hands and started pushing them together, as if he were squeezing an invisible cantaloupe. The metal grate over the grill whined and gave, caving at the sides before slamming into the ground in a hemispherical shape.

Larry smiled and dusted off his hands. "And *that* is how you make a raccoon cage."

I walked forward. Sure enough, Tony was trapped inside the bent grill cage, swallowing giant mouthfuls of the stinking, rotten meat.

"I can't believe that worked," said Tank.

"I can't believe he's eating that," said Larry.

"I can't believe I haven't ... *urgh* ... puked."

I shouldn't have said anything. With a heave and a rush, I leaned over and let 'er rip.

31

THE SUBURBAN'S HEADLIGHTS CUT A BRIGHT SWATH across the pitch black country road as I took yet another curve at a slower speed than I was used to. Despite the high-speed chase through downtown Austin and the resulting SUV aerials, the truck itself ran as smooth as ever thanks to Larry's restorative magic—which wasn't saying much. At its best, the Suburban's ride could generously be called turbulent. But the added weight had reached some nebulous tipping point, exacerbating the vehicle's existing boat-like tendencies and turning me into a more cautious driver.

Larry sat next to me in the passenger seat holding the *Librum* in one hand and Bill in the other while Dawn, Darragh, and Tank shared the back bench. Darragh, despite his momentary lapse into consciousness, had kept right on snoozing, occasionally ripping forth with a ragged snore to remind us he was alive. Tank's clothes had been destroyed by his most recent transformation. Since we hadn't thought to bring any spares with us, he'd made the best of a bad situation and stolen what he could from bikers who weren't able to tell him no. The sleeveless leather jacket that was a bit too small and showed off his bulging biceps wasn't a bad look, but the bloodstained jeans left something to be desired.

In his arms, Tank held the makeshift cage containing Tony the raccoon, which we'd bent from a hemisphere into a full one. Initially, we'd stashed the ball-shaped cage in the back, but after Betsy started growling at Tony and Tony returned the favor with a vicious hiss, we'd decided it would be better to separate the two. Personally, I would've preferred to leave the cage in the back and dealt with the sounds of aggression as a means of putting more space between me and Tony's lingering rotten meat smell, but with all the Suburban's windows down, the funk had faded beneath the gag threshold.

"Am I the only concerned about what happens if Tony reverts back to human form while he's in that cage?" I asked. "There's physically not enough space in there to contain him."

"Have you looked outside your window?" said Larry. "That full moon's not going anywhere for another—" He glanced at the radio clock. "—five and a half hours or so. The bigger problem will be getting Tony to transform back at all."

"I was hoping it would happen by accident at Bone Lickers," said Dawn. "That maybe he and Tank would transform at the same time while they were engaged in a heated wrestling match and glistening with sweat from the exertion. Could've been hot. I might've had to jump in there and... *split them up.* Or at least get in the middle." Dawn bit her lip.

"Jeez, Dawn, get a hold of yourself," said Larry. "It's been, what? A day since you and Charity hooked up?"

Dawn stared wistfully out the window. "That counts as a dry spell in my book."

"Speaking of books." Larry patted the heavy one in his lap.

"We saved Bill, we got the tome, and nobody died. At least not any of us. I'd call that one hell of a successful night."

My mouth dropped at the sheer stupidity of Larry's statement. I tilted my head to stare at him in disbelief, but the flashing lights in my rear-view mirror distracted me. I heard the siren a fraction of a second later. "Oh, you've got to be kidding me."

"Don't worry," said Larry. "I've got this. I'm friends with the police, remember?"

"The Austin, police, maybe. We're still in Driftwood, as far as I know. For the love of God, shut up and let me handle this."

"Right," said Larry. "Everyone? Act cool."

I pulled over to the side of the road, and the police car pulled to a stop behind me. A floodlight on the top of the car burst to life, and a state trooper stepped out the door.

"You want me to stay quiet, too?" asked Bill.

"*Oh, shit,*" I said. "Larry? Bill!"

"I'm on it."

As the state trooper walked toward us, Larry pressed his fingers into Bill's forehead. I heard a *whump,* and the next thing I knew, Larry wasn't cradling Bill in his arms but a watermelon instead. I heard a muffled moan—coming from *inside* the watermelon. Larry stroked it, hushing it as the trooper stopped at my window and leaned over.

"License and registration, ma'aaaaammmm...?" The word stretched as the officer glanced into the truck, his eyes darting from one person to another. He blinked, his brows furrowed.

"Right," I said, reaching into the center console for my wallet. "Larry? The registration's in the glove box."

The officer pointed at the cage in Tank's arms. "Is that a raccoon?"

I swallowed back a lump. "It is."

Betsy barked. Tony hissed.

"Do you have a permit for that?" asked the officer.

"For what?" I asked. "A raccoon in a cage?"

"Yeah."

"Do I need a permit?"

The officer blinked again. "Well... guess I'm not sure. Say, is that a midget?"

"The politically correct term is dwarf, I think, officer."

"But he's not a dwarf." Larry handed me the registration as the watermelon continued to moan softly. "He's actually a leprech—"

I elbowed Larry as I took the papers from his outstretched hand. "Right. Here you go, sir. License and registration. Can I ask what the problem is?"

The trooper couldn't stop staring. "No problem. You've got a tail light out, that's all. So... where are you folks headed?"

Dawn smiled and waved at the officer. Darragh cut loose with another snore.

"On our way back to Austin," I said. "Headed home."

The officer snorted. "Of course. *Keep Austin weird,* right?"

"You got it," I said with a smile.

The trooper grabbed my ID and the registration paperwork. "I'm leaning toward letting ya'll off with a warning, but I've got to run your license first. Sit tight for a minute, okay?"

The officer walked back to his car, and I breathed a sigh of relief. So did Larry. The watermelon didn't though. It kept moaning.

"You can ease up on the glamour," I said. "At least until the trooper comes back with my ID. It sounds like you're smothering him."

"Smothering? Yes. Glamour? No," said Larry. "I didn't trust myself after the debacle with Darragh. I took a different path."

I glanced at the watermelon with newfound horror. "Come again?"

"That's right. Go on. Touch it. We can crack it open later and have a taste, though I wouldn't recommend it. Bill's head being encased in there will probably give the fruit a sour taste. But don't worry about Bill. He can't suffocate. One of the perks of being a zombie."

"If nobody else wants it, I bet this little guy wouldn't say no," said Tank, lifting Tony's cage. "He doesn't seem to have a problem with spoiled food. Come to think of it, considering what he did to that ham, we should keep him away from Bill."

My phone rang. I pulled it from my pocket and answered, not even giving second thought to the fact that it was one in the morning. "Hello?"

The voice that responded was thick with a familiar Russian accent. "Miss Lexie. I was of hoping you'd still be awake."

I felt my cheeks tighten. *"Romanov.* What do you want?"

Everyone quieted and turned their attention to me, animals, unconscious leprechauns, and watermelons not withstanding.

"You know what I want."

I switched the phone to speaker so everyone could hear. "The tome. Well, tough luck, Romanov. We've got a pretty good idea of what you intend to do with it, and we're not in the business of enabling homicidal maniacs with delusions of grandeur."

"We're not in that business *anymore,"* corrected Larry.

"Please, Miss Lexie, there is no reason to delay inevitable. I will have tome, by any means necessary. I require it to complete magical superfecta."

"Your magical what?"

"*Superfecta*. Is like trifecta, but with four elements instead of three."

"Didn't you already obtain four items for him?" I whispered to Larry.

"Yeah, but one was that useless map. I don't know why he didn't buy it himself."

"Point," said Romanov, "is tome will be mine. But I will extend olive branch first. Bring me tome, and I will not hold offense against you. You have until dawn. I suggest you make logical choice."

My phone beeped as Romanov ended the call. I looked up at Larry. "Well? You promised me you wouldn't give in to this guy."

"I promised you I wouldn't sell him the tome, if I recall correctly."

"Stop jerking her around, Larry," said Dawn. "She's right, and you know it. Romanov is dangerous. There's no telling what he'd do with that book. It's bad enough he's in command of the items we've already sold him."

"I know, alright?" said Larry. "I may be stubborn, but I'm not blind."

"So," I said. "What do we do? Obviously, we can't risk him finding the tome. We need to either destroy it or hide it somewhere so obscure and off the beaten path that he'll never find it."

"That's one option, if such a place exists," said Larry. "But there's another method."

"Being?"

Larry smiled. "He needs all four items, right? So maybe we take back some of the ones he's already acquired."

32

I sat on the mangled couch in the Nyte Patrol living room. Tank had turned the TV—which thankfully still worked—to Food Network where Masaharu Morimoto and Bobby Flay were engaged in a heated Iron Chef showdown with currants as the secret ingredient. For once, I was the only one watching, though. Dawn sat on the armrest, running a whetstone over the edge of her katana, having already honed the wakizashi to a razor's edge. Meanwhile, Tank was methodically disassembling, cleaning, oiling, and reassembling every one of the dozen guns in his duffel bag. I felt like I should be doing something, too, but what, exactly? Tidying the living room? I didn't even clean my own dorm room. Waxing my demon tooth bat? It seemed impervious to damage, no matter what I smacked with it.

I yawned and checked my phone. Just after two. Maybe the best way I could prepare would be to take a nap.

"Well, I think I did it," said Larry.

I rose from the couch and joined the wizard as he waltzed in from the kitchen. "Did what?"

"Solved Tony's transformation problem," he said. "I cooked up a potion, convinced him to lap some of it up, and he returned to human form. Good thing I still had some eye of newt on hand, otherwise he would've been plum out of luck."

"Is it a permanent solution?" I asked.

Larry shrugged. "The moon'll still be close to full for a couple days, so we'll find out soon enough."

"*Almost full?* I thought it was an either or kind of thing."

Larry shook his head. "Common misconception. For were beasts who can't control their transformation, it's the *amount* of moonlight that hits them that's the triggering mechanism. I mean, haven't you ever seen a monster movie where it's overcast and the clouds break and suddenly little Johnny turns into a snarling werewolf? That's based in fact."

"Really?"

"Absolutely. Remember when we were listening to Mystic Radio yesterday and the jockeys mentioned the overnight were attack?"

I almost slapped my forehead. "Damn. They said the creature was *striped.*"

"Yup," said Larry. "It was Tony. Or at least I assume it was. His memory while he's in raccoon form isn't the best. But for now he's safe. He's finishing showering and getting changed. Speaking of which—can you give him a ride? He lives in one of the campus dorms, too."

"Sure. I can drop him off on my way back."

"*Your* way back? Girl, we're not done."

"Are you kidding?" I said. "It's past two. I have classes tomorrow."

Larry adopted a serious look. "Lexie, you said it yourself. Romanov's dangerous. His vampire dubstep orgy proved that, and as cool an effect as those crystals gave to the party, I have a feeling they also helped channel a more dangerous energy into the mix. If we're to steal back the items we delivered to him, there's no time like the present. He won't be expecting it, not only because it's the middle of the night but because he thinks we'll cave and give him what he wants."

I sighed. "Fine. If I miss class, I miss class. But tell me you have a plan this time. Like, a real plan that you've thought out that doesn't involve winging it with flames and balls of lightning and Tank and Dawn and me pulling your ass from the fire when everything goes to shit."

"I do," said Larry. "Together, we'll head back to Romanov's place. Tank and Dawn will venture into the back of the estate to recover the crystals. Chances are, they're still there. Nobody's going to clean up that mess until the morning. You'll come with me to take back the sword. When I delivered it, I took it under Romanov's supervision to the armory, so I know where it is. I've already explained that the map is useless, so we don't have to worry about it. The amulet is the hard one. When I delivered it to Romanov, he slipped it over his neck right away, and though I'm not a betting man, I'd wager he's still got it on his person. But the way I see it, we can let him keep that one. He said he needs all four. One won't do him a whole lot of good."

"Fair enough," I said. "And the tome? Clearly putting Bill on guard duty isn't going to cut it, and you're nuts if you think we're going to bring it with us to Romanov's place."

"I admit I may have overestimated Bill's ability to repel the enemy," said Larry. "But I've thought it through, and I know a place where the *Librum* will be utterly, unimpeachably safe. Somewhere Romanov absolutely *will not* be able to reach it himself, in the care of someone who understands the magnitude of the object they're instructed to protect."

"Oh, god. You're not leaving Betsy and that drunken leprechaun in charge of guarding it are you?"

"Betsy's watching over Darragh while he sleeps his bender off in the guest room, but no, I did not expect the police dog to guard him and the tome both."

"So who's in charge of it then?"

Larry waggled a finger. "No. It's better only I know. That way if anything happens, if Romanov captures you or Dawn or Tank, he won't be able to find it. And I can lock the information in my mind where nothing short of a nuke can dig it out. Trust me."

"You realize every time you've told me to trust you, you've later proven yourself to be totally untrustworthy."

"This time it's going to be different."

A door creaked. I turned to find Tony exiting the bathroom, his hair wet and mussed up, wearing the He-man shirt and pants we'd recovered from near the Suburban, though he'd lost his glasses. He smelled blissfully like soap.

"Perfect timing," said Larry. "Go on. Get him home. We'll be ready when you return."

I sighed and gave Tony a wave. He followed me out the back door and into my Suburban. The engine roared to life with a turn of my keys, and I turned the truck around in the driveway before heading back toward campus. Streetlights cast their yellow glows over the sidewalks, the streets empty and still.

We traversed a few blocks in silence before Tony found his tongue. "You know, Lexie," he said as I turned onto West 21st Street. "I just wanted to say... About tonight..."

"I'm sorry," I said. "That was a disaster. You shouldn't have been a part of it."

"What? No. I was going to thank you."

I executed a double take. "Thank me? Are you nuts?"

"No, really. Without your help and Larry's and everyone else's, I'd still be running around the woods right now, naked, clawing people's faces to shreds. Trust me. It's happened before."

"I know. I heard it on the news. But I'm surprised you're not upset after how many times I forgot to tell Larry about your problem, not to mention how we treated you in general. I mean, I nailed you with a demonic softball bat, for Christ's sake."

Tony blinked. "You did?"

"Right. Larry said your memory while in raccoon form is fuzzy."

"Well if you did, I don't feel it in my ribs anymore," said Tony. "But never mind. What's important is that, ultimately, you didn't forget about me. You helped me out, and I appreciate it."

Tony smiled. With his hair freshly washed and his ridiculous glasses gone, he was actually pretty handsome. I'd bet if he put on something other than a 1980's comic-themed T-shirt he might even pass for a hunk.

"If you say so. Either way, I'm glad it worked out." I pulled up outside the Jester dormitory and put the beast in park.

Tony didn't reach for the door handle. He sat there, smiling at me with that goofy, somewhat unsure grin of his.

"Well... we're here," I said, stating the obvious.

"Can I tell you something, Lexie?"

Oh, boy, I thought to myself. *Here it comes.* "Shoot."

"I know I didn't make it easy on you, what with popping up

and refusing to come meet Larry in person. Truth is social inter-actions don't come naturally to me. But there's something about you that... I don't know. Puts me at ease. It's hard to explain. Ever since I saw you standing in that doorway, I felt this incred-ible connection, like we're meant to—"

"Alright, let me stop you right there," I said.

Tony blinked, confused. "What is it? Did I say something wrong?"

"No, it's not that. But I know where this is going. The whole love at first sight spiel. That you thought we had a special moment, maybe when I stumbled into you at the library, or when I pet you on the head while you were in raccoon form trying to settle you down—but we didn't. Really."

Tony's mouth hung open. "No moment?"

I shook my head. "No moment."

"Oh." He perked. "Well—maybe there doesn't need to be a moment. You know, some fires burn slow. Lexie, I felt a spark. Honest. I mean, if you're not busy, I'd love to—"

"I am kind of busy though," I said. "I'm an engineering major. You know how it is. Plus I'm on the softball team, at least for now, and that takes up *a lot* of time. And even if I end up getting kicked off the team, I'm kind of picking up this whole Nyte Patrol thing, which doesn't leave me with a lot of time for personal relationships. No offense."

Tony sighed, and his face fell. "Right. No. I get that."

"But," I said. "You are hot. Like, *really* hot. And just because I don't have time for a relationship doesn't mean I'm busy *all* the time. I get drunk and lonely every now and then like any other girl. So... You've called me. I've got your number. We'll see."

He stared at me in shock. "Are you serious?"

"I'm not making any promises, and if you start blowing up my phone, that maybe is going to turn into a hard no."

Tony blinked and shook his head. "Right. Sure. Sure. So, uh... goodnight?"

"Goodnight, Tony."

He eyed me with uncertainty, then puckered up and leaned in.

I caught him six inches out with a finger to his lips. "Yeah. It's not that I'm against the concept, but your breath still smells like rotting meat. Next time, okay? After you plow through a tube of toothpaste and a few bottles of mouthwash."

Tony chuckled, blushing as he pulled away. "Right. Sorry."

"It's fine. *Goodnight, Tony.*"

This time he got the hint. He hopped out and closed the door behind him. I put the Suburban in drive, pulled onto the street, and headed back toward Larry's place. I glanced in the rear view mirror to make sure Tony was headed to his dorm, but I couldn't help but notice the smile on my own face.

33

I PULLED UNDERNEATH THE LOW HANGING BOUGHS OF A massive pecan tree and killed the engine. Down the street, I could barely make out the entrance to Romanov's estate by the light of the moon.

"Alright," said Larry as he turned to face Dawn and Tank. "Everyone ready?"

Dawn pulled one of her swords from its sheath and ran her thumb across the edge. "Ready as we're going to be."

Tank worked the action on his Mossberg pump action shotgun. "Roger that."

"You've got the phone, right?" asked Larry.

Dawn patted her pocket. "The best burner an all-night 7-11 sells."

"And you've got Lexie's number?"

"Larry, what do you take me for, an idiot?"

"And it's on vibrate?"

Dawn pulled the phone from her pocket and checked. She flicked her thumb at the switch on the side. "It is now."

"See?" said Larry. "This is why we have a checklist. It's not because I'm the overbearing group mom."

"Hate to break it to you," said Tank, "but shotgun fire is louder than a phone."

"Well hopefully you won't run in guns blazing," said Larry. "Besides, if it comes down to a gun fight and we need to contact you, perhaps Dawn will *feel* the phone in her pocket buzzing over the massive cacophony of gunfire."

Tank grunted and hopped out the door, shaking his head.

"Relax," said Dawn. "We'll be fine. It's your group I'm worried about."

"Our group?" said Bill. I'd propped him up in the center console. He claimed he liked the air on his face. "Are you saying we're reckless?"

"I'm saying you're the team with Larry on it. Meet you here in an hour?"

"If everything goes according to plan," said Larry.

Dawn exited, gave Tank a nod, and together they crept into the forest. I checked the clock. It was 3:15.

Larry reached under the seat for his baby carrier and started strapping in.

"So, how confident are we in Dawn and Tank's ability to sneak through the grounds undetected?" I said.

"Dawn's? A hundred percent," said Larry. "Tank? Maybe twenty. And that's only because I enchanted his shoes to keep them quiet."

"I don't think it's his *shoes* she's worried about," said Bill.

"You want to remind me why we decided to break into this place in the middle of the night?" I asked.

Larry buckled a clasp. "The element of surprise, Lexie. We went over this."

"Yeah, but at the time I failed to recognize that the element of surprise doesn't exist because Romanov is expecting us to deliver the tome."

"He's not expecting us to drop by unannounced, he's not," said Larry. "He's probably waiting by his phone, hoping we'll call."

"Not to mention everyone here is certainly on edge after our dubstep orgy battle."

"Which again works to our advantage. No one would be crazy enough to return to the scene of that crime."

"And last but not least, this place is a *vampire academy*. Vampires are active at *night*. Why couldn't we have waited until dawn?"

Larry frowned. "Okay, I may have failed to think that one through. But I still contend the element of surprise more than makes up for it."

"Oh, god," moaned Bill. "We're all going to die, aren't we?"

"Can it, watermelon breath," said Larry. "Besides, what do you have to worry about? You're already dead. Now quit whining and hop in." Larry held the side of his baby carrier open.

"Sure," said Bill. "As soon as I finish that online levitation course."

Larry snickered as he hoisted Bill into the carrier and snapped the last clasp into place. He gave me a nod. "Remember, follow me, and stay quiet. We'll make this quick and painless. Get in, get out."

"*Quick and painless,*" said Bill. "That's what the executioner told me, you know."

"Bill? The stay quiet part goes double for you."

We hopped out of the truck and headed up the road,

ducking into the forest twenty feet shy of the driveway. I stuck behind Larry and stayed silent, doing my best to avoid branches or crisp leaves that might crunch underfoot. Maybe Larry had enchanted my shoes, too, because I miraculously managed to creep through the underbrush with mouse-like stealth, but my best efforts couldn't stop a sense of dread from growing in my stomach.

We paused as the forest cleared at the edge of Romanov's circular driveway. I glanced upon the mansion's darkened windows and gothic stylings. Not a bird chirped, nor raccoon screeched. "I've got a bad feeling about this."

"Hey," hissed Larry. "What part of quiet didn't you understand, C-3PO? Even Bill shut his yapper."

Bill wiggled his eyebrows at me in a stern fashion.

I rolled my eyes, then ran a pair of pinched fingers across my lips before giving Larry a pointed glance.

He nodded his approval and took off across the lawn at a jog. We booked it to the front door, which opened without a sound under Larry's touch. I figured Romanov didn't bother with security given all the ferocious vampires he had wandering his property.

Larry continued to lead the way, through the entrance hall, taking a right at the grand staircase, then down a smaller stairwell tucked behind a sitting room. No vampires flew at us at superhuman speed, with fangs bared or otherwise, and I started to think Larry must've cast another obfuscation spell over us because I knew for a *fact* his luck wasn't good enough to produce the same result.

As we reached the basement, the gothic opulence of the upper floors turned to a cold, sterile functionality. Hardwood became polished stone, wall tapestries disappeared, and windows vanished. Even the walls themselves changed from sheet rock to a brushed steel. All we needed was a vault with a fingerprint reader and a retinal scanner to complete the *Mission: Impossible* vibe.

"The armory's ahead," whispered Larry. "With luck, the sword will be where I left it upon delivery."

"And if the door's locked?" I said.

"I'll magic my way in."

"You can pick locks with magic?"

"I was planning on vaporizing the hinges, actually."

We turned a corner and found a room protected by a heavy iron grate—which happened to be wide open.

Larry snickered. "Everything's coming up roses. Come on!"

I followed him through the door, glancing at the finely-crafted wrought iron in disbelief. "They left it open?"

Larry had already dived onto a weapon rack, sifting through a collection of medieval halberds. "Probably so they could access the weapons on short notice."

"On short notice," I said. "Which they would do if they were *expecting us to return.*"

"Damnit." Larry darted to another rack, this one with rapiers, cutlasses, and sabres. "Where is it? Romanov had me hang it up right here."

An accented Russian voice sounded at our backs. "Mr. Stuttgart. So nice of you to drop by."

My stomach sank. "I told you I had a bad feeling."

I turned around slowly to face our antagonist—only to find Cheyev standing there instead. He'd changed out of his mesh raver's gear back into a tailored suit, one that was grey and black and rippled in the underground armory's dim light. He held a four foot claymore that looked as if it had been pulled from the set of *Braveheart,* its point resting on the floor and his hands gripping the pommel. He also wore an amulet around his neck, a tangle of twisted vines and thorns that glowed with an eerie green light.

"Cheyev?" said Larry. "What are you doing here? Does Romanov know you took his sword and his amulet?"

"Romanov knows and approves because sword and amulet are in rightful place," said Cheyev. "You see, Romanov stands before you."

"What? Where?" said Larry. "Romanov, come out of the shadows! If you want to fight me, show yourself! Face me like a man!"

"No, idiot," said Cheyev. "I am Romanov. I stand before you."

"You?" Larry snorted. "You're not Romanov. I met Romanov. He escorted me down here when I delivered that sword you're holding."

"Was lackey you dealt with," said Cheyev. "A fake. I am real Romanov."

I glanced at Larry. "Well, this seems like a pointless plot twist."

"No," said Romanov defensively. "Is very important. Villain always reveals himself as someone unexpected. Is very shocking. Admit it!"

Larry's brow scrunched. "It's surprising that you're your own *butler?*"

"Cheyev is not butler," said Romanov. "Cheyev is important cog in vampire training academy. Place cannot run without him."

"And that makes this shocking?"

Romanov lifted the sword. "Enough talk. You tell me where book is, and I kill you quickly."

"Do your worst, Romanov," yelled Bill, who I'd almost forgotten was strapped to Larry's chest. "You can't frighten us with death!"

"Not you, maybe," I muttered.

"Fine. I stab you in eye socket," said Romanov.

Bill shrieked. "Give him the tome, Larry! Give it to him."

"No chance," said Larry. "I've stashed that book somewhere no one will ever find it. It's guarded by the best of the best, someone so talented and so clever that you'd soil yourself if you even knew who guarded it. You might as well give up, Romanov, because you'll never get it."

Romanov seemed to think it over. "Interesting. But I disagree. I think I kill you now."

His amulet began to pulse as he lifted his sword.

"Wait!" said Larry.

Romanov paused with the tip of the claymore in the air. "What?"

Larry shot me a glance. He was doing something with his hands behind his back, but I couldn't tell what. "Uh... Lexie has something to say to you."

Romanov pierced me with his gaze. "Yes?"

I think I got the gist of Larry's outburst. "That's right. I wanted to tell you that, ah... you can't kill us. You haven't told us about your evil plans yet."

"I do not understand. Is this American tradition?"

"Pretty much. Right, Larry?"

Larry's fingers continued to dance, half hidden behind his thigh. I interrupted him as he mumbled something to himself. "Yes. Absolutely."

Romanov sighed and lowered the sword. "Very well. As you see, I have vampire academy. I have armory. I train vampires. You get point? I need vampire army to help take over world, but is hard recruiting. Need more help. More soldiers. This makes sense, *da?*"

Larry was still mumbling to himself, so I stalled. "More or less, but I don't get the whole taking over the world thing. I mean, who wants the *whole* world? You know that includes the crappy parts, right? Like Rwanda and Afghanistan?"

"Dude," said Bill. "That's kind of offensive to Rwandans and Afghans."

"Fine," I said. "Detroit and Baltimore, then. The point still stands."

"Enough," said Romanov. "Is time to die."

"Really?" Larry smiled at the Russian, his fingers having stopped moving. "After everything we've done for you? Procuring that sword, that amulet, your crystals. And you'd kill us, just like that? I thought more of you Romanov. All that time you led me to believe you were an eccentric billionaire philanthropist when really you're just an evil, heartless murderer."

"Please," said Romanov, matching Larry's smile. "I am not *heartless*. Is why I kill you fast."

Romanov leapt at us with his sword. Larry's hand shot toward the man. An undulating globule of darkness erupted from his palm and raced toward Romanov's head, but the vampire was too fast. With lightning-quick speed, he brought up his sword. The spell bounced off its gleaming edge and flew back toward us, expanding as it approached.

34

I floated in space, surrounded by black nothingness pockmarked by distant stars and galaxies. Something in front of me crackled, a faint blue light that twinkled distinctly from the stars beyond. I reached for it, wondering what it was, but I couldn't seem to touch it, and as far as I could tell, I had no way of moving toward it. I looked up, down, and around. The pale energy was ubiquitous, surrounding me on all sides, except on the one, where a dark blob preempted it.

The blob was moving.

I screamed, and the blob swung toward me, suspended in the nothingness like I was. It shifted and I heard a voice. "Lexie?"

"Wait... Larry?" I said.

"Well, *crap,*" he said. "So it hit you, too, I guess."

"What are you talking about? *What* hit me? Larry, where are we?"

He sighed. "It's called a mind prison. It's a cage for your conscious thought. Traps all the parts that make you *you* within it, separate from your corporeal self."

"It's the spell you were working on while I stalled Romanov."

"Yeah. Except I guess it didn't hit him. Dang, Lexie, I don't know what happened. I had perfect aim, but Romanov brought that sword up and... *BAM!* He bounced it back at us somehow. I don't know how he did it. The spell should've passed through the steel like it wasn't even there."

I felt hot anger boiling inside me. "Larry, did you talk to Dawn after tasking her with studying the sword's history?"

"No. Why?"

I clenched my teeth. "It's a sword of deflection. *Deflection,* Larry."

"Ohhhhh. Well, that would do it."

I took a deep breath and let it out slowly. "It's okay. Focus on the solution, not the problem, right? So how do we get out of here?"

"I have no idea."

It took me a moment to respond. "What do you mean you have no idea?"

"Well, I've cast these things before, but I've never tried to escape from one myself."

"Okay... So how long before it wears off?"

"Well, that's the thing," said Larry. "Given that I designed this one for Romanov and that he'd proved himself to be evil and untrustworthy and what not, I sort of made it... *permanent.*"

The hot anger turned to rage. "God damnit, Larry. *GOD DAMNIT!* What the hell is wrong with you? Why would you do something that stupid? I mean, why not zap him with a lightning bolt or, I don't know, *a fireball?* Seeing as we already found out vampires don't like fire!"

"I don't know, Lexie. I—"

The anger was flowing now, and I couldn't stop it. I felt like I had my softball bat back in my hands, and Larry was the Gatorade jug. "You're an idiot, Larry! Have I ever told you that? *You're a freaking moron!* You never think ahead. You never have a plan. You always try to wing your way through everything, no matter how dangerous or unlikely the odds of survival might be. And you know what? That's a terrible way to go through life! But that's not even the worst part. The worst part is you *never learn.* I mean, shit, I've only been around a few days and I've already seen you shoot yourself in the foot at least a dozen times. Seriously, what is wrong with you? How stupid can you be?"

"I know, I—"

"And yet somehow you're the *leader* of this operation? How in the world did that happen? I get Bill, he can't move, but did you cast a spell of stupidity on Tank? Are you blackmailing Dawn with an abstinence tape? Because you sure as hell didn't earn the right. I'm surprised you haven't killed everyone around you years ago. Which brings me to your stupid spell. The one that brought me to your doorstep. For two days I've been trying to wrap my head around why it picked me. Don't get me wrong. It was obvious from the start that you were incapable of solving even the most basic problems on your own. But there's always been more to it, and I think I've finally figured it out. It's because as worthless of a leader as I am, I'm maybe the only person in the world who's better at it than you."

I paused, the anger whistling out of me, because I'd finally come to the crux of my rage.

I wasn't angry with Larry—or at least, not only with him. I was angry with myself. I was upset because I'd also behaved stupidly. Irrationally. When my hitting had suffered, when I hadn't had the power out of my shoulder I was used to, what had I done? I'd ignored it and plowed ahead anyway. I sure as hell hadn't come up with a better rehabilitation plan than the one I'd been given by the team doctors in the offseason. In fact, when they'd asked how I'd been doing, I'd lied and claimed I was better off than I was, all so my coach would think I'd be ready in time for the start of camp. Some plan that turned out to be...

And as far as leadership was concerned? I'd lost my cool in practice, made an ass of myself, and nearly hurt a teammate whose only fault was that she was a better player than me. When given the opportunity to rectify the situation, I'd hidden. I'd run away and immersed myself in this, trying to find a new home among the Nyte Patrol when a solid apology, some humility, and self-reflection would've rectified matters all along. I'd even made the problem worse by repeatedly lying to my best friend about my intentions to improve my behavior. I'd let my team and my friends down. I'd abandoned them. Me. Their co-captain. The one person they were sure had their best interests at heart.

Everything I'd accused Larry of, I was guilty of the same. The only difference was that at least Larry's intentions had been in the right spot.

I took a deep breath, feeling even worse than I had after my talk with Heather. "Look, Larry. I'm sorry. I shouldn't have said any of that. I crossed a line."

Larry responded in a calm, self-aware tone. "What? No. Don't be sorry. Fact of the matter is you're right. I screwed up. Perhaps more than anyone in the history of screwing up has. I deserve to be chewed out."

"No. I mean, yes, you did screw up. I won't sugar coat that. But you're not the world's biggest screwup, not by a long shot. I should know. My anger is about my own personal problems, not any issues I have with you."

The blob shook. I think Larry was nodding. "Yeah. I know."

I peered at him—not that it helped me see him any better. "You do?"

"I've always been cursed with the ability to read people. Not in a magical or mind reading sort of way. Just the regular kind. I know most people think of me as a gump or a goof. It's okay. I'm both, to be honest. But I read you the instant you showed up at our door. I knew you were running away from your problems. I could see it in the way you stood, the way you talked back when I asked you questions. Everything about you screamed troublemaker with a chip on her shoulder. But I trusted my own magic. I trusted that the spell picked you for a reason, and you know what? None of that has kept you from doing a good job. Honestly. You've been a valuable addition to our team, and yes, you *are* a better leader than I am despite your lack of relevant experience. I don't for a second regret bringing you on."

"Thanks, Larry. I appreciate that."

We floated in silence for a moment.

"Do you mind if I give you some personal advice, though?" said Larry.

"Not at all."

"As useful as you've been, and as much as I've enjoyed having you at my side these past few days, don't give up everything you've ever worked for to join us. Dawn, Tank, and I, for all our powers and abilities—we're just a bunch of washed up hacks. We rarely get anything right. And the reason Dawn and

Tank follow me? It's because we've been through a lot together. They trust me because we're friends, although thanks to you I've realized I haven't been treating them as such. But you have friends, too. Teammates. People you've spent years with, training by their sides, cultivating relationships with. I may not know much, Lexie, but I know the most important thing in life is the people you spend it with. And even though it might not seem like it at times, no relationship is too broken to be repaired."

I shook my head. "I'm not sure I believe that last part."

"Have you tried to fix it? I mean, *really* tried?"

I sighed. "No. I haven't. And I should. You're absolutely right about that. But it's not as if I can go back to the way things were, either. Even if I can patch things up with my coach and teammates, *I'll* never be the same. Knowing what I know about the world? How can I focus on softball and engineering with vampires and demons on the loose? I mean, you're selling yourself short, Larry. You, Dawn, Tank, and Bill? You're out there saving the world!"

Larry snorted. "When we don't make it worse, you mean. But I'll let you in on another secret. The world's always in need of saving, but somehow it always manages to survive, regardless of what we or anybody else does. And like the world, a good friendship lasts forever."

"Both can also end in an apocalyptic catastrophe, though," I said.

"Come on," said Larry. "What happened to you? I thought you were the optimistic one."

"*Me?* What ever gave you that idea."

"Well, it sure as hell isn't Bill. And Dawn—"

The faint blue light of the field around us wobbled and

shook. The stars and galaxies shifted and spun, turning into blurred streaks. Someone crashed a cymbal over my ears, or perhaps imploded a sun. My head felt like it turned inside out, and with a mind-bending thump, I found myself back in Romanov's armory, with Dawn and Tank standing over us, the latter of the two holding Bill. All three of them were smiling.

35

"Dawn. Tank. Bill," I said. "What are you doing here?"

"Saving you, clearly," said Dawn. "What else would we be doing?"

"You came back for us?"

"Of course we came back for you." Dawn offered me a hand and pulled me to my feet. "You're part of the team. We don't leave teammates behind."

"Or friends, either, for that matter," said Bill.

"See?" said Larry as Tank helped him to stand. "Told you, Lexie."

"That the rest of the gang would save us? You had no confidence in that whatsoever."

"That good friendships last forever," said Larry. "Speaking of which, how *did* you save us?"

Bill smiled. "I'll take the credit for that. You see, while you were busy crafting that spell you shot at Romanov and Lexie was stalling the guy, I'd been plotting my own attack. I figured if I timed it right, when the shit hit the fan I could dive bomb

Romanov and give him a good old bite on the arm. So I chewed through the side strap of the baby carrier and waited for the right moment to strike."

"No way," I said. "So when Romanov leapt at us with the sword, you jumped out, savaged him with your teeth, and drove him off?"

"Not exactly," said Bill. "I tried to jump but I sort of rolled out and fell. But on the bright side, I did it fast enough to avoid the spell Larry cast, which bounced off Romanov's sword and slapped the two of you in your mugs."

"So how'd you fight Romanov off?" asked Larry. "Did you bite him on the calf?"

"Well, I didn't precisely *fight him off*, per se. When the two of you slammed to the ground after being struck by the spell, Romanov pulled back on his sword. He stepped over the two of you with this shocked expression on his face, like he couldn't believe his own luck. He leaned over and touched Larry's head to make sure he was really out, I guess. His eyes widened, and he started laughing maniacally. Then he ran off abruptly."

"So there was no fighting at all?" I said.

"None," said Bill. "But I didn't give up, and this is where my heroism really shone through. I knew I had to get ahold of Dawn and Tank, so I chewed through the outer pocket of your pants, Lexie, to get at your phone to give them a call."

I glanced at my jeans. True to Bill's word, the outer part of them had been chewed off over my left hip, and the surrounding material was wet and slimy to boot. "Eww. Gross."

"*Heroic*," corrected Bill. "But it gets better. You see, I actually couldn't call Dawn using your cell phone because I didn't know your passkey to unlock it."

"Couldn't you have pressed it against my thumb?" I said.

"Well, I could've if I had arms," said Bill. "*You* try dragging yourself by the tongue and holding a cell phone between your teeth at the same time."

"So how did you contact Dawn and Tank?" asked Larry.

"I did the only thing left that I could," said Bill. "I went out in search of them myself. With my tongue as my only means of propulsion, I dragged myself inch by painstaking inch back to the stairs, swallowing roughly half a pound of dust and cat hair along the way. Then I tongued my way up to the main level and back to the car where I found them waiting."

"Or at least that was his intention," said Dawn. "In reality, we found him panting at the base of the lowest basement step having not made an inch of progress for the previous two hours."

"*Two hours?*" I said.

"About that," said Larry. "The mind prison is a construct completely separate from the space time continuum. The concept of time doesn't exist there. What for us seemed like a few minutes clearly was a lot more. But what I don't understand is how you all managed to free us from its confines."

"Bill can't take credit for that one," said Dawn. "I was the one who sprung you loose."

"But how?" said Larry. "Last time I checked, you can't slice a metaphysical mind prison open with a katana."

"I didn't cut it open. I used magic to free you."

"*Magic?*" Larry laughed. "You're not a witch. There's no way you've been hiding that from me all along. I would've smelled it."

Dawn fixed Larry with a scornful look. "I'm not a barista either, but I can still brew a mean cup of coffee. You think I haven't been paying attention to the way you operate for the past several years?"

"I'm not buying it," said Larry. "You couldn't untangle a spell of that complexity on your own, not without the proper training."

"Well, not on my own, exactly," said Dawn. "Lucky for me you talk in your sleep."

Larry squinted, confused. "So?"

"So, that one time we slept together wasn't a total waste, as disappointing as the experience was. You mumbled one of your four hundred middle names to yourself in the middle of the night. For the record, the demons now have possession of 'Archibald.'"

Larry blew a raspberry. "I never cared for that one anyway. Nice work, though. I'm proud of you."

Dawn smiled. "Thanks."

"Yeah, well, Dawn and Tank might've done good work," I said, "but we sure as hell didn't. In case it wasn't obvious, Romanov got away, and he has both the sword and the amulet."

"Yeah, Bill told us," said Dawn. "But don't praise us too much. We weren't successful in our mission, either. The crystals were gone from the clearing. Romanov must've collected them and stashed them somewhere after we crashed his rave."

"And the map," said Bill. "Don't forget he's still got the map."

"Right," I said. "So Romanov still has four of the five objects, making this excursion a complete and total failure."

"Could've been worse," said Larry. "At least Romanov didn't kill us like he threatened to."

"Yeah," I said, scratching my head. "I wonder why he didn't?"

"Maybe because he knew that if he did, he'd never find

where I'd hidden the tome," said Larry. "Remember, I've locked away the secret to its location deep within my mind."

I pursed my lips, thinking about Bill's recollection of the events. How Romanov had stepped over us, touched Larry's head, and then broken out in laughter. "Larry? How does that mind prison spell work, exactly?"

"Well, it traps the victim's mind in the prison, cutting it off from the corporeal self as I mentioned, giving only the spell's caster access to the mind that was—*oh, crap*. Romanov knows where the *Librum* is, doesn't he?"

"You gifted Romanov the means with which to read your mind and discover the location of the tome?" said Tank.

"Calm down," I said. "Larry and I already had a moment in the mind prison where I called him a lot of names and subsequently forgave him for his idiocy, so let's extend that feeling of charity to the present."

"It's okay," said Larry. "Even knowing where it is won't help Romanov. I made sure to put it in a place where he wouldn't be able to reach it, just as I promised."

"And where is that?" asked Dawn.

"In a book."

I blinked. "You put the book in a book? Like, you swapped the cover out?"

"No," said Larry. "I gave it to Adric. The bibliomancer. I told him to store it in one of his texts. He's the only one who can get it out."

Dawn frowned. "So let me get this straight. You gave the book of power to a sorcerer who can read latin and specializes in books."

"That's right."

"Someone who, if threatened with torture or death, could

easily remove the *Librum* from its literary confines and furthermore could help Romanov interpret and use the mystical powers held within the tome."

Larry smiled nervously. "Well, when you put it that way..."

"Larry, I'm finding it harder and harder to keep our mind prison moment going," I said.

Larry swallowed hard. "Yeah. I'm thinking maybe we should pay Adric a quick visit."

36

THE SUBURBAN'S TIRES SCREECHED AS I SLAMMED ON THE brakes, pulling the beast onto the sidewalk outside PCL. Larry, Dawn, Tank, and I jumped out of the truck and raced toward the library. Larry cradled Bill under his arm, his leather duster flapping in the breeze. Dawn's swords swayed as she ran, but it was Tank who'd channeled his inner commando. He'd strapped a bandolier filled with 40 mm grenades to his chest. He held a grenade launcher in one hand, a sub-machine gun in the other, and had multiple pistols, shotguns, and assault rifles attached at his hips and back. He'd also pulled a red bandana from somewhere and wrapped it around his forehead to complete the look.

We tore across the plaza in the pre-dawn darkness and skidded to a halt in front of the doors. The library wouldn't open for another hour, but we didn't have to worry about how to get in. Someone had already taken care of that for us. Shards of glass littered the concrete alongside twisted metal frames.

Glass crunched underfoot as Larry stepped cautiously through the carnage. "Crap. *Crap crap crap.*"

"Move!" said Dawn. "He might still be here."

We barged in, oblivious to security systems or cameras or anything of the sort. If Romanov hadn't tripped any alarms on his way in, I figured we were safe for the time being. Even if we weren't I had a feeling the enormous black man carrying fifty pounds of firearms would be the first person the police would target, assuming they weren't too busy fighting off an apocalyptic catastrophe of Romanov's creation instead.

We skirted the elevators, instead racing up the stairs as fast as our legs could carry us all the way to the sixth floor. The stairwell door nearly burst off its hinges as Tank crashed through it first, then we dashed past the staff office and through the book stacks en route to Adric's converted janitor's closet. The door was closed as we approached it, and for a moment my heart soared with unexpected hope, but it didn't last.

Tank kicked the door open, and we all let out a collective sigh of defeat. Adric's closet had been trashed. Books littered the floor, his cot had been overturned, and the first generation iMac Adric had recovered from the pages of the old Macworld magazine had been crushed as if by a giant fist. Beyond that, a twelve foot gash split the wall, leaving behind a gaping hole edged with crumbling mortar that peered out over the southern edge of the University of Texas campus, but even that wasn't the worst part. The worst past was that Adric was gone.

"Damn," said Larry. "This is bad. This is really bad." He darted forward and started sifting through the books on the floor, tossing them to the side as he scanned the covers. "*The Count of Monte Cristo?* Good, but no. *Javascript for Dummies?* Definitely not. *Ranma ½?* Didn't realize Adric read manga. Also no."

"What are you looking for?" I asked.

"The book Adric stashed the *Librum* inside of," said Larry.

"A book so boring, so godawful that no one would ever bother opening it. *The Canterbury Tales*."

"*The Canterbury Tales* is a classic of English literature," I said. "What do you have against it?"

"Nothing, really," said Larry. "But Geoffrey Chaucer has been dead for over six hundred years, so he's not likely to sue me for libel for insulting his baby."

"If it's a spoken insult, it's considered slander."

"Trust me, it's libel we need to worry about," said Larry.

"Would you cut it out?" Dawn stood by the mangled outer wall. "Arguing over minutiae isn't going to get us closer to Romanov."

"Then help me look through these books, will you?"

"It's not here, Larry," said Dawn. "Or if it is, it doesn't contain the *Librum* anymore. That should be obvious. Do you really think Romanov would've left with Adric in tow but not the tome?"

"We don't know for a fact it was Romanov who broke in," said Larry.

"Of course we do," said Dawn. "Who else would've kidnapped Adric? Not to mention this gash in the wall is clearly the work of a magic sword. Trust me, I know blades."

Larry sighed and collapsed against the wall, dropping the book he held in his hands. "Damnit. You're right. I know you are, I just didn't want to admit it. I'm sorry, guys. I screwed up again, and now Romanov has all four of the objects of power, five if you include that stupid map. With the power of the tome added to what the sword, amulet, and crystal already grant him... I'm not sure there's any way we can stop him."

"Hey," I said, stepping over a pile of discarded books to stand over Larry. "What kind of attitude is that? In the past three days we've managed to survive getting jumped by angry bikers—twice I might add, fought our way through a horde of demonic nightmare beasts, survived an attack by a pack of horny ecstasy-addled vampires, and made our way out of a supposedly permanent mind prison, thanks to Dawn and Tank. So unless we're actively getting cut in half by a magic sword or having our faces torn off by angry vampires, I'd say there's still time to avert the apocalypse, especially if we work together. What was it you said while we were trapped in your spell? *That the bonds of friendship are the most powerful force on Earth.* Together, we're unstoppable."

"Actually, I'm pretty sure I never said that," said Larry.

"Well, you should've," I said. "Because that's the assumption I'm going to proceed on until proven otherwise. We're a team, and we're going to save the world. Right? Who's with me?"

I stuck my hand out and waited, fierce determination burning in my heart. For a moment, I thought I'd made an ass of myself and everyone would walk away, heads hanging low, but then Dawn placed her hand over mine.

"I'm with you, girl," she said. "You're a badass, and I'll fight by your side anytime."

"Thanks, Dawn," I said. "Right back at you."

"Back at both of you." Tank slapped his hand over the top. "You're the fiercest pair of skinny chicks who don't use guns I've ever met."

"Really?" I said. "You think I'm skinny?"

"Everyone seems skinny to me."

Larry shook his head as he picked himself off the ground. "Damn, Lexie. I know I already told you this, but from the moment we first met I knew you had it in you." He stuck his hand out and grasped the rest of ours. "All right. I'm in, all the way. But from now on, Lexie's in charge. I think she's earned it."

"Hell yeah!" screamed Bill. "Larry! Hold me out. Let me get my tongue on the pile."

I shrugged. "What the hell. Why not? Let's get him in here."

Larry held Bill out, and he licked the top of our hand quartet. Thankfully, it was Larry's hand on top, so he got the worst of it.

"So," I said as we pulled our hands back. "Our number one priority—hell, our *only* priority—is stopping Romanov before he can unleash the power of his artifacts. All we have to do is find him first. Larry? Can you track Adric? I know you couldn't track Tank through the woods, but Adric's a fellow magic user. Surely you can follow his scent."

Larry shook his head. "I could if I were close. As things stand, that's a no go."

"We could call the police," said Tank. "Have them put an APB on Romanov."

"That's not a bad idea," said Larry. "Frank was kind of a dick when I talked to him last, but he did say to call him when we were in his jurisdiction."

"And we still have Betsy," said Dawn. "We could bring her here. Have her get a whiff of Adric's scent. His real one, I mean."

"Guys. *Guys,*" said Bill. "If I had a hand, I'd be raising it."

"Yes, Bill?" I said. "You have a suggestion?"

"This isn't rocket science," he said. "We gave Romanov a *map*. It even had a location circled on it."

I blinked. "Oh my god. He's right. The South Congress Bridge. Let's go!"

37

THE SUBURBAN ROARED AS I PUNCHED IT DOWN CONGRESS, the speedometer pushing against the stopper at the far right of the gauge thanks to another jolt of Larry's magical power. The side streets ticked down mere seconds apart: 8th, 7th, 6th, 5th. The skyline expanded as I cleared the last of the skyscrapers on 2nd, the faintest hint of purple and blue brightening the sky. Somehow the roads remained miraculously empty even as dawn approached. I didn't think it was a good sign.

I blasted through the red light at Cesar Chavez and slammed on the brakes. The 'burban shuddered as we skidded two hundred and fifty feet to a stop. I didn't even bother to kill the engine as I hopped out. If I was wearing sunglasses, I would've taken them off dramatically while muttering something pithy, like *"Good god..."* Instead, I stared, slack-jawed, at the scene before me.

Romanov stood in the center of the bridge, his amulet glowing bright green, ten times as bright as when I'd seen it in the armory. He'd sheathed his sword across his back and rearranged the crystals into a pentagram around his feet, the latter of which were glowing with a potent pink light. He held the *Librum de Virtute* open in one hand while he gestured in the air with the other. I was too far away to hear him, but his lips were moving in tandem with his waving hand.

Beyond him, in the air over the Colorado River, hung several midnight black portals, the edges crackling with a mysterious purple energy. Two already occupied the air on the east side of the bridge and another to his left on the west side. As I watched, a fourth formed. It started out as a bright purple speck in the pre-dawn sky but quickly spiraled and expanded to the size of a pickup truck. Tendrils of the purple energy trailed from the far sides of the portals, dancing in the air like jellyfish tentacles.

Adric hovered in the air behind Romanov, bound by glowing blue ropes that twisted around him. He struggled against them, but the sound of the Suburban's screeching tires must've drawn his attention. His eyes widened at the sight of us, and he started screaming. "Help! Help me! This psycho's going to kill me. *He'll kill us all!*"

We all raced forward, coming to a stop some thirty feet from Romanov as the Russian turned to face us. "Well, if it isn't Nyte Patrol," he called. "I was expecting you, but thought you would be faster. Is disappointing, really."

"Well, prepare to be even more disappointed, Romanov," said Larry. "Because we're here to stop your evil plans once and for all. You should've killed us when you had the chance."

"Yes, I think about that," said Romanov across the expanse of concrete. "But delivering monologue felt so good, I could not bring self to kill you, not until you see means of ultimate destruction, *nyet?* Victory so much more satisfying when you see knowledge of inescapable defeat in enemy's eyes and hear fear-filled cries."

"Too bad that won't happen." I pulled my demon tooth from my pocket and gave it a good squeeze, growing it to bat length in the blink of an eye. "What you don't understand, Romanov, is that we're prepared this time. We're confident. We even had a group meeting. Not to mention this is like the third time we've faced you, and I'm pretty sure we're up for a run of good luck around now."

"Perhaps you miss moment when I say I expect you here sooner," said Romanov. "That imply you are late. In fact... I think I hear means of your demise coming as we speak."

I perked my ears, but I couldn't hear anything but the faint crackling of Romanov's floating portals. Then something joined in. A faint humming coming not from the portals or Adric's glowing bonds or the rumbling engine of the Suburban but from the air, instead.

The crackling purple energy at the edges of one of the portals flashed. Something whistled and flew from the center of the hovering darkness, landing on the concrete bridge with a thump. A young man, crouched on one knee. He unfolded and stood, like Arnold Schwarzenegger in *Terminator,* with the same death stare locked onto his face and his body just as free of clothing.

"Ugh," said Larry. "I was fine with it before, but now I'm with you. This nudity is gratuitous."

Two more portals crackled, and two more individuals, one man and one woman, landed on the bridge. I glanced at the portals, seeing the purple tendrils dancing, flicking at speedy black blurs that whipped through the air just out of reach.

"Oh, shit..." I said.

Romanov smiled and started to laugh. "Ah, yes! I know look. Softball player has deduced plan. Go on, share. I wait."

I spun to the rest of the Nyte Patrol. "It's the bats. *The bats!*"

"What bats?" said Tank.

"The ones that live under the bridge," I said. "Remember how Romanov said he wanted to build an army to take over the world, Larry? The tome gives him the power to imbue items with power. Not just items. Non-sentient beings, too. Like bats!"

"Hold on," said Larry. "Are you saying he's turning the bats under this bridge into an army of vampires?"

"They leave to hunt bugs at dusk," I said. "They return at dawn. All of them."

"And how many roost under this bridge, exactly?" said Dawn.

"I don't know. A million? Maybe more?"

Larry's eyes widened. *"Holy..."*

Romanov's laugh grew. "Yes. *Yes!* That is look of fear and despondency I hoped for. Is perfect!"

"There's no time to waste," I said. "We have to stop Romanov before more of those bats make it to the portals. Dawn? You and I will take Ivan on head to head. Tank? Keep the vampires off our backs. Larry? You need to shut down those portals."

Dawn nodded. Tank switched off the safety on his grenade launcher. Larry gave me a thumbs up. "You've got it, boss."

"Hey, what about me?" said Bill.

"You're good at chewing, right?" I said.

"Better believe it," he said with a smile.

"Great. Then your job is to free Adric. Fly like the wind, Bill!"

I'd never been much of a pitcher, but I did my best. I grabbed Bill by the hair, whipped my arm underhand, and released. Bill flew threw the air, screaming a battle cry the whole way. *"For Sparta!"*

I gave Dawn a nod and we raced toward Romanov. The Russian smiled and pulled the claymore from its sheath. As he did so, the *Librum* spun and grew, glowing with the same green light as the amulet as it transformed into a book-shaped shield. A grenade screamed across the sky, blasting one of the vampires to pulp as Dawn and I made contact.

Despite my athletic background, Dawn was a step faster than me. She spun through the air, her swords whipping around in a tornado of sharpened steel. Sparks flew and clangs filled the air as Romanov parried the blows, moving with vampiric speed. I lunged in beside her, slapping my demon bat at Romanov's midsection, but he pulled his shield back at the last moment. My bat hit the leather cover with a thud, pushing him back mere inches instead of launching him into the surrounding river.

Dawn intensified her attacks, as I did mine. Romanov kept blocking my blows with the book shield, but I didn't let it phase me. Despite the fact that I was a college student with absolutely zero martial arts or combat training whatsoever going up against a potentially millennia old vampire armed with multiple pieces of magical weaponry and armor, I never once lost confidence in my abilities, even when it was warranted.

Romanov punched with the *Librum,* sending me skidding across the pavement thirty feet until my shoes snagged, I toppled, and fell. I rolled and bounced to my feet as Dawn continued to battle Ivan, glancing at the mangled, glowing blue ropes that had tripped me. "Hey, way to go, Bill!"

"Thanks!" Adric cradled him under his arm, standing in the middle of the chaos as he looked about him in fear.

"What the hell do I do?" cried Adric.

Tank ran past, his grenade launcher thumping as he fired missile after missile. "Help fight the vamps. How are you with a shotgun?"

"Dreadful!" he said.

Larry darted into the fray, firing bursts of bright white light from his palms. "I got your back, Adric. I packed a crate of books into the Suburban on our way out of the library just in case. Get to it!"

Adric took off while Larry fired more light at the portals. The inky black masses swallowed the beams whole. "Damn! Guys? I'm not having a lot of luck."

A dozen more vampires flew from the portals, landing on the bridge in coiled crouches. Tank fired several more grenades before ditching his launcher, pulling his SIG Sauer tactical patrol rifle, and cutting loose with a hail of gunfire.

I stood and dusted off my pants. "Well, try something else."

Larry mumbled something under his breath. "Fine. Here goes nothing. But if you see any demons, don't kill them. They're on my side. *Balthazar! Murray! Horatio!* Hah! That's been my least favorite name for two decades!"

Red light flickered across three of the portals, and they started to shrink. I darted toward Romanov, whose sword continued to ring and spray sparks under Dawn's unrelenting onslaught. I swung my bat at him with wild abandon, even catching him once across the ribs. I think it was only because he was distracted, though.

He glared into the sky and roared in anger. "I think not!" He spun, blasting Dawn and me through the air before turning his attention to the shrinking portals.

This time, pain blossomed in my shoulder as I hit the concrete and rolled to a stop. Gritting my teeth, I pushed myself up only to have Adric race by me with a crate in his arms. "Damnit, Larry! What is this? I thought you'd grabbed one of *my* boxes. These are all Harlequin romance novels and chemistry textbooks."

"I thought you'd be happy I remembered at all," called Larry. "Come on. Work with it."

Romanov lifted his arms to the air, the heavy claymore pointing toward the nearest portal. More of the mysterious purple energy rippled along the blade before shooting into the void. The purple energy mixed with the red from Larry's middle name-powered spell. Unseen voices shouted in anguish, filling the air with demonic screams. Romanov's arm shook with exertion, but the portal reversed course and started to grow again.

Two dozen more vampires poured through the existing portals. Tank's assault rifle clicked empty as he switched to his submachine gun.

"Now, Adric." Fire and lightning shot from Larry's fingertips. "We need help. *Any help.*"

Adric looked terrified, but to his credit, he didn't let that stop him. He overturned the crate of books and tossed several of them in the air. With a speed he hadn't shown the first time I'd met him, he plunged his arms into the books as they spun around him, brilliant flashes of the familiar radiant blue light shooting from their pages as he did so. As I wondered about the color-based properties of everyone's magic, Adric ripped his arms free and began tossing people onto the battlefield.

Yes, *people*—or at least stereotypes. From the pages of the romance novels he summoned a buff, shirtless cowboy, a buff, shirtless firefighter, a buff, shirtless sea captain, a buff, shirtless prince, a buff, shirtless billionaire bad boy, and at least a dozen other buff, shirtless guys whose faces seemed nebulous and indistinct. Then from the chemistry texts he ripped free a pile of lab coats and goggles. "Safety first! Put these on. And soft hands for this next batch." Barely had he flung the apparel before he started tossing bunsen burners, graduated flasks of bubbling liquid, and packets of powder wrapped in twine to the waiting beefcakes. "Go. Go!"

The romance guys surged into the fray, punching vampires, searing them with flames from the bunsen burners, and tossing the chemicals into their midsts, alternatively blowing them to pieces or melting them with strong acids. Of course, they weren't ideal soldiers. Many of them got distracted and went after the naked female vampires, abandoning their weapons and lab coats alike to wrap them in fierce embraces and try to make passionate love to them. Those guys got their faces torn off.

"Damnit." Dawn raced up beside me, panting hard. "Why is it every fight we're engaged in is so *freaking hot?*"

"Never mind that," I said. "We need to come up with a new strategy for Romanov. With that sword of deflection of his and his book turned shield, I can't land a decent hit on him."

"Me neither," said Dawn. "Larry? You have any ideas?"

Larry froze a vampire with a spray of super chilled frost. *"Archer!* Damn. I actually liked that one. Do I have any ideas about what?"

"Stopping Romanov."

"I'm a little busy keeping these bat-to-vampire portals under control. Maybe get Tank to help?"

Tank rushed by in full bear form with the red bandanna still wrapped around his forehead and a mini gun in his massive paws.

"Tank?" I said. "When did you transform? And where did you get that gun?"

"Gruh rah rur gruroo."

"From a Gulf War themed romance?" said Dawn. "They make those? Never mind. Unload on Romanov while he's distracted by Larry's anti-portal magic."

Tank depressed the firing mechanism on the mini gun with one of his gargantuan claws. The barrel spun up, and a second later the machine filled the air with high-speed lead and ferocious sound. Romanov jerked and spasmed as the barrage hit him, but Tank kept right on firing. Bullet casings choked the air, shimmering as they flew, the multicolored magics playing off their shells.

After thirty seconds, the hammering rattle of gunfire ended, replaced instead with the metallic melody of the last bullet casings bouncing off the concrete. Romanov turned toward us, his clothes ripped to shreds but his body seemingly intact. He scowled and threw down his sword.

"Well, that didn't work," said Dawn. "Anyone have any other ideas?"

Larry stopped another naked attacker dead in his tracks with a burst of some sticky, tar-like substance. "Come on, guys. Think. He's a vampire overlord, and beyond that, he's an evil supervillain. He's got to have a secret weakness. They all do."

"Like what?" I said. "His love of cheap Russian stereotypes?"

"No," said Larry. "Something obscure, but something he'll have hinted at during our interactions with him. Maybe during one of our calls or his monologue. It's classic villain behavior."

The world around me slowed, and my eyes widened with sudden realization. "That's it. He's a vampire. We can stake him!"

"Or that," said Larry. "Assuming you can find a stake."

The burly, shirtless eightieth century sea captain approached. "Yar. Did someone call for a harpoon?"

"Close enough." Dawn grabbed it from the man's outstretched hands, wound up, and threw it with all her might. It sailed through the air and plunged straight into Romanov's chest, right over the heart.

Romanov looked down at the weapon, put a hand on it, and ripped it out. He roared with anger and started stalking us from across the battlefield.

"Strike two," said Dawn.

"That's impossible," I said. "I was sure that would be it. Romanov even alluded to it during his monologue, just like you said, Larry. Remember? He emphasized the fact that he wasn't *heartless*."

Larry froze in mid step. "You're right, damnit. He *did* emphasize that. But if that harpoon didn't stop him, that can only mean..."

"What?"

"That he's moved his heart to prevent himself from being staked."

"*What?*" I said. "That's insane."

"It's not insane," said Larry. "Lots of people have tried it. Davy Jones did it in *Pirates of the Caribbean: Dead Man's Chest,* and the Tzimisce clan from the *Vampire: The*

Masquerade role-playing game can do so via the vicissitude skill."

"Well, if you say so." Romanov batted a pair of battling vampires and buff dudes off the bridge with a casual swipe of his hand.

"Plus there were episodes of *Buffy the Vampire Slayer* where vampires got dusted after failing to get hit in the chest, implying their hearts were in the wrong spot. Not to mention the Simpsons *Treehouse of Horror* episode where Homer stakes Mr. Burns in the crotch, though that was more for comic relief. Heck, even Tony Bennett wrote about leaving his heart in San Francisco, though I think he meant it in a figurative sense."

"Whatever, Larry!" I screamed. "None of that helps us unless we know where his heart is now!"

"Well, for all our sakes, we'd better hope it's somewhere in his body," said Larry. "Otherwise we're in a world of hurt."

"Got anymore harpoons, handsome sea captain guy?" asked Dawn.

He didn't respond because there was a vampire perched on top of him, tearing open his throat with its bone white fangs.

"And I think that's strike three," said Dawn.

"Not on my watch!" said Larry. "Adric. Quick. What do you have in hand right now?"

The bibliomancer was elbow deep in a pair of floating books, one a thick softbound volume and another a small paperback. "A McMaster-Carr catalog and a quaint nineteen-fifties suburban romance. Why?"

"Perfect," yelled Larry. "Picket fence me!"

Adric was either smart enough or scared enough not to ask. He ripped a length of white picket fence from the paperback and chucked it at Larry. Larry's hands whipped in front of him.

Air rushed and swirled, catching the fence in a nascent cyclone. "More! *More!*"

Adric chucked more pieces toward Larry as the maelstrom grew in power. It swirled faster and faster, ripping the white-washed pieces of hardwood from their supports and accelerating them to category five speeds.

Romanov, still some thirty paces away, glanced at the cyclone. His eyes widened, and I knew we were on the right track. Of course, he was also supernaturally fast.

"Now!" I screamed.

Romanov blurred as he leapt toward us. At the same time, Larry unleashed the cyclone, sending it crashing into Ivan's path. Wood cracked as fifty feet of white picket missiles pounded Romanov in mid air. I lifted my arm to shield my eyes from the debris.

The wind howled mercilessly, but I still heard the thump as Romanov landed next to me. I screamed and pulled back on my demon tooth bat, but I couldn't beat his speed. Not one on one. Thankfully, I didn't have to.

The Russian wobbled and nearly fell. His body was mangled, covered in scrapes and dotted with thousands of tiny splinters, but it was the lone fence post protruding from his kidneys that gave me hope.

"You... *you fools,*" he said. "You think... you can stop... *me?* You're only... making things worse for yourselves... in the end."

I smiled. "That fence post looks a little wobbly, Romanov. Let me help you with it."

I swung my bat at full force into the end of the post, driving it another two feet into Romanov's stomach and out the other side. Ivan screamed, an ear-piercing death howl that heated the air and shook the bridge underneath us. He fell to his knees, and his entire body burst into flames. I put an arm up to shield my face from the sudden heat only to hear Larry's voice over the searing crackle.

"Run, Lexie. *RUN!*"

I felt his hand on my arm and together we raced away from his flaming corpse, the heat growing more intense, his death scream more violent. Out of the corner of my eye, I saw Dawn running. Tank, too. Even Adric. I felt a wave of air rush in, trying to force me back toward the vampire overlord, but I fought it and kept churning my legs. Larry screamed something in my ear. To jump, I think, so I did.

That's when the explosion lifted me into the air.

38

I BOUNCED ACROSS THE PAVEMENT, MY EARS RINGING AND the smell of smoke thick in my nostrils. I didn't fight it, keeping my arms tight against my body to avoid further injury. Eventually, the blast's momentum dissipated, and I rolled to a stop. I felt heat on my leg. Looking up, I saw that my jeans had caught fire, but only a little. I slapped at them with an open palm, smothering the flame with a few well-timed strikes.

Larry skidded to a halt beside me. He wasn't on fire, but he groaned as he pushed himself to his knees. "Son of a bitch. I think I shattered a femur."

I looked past him to where Romanov had fallen. Instead of a corpse, there was nothing left of him but a smoking crater. Dead and dying bats littered the roadway around him, some of them on fire, others merely steaming. The midnight black portals and creeping purple tendrils had vanished from the now orange sky. The romance novel army lay on the pavement among the bats, winking out of existence into streams of blue light that whirled in the air, twisted together into ropes, and drained into the smoldering remains of Adric's books.

I winced as I sat up. "Since when do vampires explode? I thought they turned to dust or decayed really fast when you killed them."

"Normally, yes," said Larry, grunting as he limped to his feet. "I think *that* had more to do with the concentrated, high-pressure evil inside of him."

Dawn walked over, her black tank top torn in at least three separate places. She wiped sweat and soot from her brow with the back of her arm. "Well, I'll be damned. We actually did it. We stopped Romanov."

Tank was still in bear form as he lumbered up beside us. "Gruh rah ruh!"

"I know," said Dawn. "And none of us died. Not even Adric. It's a miracle."

I looked behind me to find Adric pushing himself to his knees. He shot us a thumbs up. "I'm good. Just need a minute... and maybe a fresh set of underwear."

"Wait... Bill!" cried Larry.

He hobbled toward the smoking crater, and I took off after him. Larry limped to a stop as he reached the epicenter of the blast, casting his head about frantically. "Bill? Bill! Oh, god. There he is!"

Larry kicked a dead bat to the side and staggered to Bill's side. The poor guy lay on his ear, his eyes closed, his skin bright pink, and his hair totally gone. His tongue lolled out of his mouth across the pavement.

"Oh, dear lord. No," said Larry. "Not Bill. *Please, no.* Bill. God! Why?"

Bill's eyelids snapped open. His eyes darted about wildly before resting on the man before him. "Larry?"

Larry's face brightened. "Bill! You're alive!"

"Technically, I'm still dead," he said. "What the hell happened? Last thing I remember I was hanging out next to Adric's book pile, trying to hand him novels with my teeth, when Adric took off and I saw a bright flash and heard a bang."

"Romanov exploded," said Larry. "It's weird, I know. But buddy—I've got some bad news."

"Oh, no," he said. "It's Dawn, isn't it? She bit the dust, and I'm the only one who never got to nail her."

"No, she's fine. Everyone is." Larry pointed out her and Tank approaching on foot. "It's you. You were too close to the blast. I don't know how to break this to you, but... you're bald."

"Son of a...! Do you know how long it takes to regrow zombie hair?"

"Don't worry, pal," said Larry. "I'll cook up a potion for you. Little bit of ragweed and powdered goat's hoof in some Rogaine and you'll be good as new."

I heard a siren in the distance—several of them actually. I stood to find a trio of police cars with lights flashing tearing down Congress toward us. The caravan swerved around the Suburban. The lead car screeched to a halt some twenty feet from us.

A familiar cop jumped out the passenger side door.

"Jesus H. Christ!" yelled Frank Connors. "What the hell happened here?"

"Nothing much," said Larry, picking Bill up gently. "Just stopped an evil mastermind from turning a million bats into an undead army that would take over the world. We're back in your jurisdiction, by the way."

"My jurisdiction? You just *blew up* my jurisdiction!"

"It wasn't me," said Larry. "It was Romanov. He was a

vampire. How was I supposed to know a fencepost through the kidneys would cause him to spontaneously combust?"

"And him! *He's in bear form?* Doesn't he know the rules? It's light out."

While Larry and Frank argued, I pulled my phone from my pocket. Amazingly, it hadn't been destroyed or even cracked in the fighting. I checked the time. Just after seven.

I put a hand on Larry's free arm. "Larry? I need to make a call, okay?"

"Yeah, sure. I've got this."

I wandered off toward the smoking crater. First, I sent a short text. Then I went into my friends list and hit the name at the top.

The phone rang four times before eventually picking up. "Yeah."

"Heather? It's me. I need to talk to you."

"At seven in the morning? This better be good."

"It is. I'm sorry. Okay? *I'm sorry.* For everything. I've been a colossal asshat, an awful teammate, and a worse friend. I let you and everyone else on the team down when I went psycho at practice, then I made it worse by hiding from what I'd done like a coward, and then I made it *even worse still* when I lied to you about coming and talking to the team at practice yesterday. Well, actually, it wasn't a lie. I was just too scared to do it, too scared to face the fact that maybe I'm not as good of a softball player as I've always thought I was. But I'm not going to make excuses. I've screwed up. I don't know if I can make things right, but I'm going to try."

The line was silent. Eventually Heather responded in a softer tone. "Okay."

"I mean it, Heather. I'm taking action, today. But the most

important thing is you. What do you say? Are we still friends? Because I really don't want to lose you."

Heather's sigh tickled my ear. "Yes, Lexie. We're still friends. God, don't be such a drama queen."

I laughed, feeling a pressure I didn't even know was there lift from my chest.

"But," continued Heather, "I don't know if apologies are going to cut it with everyone else—especially Coach."

"I just sent her a text telling her I needed to talk to her in person," I said. "But I know I can't fix everything with words. Maybe I can't fix everything, period. That's okay. I'm still going to be there at practice to confront this head on. Pointless or not, I'm going to try to make things right."

"Good," said Heather. "I'm glad to hear it. And for the record, I hope you *can* fix it. You're not just my friend. When you're on your game, you're still the best hitter we've got."

I thought about my demon bat and smiled. "You don't know the half of it. So... practice?"

"Practice."

Heather hung up. I smiled as I slipped my phone back into my pocket.

I felt a soft pressure on my shoulder and turned to find Larry standing next to me. Behind him, Tank was grunting and gesturing at Connors while Dawn interpreted. Some of the other cops grilled Adric and Bill.

"So," I said. "How long have you been standing there?"

"Long enough to get a gist of the conversation," said Larry. "You know, I was coming over to tell you I was proud of you for taking charge, and beyond that, for coming up with a way to take down Romanov. Instead, I find myself being proud of you for doing your best to be a good person."

"Thanks, Larry," I said. "And I know I already apologized, but you're really not the hopeless, incompetent schmuck I painted you as. You're actually a pretty decent guy, yourself."

"Please. I'm blushing."

I heard a distant rumble, then the ground under my feet started to vibrate. I thought it might be a heavy truck approaching, but the rumbling grew. My whole world started to shake.

"My god," I said. "Is that an earthquake?"

I fell to the concrete as the bridge continued to dance, and then I heard something over the rumbling. A laugh—impossibly deep, dry as dust, and painfully ancient. It grew in intensity. I plugged my ears as I bounced over the pavement. And then I saw it. A nebulous spirit, barely discernible from air, emerging from the crater left behind by Romanov's explosion.

Words formed on the wind. "Free. Free. *Free at last!*"

The spirit rocketed into the air with a whoosh, the scream fading as it went. The laughing ceased, and the bridge stilled.

"What the *hell* was that?" I said.

Larry picked himself off the ground. "I don't know. Probably nothing to worry about. The important thing is Romanov's dead."

"Nothing to worry about?" I said. "That spirit just few out of Romanov's crater, laughing as it sped into the sky! Of course we should be worried. Wait... What was it Romanov said as he was dying? Something about us being fools, and us only making things worse for ourselves?"

"Lexie, Lexie," said Larry, as he helped me off the ground. "Stop obsessing over this. The important thing is we stopped the bad guy and we all lived to fight another day. Trust me, that's the best you can hope for in this line of work. Now, what do you say we go celebrate?"

I glanced at the sky, a frown on my lips. "What did you have in mind?"

"Well, I know a guy who makes a mean Mountain Dew Baja Breeze-a-rita."

"It's seven in the morning, Larry."

"Or we could just get breakfast burritos. I know for a fact Tank wouldn't say no to those."

Despite the circumstances, I couldn't help but laugh. "Alright. Breakfast. And then I'm going back to my dorm to take a nap. Something tells me I'm going to need it."

ABOUT THE AUTHOR

Hi. I'm Alex P. Berg, author of *The Nyte Patrol*. Hopefully, you laughed your head off in this off-the-wall, urban fantasy spoof, but Lexie, Larry, Dawn, and Tank's adventures are just beginning. Be sure to pick up the sequel, *Nyte Terrors,* in which Lexie joins the Nyte Patrol full time and gets more than she bargained for.

Need more adventures, mysteries, and laughter? Try my Daggers & Steele series, featuring homicide detective Jake Daggers and his clever new partner, Shay Steele. The complete ten book series is now available on Kindle Unlimited. Read it now!

Word of mouth is **critical** to my success. If you enjoyed this novel, please consider leaving a positive review on Amazon. Even if it's only a line or two, it would be a *huge* help. Thanks!

Want to connect? Visit me at www.alexpberg.com or contact me on social media.

For a complete list of my books, please visit: www.alexpberg.com/books/.